Surfer's Edge

A Novel

By

Hannah Shelton

Surfer's Edge
By Hannah Shelton
Published by Hannah Shelton Copyright 2011 by Hannah Shelton
Cover Illustration Copyright 2011 by Leanne Roberson Sargeant
www.sergeantphotography.com
Graphic Design Copyright 2011 by Adam Sexton
ansexton@live.co.uk
Edited by Lauren Wise at Midnight Publishing, LLC
www.midnightpublishingllc.com
This book is a work of fiction. Names, characters places and incidents are either products of the author's broad imagination or used fictitiously. All rights reserved. This book is licensed for your personal enjoyment only. If you would like to share this book with another reader, please purchase an additional copy for each recipient. Thank you for respecting the HARD work of this author.

For Momma

02/03/48-06/30/10

Chapter Guide

Preface
Chapter 1: Monotony's a Bitch
Chapter 2: Chicken-Fried Friends
Chapter 3: Ear for the Ramblings
Chapter 4: Ambiguity
Chapter 5: Waiting…
Chapter 6: No Reason, Other Than the Obvious
Chapter 7: Reunited
Chapter 8: Surprises Abound
Chapter 9: The Thing With Tragedy Is…
Chapter 10: Some Answers are Better Not Knowing
Chapter 11: The Shore's Awash with Aussies
Chapter 12: More Than Just One Good-Bye
Chapter 13: It's a Good Day for G'day
Chapter 14: Some People Know How to Make an Entrance
Chapter 15: The Unwelcome Visitor Visits
Chapter 16: Screw Reality
Chapter 17: When the Shit Hits the Fan, You Better Have a Poncho
Chapter 18: The End Is Near…
Epilogue
About the Author

Preface

I felt like puking.

I wanted to breathe, but I couldn't. Up was nowhere to be found. It was pitch-black and I was starting to lose air.

Focus, Sam.

Finally, my hand hit the hard bottom; a good sign. That meant I just needed to flip around and kick back up. But in the darkness, I wasn't sure which way that was. I felt panic start to creep in.

I remembered my mantra: calm, calm, calm. After an interminable silence of kicking into nothing, I finally broke the surface, gasping for air. For a moment I just tread water, regaining my equilibrium.

That was a close one.

I heard a sharp whistle in the distance. Paddling doggedly in a circle, I finally spotted the on-shore lights of my hometown, Huntington Beach, California.

Somewhere in the mad rush of being plunged underwater I lost my board, because the leash hung helplessly off my ankle as I swam toward shore. Despite my fatigue, I couldn't help feeling accomplished, thinking of all the hard work I had put in to prepare for the US Open of Surfing, one of the largest local surf competitions and the most opportunistic platform for someone like myself to break onto the coveted professional surfing scene.

As I swam with the waves back toward shore, I finally caught sight of my father, best friend and mentor, Darrell Dane, or as I called him, "Pop", waving at me from the very spot he had been standing in for the last three nights since I had started my twice-daily (sometimes thrice) surf sessions to prepare for the Open. I didn't surf much at night and, over-protective father that he had always been, he insisted on joining me.

"You sure did give me a scare there, honey," he said, holding out a thick beach towel for me as I pulled myself up out of the water. "I was about ready to jump in and go after you."

"Haha," I said, shivering as I quickly toweled off and threw on the sweat-suit I had packed in my beach bag. "I scared myself for a minute there, too."

"C'mon, let's get out of here before some overzealous cop tickets us." He clapped me on the shoulder, and together we walked the two blocks home. Although I was nearly twenty-one, I was one of the few people I knew my age who didn't mind still living with their parents. In fact, most of my friends actually liked hanging out with Pop.

"By the way, that last bottom turn was awesome. Even if you did lose another board, and a good one at that." He scowled good-naturedly.

I was notorious for breaking and losing surfboards, so Pop had started shaping as a hobby to repair them for me in an effort to save money. But as I had gained notoriety in the surf community and started competing in local heats (and breaking and losing more and more boards), Pop had taken it upon himself to be the shaper of all of my boards.

"What time shall I see you at the breakfast table?" Pop asked, poking his head into the open bathroom door as I brushed my teeth.

"Five-thirty?"

He smiled. "You know that's only six hours from now."

I spit the toothpaste out of my mouth and grinned at him. "That's alright. I can sleep when I'm dead."

*

The alarm went off at five-thirty. Sleepily, I rolled out of bed and padded to the kitchen where I found Pop already awake, putting together a pot of coffee.

The enormity of the forthcoming competition was really starting to hit home, for me and for Pop. Our light-hearted banter from the previous evening was gone as we discussed time slots to meet at the beach, in between my work schedules.

A couple of Pop's old surf buddies were down at the water when we arrived, coffee mugs and wetsuits in tow. I had known most of them since before I could remember, and they knew how important the forthcoming competition was, for Pop and I. They extended their well wishes to me before moving on to making small talk with Pop. I hurriedly pulled my wetsuit on and charged toward the water, not wanting to waste any surf time.

Before I knew it, it was time for my morning job at the local surf shop, a place I had also called home since I was sixteen-years-old. Not only did it afford me a chance to hob-nob with some of the globe's best surfers, but it also inspired me to keep pushing forward in my own pursuit of becoming a professional surfer. Though I knew the pro-surfing industry could be downright cut throat at times – not to mention incredibly competitive - it was the only thing I had ever wanted to do with my life, the only thing I had ever planned to do with my life. Unfortunately, it had yet to pay the bills, so four nights a week I also worked at a small restaurant. Between the two, every extra penny earned was set aside. Surfing could be a very expensive sport, and you never knew what could happen: one day your board might hit you in the face and your nose breaks, the next you could tear your wetsuit on a rock.

I had a couple of free hours until my night shift at the restaurant. So, as usual, I snuck off to the beach, dropping in and catching airs until my watch yelled at me to get to work.

*

I walked through the back entrance of the restaurant to my locker, amidst the usual unabashed stares and 'Ola bonita!'s' from the kitchen staff. I felt myself tense up immediately like I always did, pushing my purse into the locker and exchanging it for my waitressing apron and notepad. I hadn't even made it to the hostess stand before I passed a new girl having a meltdown into her cell phone and a manager begging me to stay on later that night because apparently, "two girls had showed up to work drunk and had to be sent home immediately", not to mention that we were "short staffed" and "particularly busy" – two phrases I had come to hate. Sadly, I was used to it. Even at barely twenty-one, I was the veteran of the place and as usual, had to take up the slack and do the work of two.

Not much longer, I told myself, thinking of the competition and envisioning walking away with the $25,000 purse.

If I had only known the next few hours would change my life as I knew it.

We were knee-deep into the 'rush'. It was a small restaurant, one where you were pretty much responsible for everything – meaning no bussers and no food-runners. No support staff. I had eleven-teen tables and could barely prioritize what needed to be done next. The line cooks were yelling out, "pick-up!" at a frantic rate and the manager was busy watering tables and putting out plates of bread. I stopped for a minute and rubbed my eyes, before slapping my forehead as I remembered the lady's tea at table eleven.

I ran through the service area, ignoring the calls of "miss!" from the grumpy old men at the bar, waving their empty coffee cups at me. I grabbed a pot of hot water, turned around, and ran back past them, dodging more waitresses and "pick-up!"'s. I was half-way past the salad bar when all of a sudden I slipped. My hand jumped reflexively, and I felt a couple of scalding hot drops of water slosh off the rim and onto my leg, burning me.

I cried out in pain, bumbling forward and crashing down on my knees. The pot of water shattered, sending glass and hot water everywhere, but by then I couldn't feel anything but the pain searing through my knees. The manager ran toward me, and even a couple of the grandpas ducked behind the bar to check on me. But I was embarrassed, and more importantly, busy. Thankfully, there was no blood, and I was able to reassure the bystanders that I was fine. I got up, limping around to clean up the mess.

But an hour later, the manager finally made me stop working and tried to get me to go to the hospital. "I'm fine," I said, "I just need to go home." The pain was excruciating.

Since I really couldn't walk, Pop picked me up, bombarding me with questions as he too tried to convince me to go to the hospital. But I just wanted to down some painkillers and go to bed, assuring him that we could go in the morning if I felt worse. But all I could think about was the Open, less than two days away by that point.

That night, I cried for the first time in a really long time.

It turned out I was in bad shape. There would be no competition, no more surfing (until further notice, I was told) and no more waitressing (though that I was happy about). Pop's unfinished surfboards gathered dust, and my dreams shattered the moment my kneecaps did.

Two-and a half years, five knee surgeries and countless days, weeks and months of grueling physical therapy later, my prognosis remained bleak and the hope of a full recovery diminished by the day.

Worst of all, I still couldn't surf. And I didn't know if I ever would again.

Chapter 1: Monotony's A Bitch

It was just another Wednesday afternoon at Scarpulli's Flooring Systems and I had once again run out of stuff to do. I sifted through online internet quizzes, from "What Nintendo Character Are You?" to "What Country Do You Belong In?" to take me away from the brown, fabric-covered walls and boring emails that intermittently popped up in my inbox. Ninety-nine percent of the time they had absolutely nothing to do with me, anyway.

I was storming through the quizzes, answering manipulatively so as to get the responses I wanted to receive when a faint whoosh graced the otherwise silent lobby. I double-clicked the envelope icon, my finger habitually moving to the delete button when I stopped, just short of trashing it.

Images of huge, crystal-clear barrels, blinking lights and bright, colorful banners inviting me to click their links, filled the screen. This time, the email wasn't from Scarpulli's - it was from Surfline, one of the many surf-related websites I used to subscribe to - and thought I'd unsubscribed from.

LIVE FOOTAGE: 16TH ANNUAL J-BAY-

"Samantha?" a dull voice said, piercing the silence. I jumped, my finger instinctively hitting the cursor trained on the 'X' in the corner of the computer screen. But I knew it was my boss before I even turned around. I took a deep breath and, with all the sweetness I could muster, said "Yes, Maria?" as I swiveled around.

There she stood: stick-straight, regarding me with a glare through cheap drug store eyeglasses. "How are those quarterly reports coming along that I asked you to input this morning?" she asked, her arms folded across her chest.

"Oh, yes, those reports. I'll have them ready for you in just a few moments," I replied, painting a bored look on my face.

Truth was, I had completely forgotten.

She glared at me, and I knew that she knew I was lying. "Could you follow me, please?"

I sighed, grabbed the crutches that were leaning against the desk and pulled myself out of the chair. Maria was already halfway to her office and I hurried to catch up. I could feel the Engineering Assistant's scrutinizing my every move as I followed her. Their hawk-like eyes caught everything, and they were at attention, ready to jump on their keyboards in the event of even the faintest whisper of gossip. Seeing me beckoned into the boss's office would be big news, and the first person to report it would be the days' hero, saving them all from another afternoon of monotony.

Sitting at one of her guest chairs was Martin the Controller, the overseer of all operations. He was both rail-thin with thinning hair (an unfortunate combination), and he had a sallow face, with this chin that sort of morphed into neck. He was unattractive on all levels, a waif of a man both in looks and demeanor. While Maria could command a room with one look, Martin was impish, a mumbler, with his eyes constantly downcast. Though both had a title and a big paycheck, Martin was about as disarming as a kitten. Looks and manner aside, Martin's presence in the meeting meant that I was definitely in deep shit about something.

"Please sit, Samantha," Maria said, motioning toward the open chair next to Martin. She sat down, deliberately moving her water glass and keyboard aside to create more space to lean on the desk.

"This is just a coaching today," she began. "But we feel there are a few problems we need to address here. First of all, your tardiness is getting out of hand. I know your commute is far, but we all have to deal with traffic. This is Los Angeles, after all, and your problem," she jabbed her finger at me, "Not mine," she gestured towards herself, "Not Martin's," she waved towards Martin, "or Scarpulli's Flooring Systems." She grandly motioned above her, circumnavigating around her point. "Period."

I stared at her, so distracted by the motioning that I couldn't focus on what she was saying (not that I would have even if I could), and tried to think of any reason why she would be waving her hands around so much.

"....There are too many personal emails coming and going, and you are not being paid to socialize. I'm sure it can get boring at times," she suppressed a little smile, "but you are a receptionist, and maintaining the reception area is your main priority. Third...."

I sunk lower in my chair, wishing I was anywhere else in the world.

".... do we make ourselves clear? The next time we have this meeting you will no longer have a job." She folded her hands together and raised her heavily penciled eyebrows.

"Yes, ma'am. I understand. Won't happen again." I responded robotically, imparting the words I knew she was dying to hear.

*

I returned to my desk, willing myself to focus on one of the mindless tasks I could occupy myself with for the remainder of the afternoon. I didn't have to wait long; just as I sat down, one of the ubiquitous Engineering Assistants passed and dropped a thick stack of envelopes into my inbox, not even bothering to look at up as she passed. I looked at the clock: they would need to be sealed and sent off before the 3:00 mail pick-up. I picked up the stack and was just about to start sealing them when Maria's loathsome face came to mind. Remembering the email from Surfline, I realized that a world where my dreams were shattered was better than a world where dreams didn't exist. Screw these people and their rules, I thought, chucking the stack back into the inbox.

*

I heard the click-clack of heels and grabbed an envelope from the inbox just as Maria appeared.

"Samantha," she said, feigning disinterest. "It seems the plant service workers are on strike, so I'm going to need you to go around the office and water all of the plants before you leave today. Maybe you could prune them a little as you do so? God knows when the strike will end. Thanks." She gave me a little wave and turned on her heels.

"Bitch," I muttered, when she was out of earshot.

"I'm sorry?" she asked, whipping around.

How could she hear that!? "Switch," I said, quickly. "I was just talking to myself about switching the phone over."

She held my gaze for a moment, but I turned around and busied myself with the phone. Once she was gone, I sighed with relief, putting my head in my hands.

I should have gone to college.

*

An hour and a half later, I hobbled up to my old Saturn. I threw my crutches into the backseat, took off my shoes and pantyhose, and stripped down to my tank top and skirt to make myself as comfortable as possible for the long drive home. Between the lack of air conditioning, smog and standstill L.A. traffic, it made the moderate June heat feel like I was driving through Death Valley.

I pulled out of the underground garage, rolled down my window and lit a cigarette, hating myself as I did every time I lit up. A piece of paper from the passenger seat flew into my face as the hot wind soared through the open window. I pulled it off and discarded it onto the passenger seat, about to avert my eyes back to the road when a paragraph toward the bottom of the page caught my attention: "Families, gather your pails and shovels and come out for the annual Grunion Run! Contests! Prizes! Fun for the whole family!"

The Grunion Run? I thought, the event I had looked forward to every June for most of my young life coming to mind. I remembered digging my hands into the sand and feeling the slippery fish squirm between my fingers, laughing and screaming when the cold, salty water got just a little too close, and begging Pop to stay out 'just a little bit longer'. The event wouldn't have been anything special to an outsider, but for us HB locals - especially Pop and I - it was a tradition. Even as I grew older, Pop and I continued to go down to the beach every June to watch the Grunion take their improbable ride at high-tide to spawn on the beach at night.

It also reminded me that I hadn't called my dad in a few days. I picked up the phone and dialed the familiar numbers. The phone rang once, twice, three times. By the sixth ring, I was about to hang up when he finally answered.

"Yello?" he called into the receiver. I smiled at the familiar greeting.

"Hey, Pop. How's it going?" I asked, exhaling smoke as I spoke.

"Sammy! Hi, honey. What are you doing? It's hard to hear you. You're not driving without your headset on, are you?" I could hear the frown in his voice.

"Sorry. Hang on." I held the cigarette in one hand as I searched my passenger seat for the crappy ear buds and plugged them into my ears, my knees the primary means of operating the steering wheel. After nearly veering into oncoming traffic, I threw the cigarette out of the window and grabbed the wheel.

Straightening out the vehicle, I asked, "Do you know what tomorrow is?"

"It's not your birthday is it?" he pretended to guess.

I laughed, missing our goofy rapport. "It's the Grunion Run, Pop!"

"Ah, it's that time of the year again, is it?" An unfamiliar tone of weariness seemed to slip into his tone but I brushed it aside.

"Yep, sure is," I blurted on, pretending I didn't hear it. "What time should we head down?" Even though we only lived a few streets apart, it seemed like we rarely saw one another anymore. He had submerged himself almost obsessively into his surfboard shaping, preferring to spend time alone rather than in the company of others, and I…well, I didn't know what my excuse was. But it didn't matter – it was the Grunion Run we were talking about. We just didn't miss something like that.

"Hm," he mused. "I don't know, sweetheart. I'm getting a little old for stuff like that. You're not a kid anymore. It just isn't as much fun for me."

"Pop, I haven't been a kid for years, and we always go." I heard myself pleading.

"Go where?" he asked, sounding strangely confused.

I cleared my throat awkwardly. I wasn't sure why I needed to repeat myself, so I let it go. "How about I call you tomorrow on my lunch?" He agreed, and we hung up.

I wondered if he was depressed again. Pop had never really recovered from my mother's car crash and sudden death when I was a baby. He and my mother had been the love of each other's lives. They were everything that encompasses first love and when she died, something in Pop did, too. While raising me had been a necessary distraction, once I grew older and Pop's responsibilities had waned, his spirit seemed to follow suit. For me and those closest to him, it had become harder and harder to be his cheerleader. I rarely saw any of Pop's surf buddies anymore - though it probably didn't help that he never answered his phone and stayed holed up in the garage, constantly.

No matter how long it had been, no matter how much time passed, she was always there: like a sooty footprint you couldn't quite remove, her presence seemed to supersede death.

*

Two hours later, I pulled up to ECM Physical Therapy, late, sweating and cursing my reflection as I glanced in the mirror. When I arrived at the receptionist desk, Cara was already calling the back office for Brian, my physical therapist.

"Dr. McVogle? Ms. Dane is here for her five o'clock appointment." She hung up the phone and looked me over. "Long drive today, Ms. Dane?"

"Call me Sam, Cara," I said, for the umpteenth time. I was the same age as most of the staff at ECM; I found it disconcerting when they called me by my last name.

I took a seat and picked up a tattered copy of Car and Driver magazine, flipping impatiently through the pages. Ten minutes later, Brian called my name. I tossed the magazine, delightedly.

PT with Brian was my favorite part of the week. From his athletic build – short and muscular, but not stubby or un-proportioned- to his contagious laugh – he laughed at anything, a goofy high-pitched sound, that made me grin every time I heard it - he would have been my dream guy had he not been married. But most importantly, he was a good doctor. He wanted full reports, considered every ache and pain I commented on, offering insight or an anecdote every time. He had this way of making you feel like you were his most important patient, like nothing else mattered until he finished working with you.

I grabbed my crutches and rose from my seat. "Hi, Brian,"

"Why are you still using those crutches?" he asked, ignoring my greeting.

I avoided his gaze, cursing myself for forgetting to leave them in the car. "Cause," I said, lamely.

He didn't say a word, just gave me that look that seemed to say, 'I'm not mad, I'm disappointed'.

I immediately became defensive. "My knees still hurt too much when I walk, Brian," I argued, sounding like I was twelve again.

"That's because you aren't walking without the crutches enough." He softened his tone. "Come on back, let's talk."

Once I was lying on the exam table, he began his usual line of questioning. "On a scale of one to ten, where would you say your pain level is?"

I squinted, trying to look serious as I pondered his question. "A six, maybe?"

He raised his eyebrow, knowing I was exaggerating. I honestly didn't know why I lied, and for the second time that day I regretted the lie once it came out.

Thankfully, he didn't press it. "Okay, lie on your back. Let's check the swelling."

I lay back obediently, hoping that it would be one of the days I only had to receive a sports massage and use the Tens Machine, a device used to encourage muscle stimulation. I just wasn't up for hard labor- though that wasn't much different from any other day. Somewhere along the way, I had lost my vigor to get better: every time I got pumped up, thinking it would be the final surgery, the final recovery, the final round of PT, the doctor would find something else wrong and the next thing I knew I was checking in for another pre-op appointment. By that point, I was recovering from the third surgery on my left knee (my fifth between the two collectively) and supposedly it was to be my final go-around. But I knew not to get my hopes up. After two-and-a-half years, the routine had become as familiar as brushing my teeth.

He examined my knee, gently pushing the kneecap this way and that to check its flexibility and to test my pain limits. He scooted his stool to a drawer and removed a jar. "It's pretty swollen, and that scar tissue needs some work. I'm going to do a massage today but you're going to have to get on the elliptical."

I started to protest, but Brian wasn't having it. "Not today, Sam."

We were both silent as he slathered my knee with cream, the nasty, orthopedic odor making my nose crinkle. He was deep in thought, slowly pushing swollen knee-meat in circles while I held on to the table for dear life, trying not to scream. The pain was nearly unbearable.

"When do you see your doctor again, Samantha?" he asked, after a few minutes.

"Next week," I squeaked.

"And that will be your first month's check-up?"

I barely nodded my head, keeping my teeth tightly clenched. He dug deeply into my thigh, making me jump with pain. "Ouch!" I said, wincing.

He didn't seem to care about my reactions. After another long silence, he stopped and wiped his hands on a towel. "I think we have our work cut out for us, Sam. You've got quite an uphill battle ahead. Your journey is going to be much more arduous than the others."

I opened my mouth to speak, but thought twice and shut it again.

"We'll keep working at that scar tissue over the next few sessions." He stood up. "Let's get you started."

I followed him out of the room and to the Elliptical machine. He adjusted various buttons and dials before I stepped on it, rolling backward as he instructed me to do. It was less painful than I expected, but I was incredibly weak.

He watched me for a minute then asked, "How does it feel?"

"I'm fine."

He started to walk away, but then came back over. "I want you off those crutches, immediately." I shot him a defiant look, but he held his ground. "I mean it, Samantha. You should have stopped weeks ago, and in finding out that you're still using them it's evident to me why we're not making the progress we should be."

I flushed. He wasn't usually so harsh.

"Maybe water therapy would work a little better for you," he said, thoughtfully.

I stopped rolling and stared at him, appalled at the suggestion. Water therapy was for old people or worse, people with severe disabilities. I wasn't in such bad shape that I needed water therapy.

Or was I? Had my lackadaisical approach to recovery really set me back so far?

*

I made the last turn home and felt the familiar sense of calm as I caught sight of the ocean. It was a beautiful day, and for a couple of minutes I sat in my parked car just taking it all in.

I didn't live in the greatest complex ever - it was old and needed a lot of upgrades, but it was home. It was also cheap, or as cheap as living by the beach could get. The thing I had always loved about Huntington Beach was that it wasn't pretentious or snobby, like neighboring Newport Beach or Corona Del Mar. Like the other beachside communities, it had its multi-million dollar homes but for the most part it was just working class people who enjoyed the sea and the lifestyle that accompanied it.

My thoughts lingered on the water as I trudged up the ancient granite stairs. What I wouldn't give to go surfing right then. To feel the cold salt-water wash over my face, to hear the sand crunch beneath my feet, to feel my eyes tear up as the cold wind whipped around my face and through my hair.

If I couldn't be in the water, I needed to at least be right next to it - being a block away still wasn't close enough. I panted as I hit the fifth stair, feeling fatigued already. Brian's words immediately sprung to mind, and I begrudgingly admitted to myself that he was right. I wasn't making progress. It was time I took things a little more seriously, so I pushed harder and climbed faster until the staircase shook in warning but I just tightened my grip on the rusted metal railing and prayed that it wasn't the day the whole thing decided to fall apart. I reached the last stair, staggered into my house and collapsed on the couch.

I was quitting smoking, effective immediately.

I sat in silence for a couple seconds, not even hearing the sound of my roommate Dixon's TV which was usually a constant. He must have still been sleeping - he worked nights as a deejay and was oftentimes wasn't awake until it was dark. .

"Knock, knock."

I looked up and saw my next-door neighbor and good friend, Crystal. It wasn't uncommon for her or her roommate, Rachel to stop by unannounced. When you lived in such close proximity there was no hiding from one another - if I'd wanted privacy, I moved into the wrong place.

"Ciggie?" She held up a pack of Camel Lights.

I'd lived in the complex for three years. I had been injured for the last two and a half. And I had been smoking for two years and five months. It was one of the things I hated the most about myself, something I completely regretted picking up. Again, I thought of Brian's words and shook my head no. No time like the present to turn things around.

She lit a cigarette and sat down on the adjoining couch. No sooner had she moved the ashtray near her than a loud banging came from outside the door and Rachel appeared, a lit cigarette between her lips and three beers in her hands.

"Guess what?" she mumbled, ash depositing on the carpet as she placed the beers in front of us.

I frowned. "Watch the carpet, will ya?"

She cocked one expertly waxed eyebrow. "Since when do you care about the carpet?"

She was right, I normally didn't care. The place was a dump, and I wasn't getting a deposit back. But that day, it just wasn't about the carpet; it was her complete and constant disregard that irked me. I crinkled my eyebrows and said, "It's gross. I mean, we walk around here barefoot."

She plopped down next to me, pointedly flicked her cigarette over the ashtray and settled back into the couch, placing her foot on the coffee table. "An-y-ways, as I was saying, I was just at the market buying cigs and guess what? I saw a flier taped to the counter and it said there's a contest coming up next week. I'm sure you already knew that, Sam, but you know what this means, ladies..." she paused, taking a long drag off of her cigarette.

In fact, I didn't know there was a competition coming up. Remembering the Grunion Run, I thought of the date. I realized she could only be referring to the Tim Howard Leukemia Foundation Open. One of the biggest – and most personal – surf competitions held in HB. I had totally forgotten, and it bothered me even more hearing it from Rachel.

"The season has arrived, ladies!" she concluded, chinking our beers and bringing me out of my thoughts.

The cigarettes, beers in the daytime, and now, reminder of my former employer's annual surf competition - something I used to not only help work, but had competed in – combined with my latest prognosis from Brian and strange conversation with Pop, set something off in me. I felt inexplicably angry, embittered. Once the happiest person I knew, I had come to a place where I loathed my life.

"Well, thanks for the update." I said, standing up. I went into my room and changed, coming out a few minutes later in yoga pants and a sweatshirt. "I'm going to the beach."

"How?" Rachel asked, exchanging a look with Crystal.

"I'm going to walk there, Rach." I controlled my voice, trying not to sound snappy.

"But you're not ready for that yet. Look, you still have the straight-leg-thingy on."

My moodiness simmered a bit with her concern, but I knew it wouldn't last. I needed some 'me time': I needed to decompress, alone.

"Look, I just really want the exercise," I said wearily.

They looked at one another again but didn't say anything. I knew I had lost them. Rachel's figure came from diets and starvation, Crystal's from Jack Daniels and cigarettes. They weren't healthy, and they didn't understand my obsession with the ocean.

Not many people did, really.

*

Walking without the crutches was a lot harder than I thought it would be. I couldn't put much pressure on the bad knee, and the strong one tired quickly from the extra effort it was making. By the time I made the one block walk to Pacific Coast Highway, waited for traffic to clear, limped through the crosswalk and finally descended the stairs, I just plopped down on the last stair from the bottom. But by that point, I didn't care where I was sitting. I was there, where I needed to be. Dusk was settling over the ocean, faint shades of pink, purple and orange taking over the clear blue sky. It was a tonic like no other, the California sunset. I immediately felt my woes dissipate as I snuggled deeper into my sweatshirt.

I observed the last remaining people on the beach. Two wetsuit-clad figures were running across the sand toward the water. A couple strolled hand-in-hand in the surf. A family with ruddy faces that matched their colorful bathing suits packed up the remnants of their beach supplies. As the sun continued its steady decline, I thought about how much I missed surfing.

Surfing had always consumed my life. Aside from Rachel and Crystal, nearly every person I knew surfed: from my family - Pop and my Uncle Chuck, who lived on the North Shore in Hawaii- to my closest friends from high school, who were gone traveling and surfing, as I had intended to do. Ever since Pop had taken me out for my first lesson at five-years-old, being a surfer had been all I ever wanted to be. As a kid, I attended surf camp each summer; when I grew older, I became a Junior Lifeguard, honing my speed and discipline as a swimmer, knowing even then the mental toughness required to be a good surfer; I grew up poring religiously over surf magazines, idolizing the greats like Sunny Garcia, Kelly Slater and Tom Carroll. I was even on the coveted HBHS surf team, a program that very few high schools offered and even fewer women were a part of.

I had grown up wanting to compete professionally, to be one of the leading ladies in the water like Malia Jones, Lisa Anderson and Lane Beachley. I ditched morning classes with the guys in favor of surfing. After high school, I didn't waste my time with college. I had no interest in school.

I took the waitress job as a means to make ends meet. Success started to slowly come through low-level heats, and I earned minimal anonymity in my community. It even began to look like I just might have a shot at gaining some pro-surfing experience, with the possibility of being able to subsidize my travels through surfing – my dream come true.

In hindsight, sticking around had been a mistake. I should have followed everyone else's suit and took off right after high school. I could have worked odd jobs as I traveled the globe – teaching surf lessons in France, bartending in Bali, maybe leading yoga classes on the beach in Costa Rica, as I progressed from amateur to pro. I trailed my fingers through the sand, picturing myself on the beach in Tamarindo. How different my life could have been.

And then the injury came. I had done as I was told and sued the restaurant I worked for. But it could take years for the lawsuit to go to trial – after two that had already passed, I wasn't sure I had the patience to wait much longer.

I thought of Pop and the pain that surrounded him that he clutched on to like a security blanket, something to comfort him on the journey he elected to travel alone. I was beginning to understand that the more he had closed up, the more I had given up. I had not only pushed him away, unable to bear the sadness of the both of us, but I had also given up on myself and my dream to be a Surfer.

Right then and there, I made a vow that I would surf again - for me and for Pop. It had been a source of life for the both of us. No matter what it took, I would get there again.

Chapter 2: Chicken-Fried Friends

Despite my trip down to the beach I still wasn't in the mood for my usual hump-day, trip to the grocery store, chicken and veg dinner, cup-of-tea, and bed at eight-thirty, garden variety culmination to a Wednesday. I pulled my cell phone out of my pocket and called Rachel and Crystal's house phone.

"How about going out for dinner?" I asked, when Rachel answered.

*

We drove to the social hub of the city, Main Street, situated a little more than ten blocks from the duplex we lived in. Having lived in HB my whole life, I was surprised to see how quiet it was, especially for a summers' night. We selected a restaurant just far enough away from the tourist trap, but found that even there wasn't much activity – not even any locals. The lone waiter sitting up front rolling silverware let us pick where to sit, and we selected a table by the window.

After we looked over the menu, I asked Rachel, "How's production going on the new film? It's an Indie, right?"

Rachel was a Professional Extra. She got paid for her acting gigs – usually a paltry sum – and she managed to get film work, nearly full time. I wouldn't have quite called her an actress, but she hadn't stooped to porn-star lows, either. She remained somewhere in between. None of it mattered, however, because she was happy - and following her dream. A satisfactory-glow passed over her face as she went into detail about her small part in the film. And though it made me happy to see her so happy, I couldn't help the tinge of jealousy I felt. The only time I ever wore that glow, felt that kind of breathless anticipation she had as she described an upcoming scene, was when I returned from a really good surf session.

I listened and tried to stay attentive as she talked, but between the comfort of the cushy booth and the warm glow of the overhead lamp, I grew drowsy. My eyes drifted out the window and I lazily played with a strand of hair, twisting it around and around my finger as my eyes thickly opened and shut.

I watched as two guys approached the restaurant and seemed to consider it, conversing with one another. I leaned forward to get a better look – and suddenly I was wide-awake.

Both were tall, lean and tanned with shaved heads. As they got closer, I scrutinized the taller of the two - there was something about him that seemed familiar, yet I couldn't think of anywhere I knew him from.

"I'm thinking of getting rid of my old dresser," Crystal said. Rachel responded with something, but I didn't hear it.

"Mine," I whispered, quickly.

"Didn't know you had any interest in it. I was just going to throw it away," Crystal said.

"No- what? What are you talking about? The guys at the door," I said, pointing impatiently.

They looked over, barely taking a second before Rachel shook her head and said, "They're your type, Sam, not ours," and resumed their conversation.

I watched the two walk in. They talked with the host, turning around at one point and looking our way. The tall guy stared back at me, and I busied myself with the nearest item - a sugar caddy – picking out a Splenda packet and studying it, pretending to be engrossed in the nutrition information.

Thankfully, the waiter arrived and placed our plates in front of us. I picked up my fork and steak knife, ready to start cutting into my dinner when a deep, gravelly male voice from over the waiter's shoulder said, "Excuse me."

We all looked up.

"What is that you're eating?" he asked, in an accented voice.

I swallowed, my mouth pathetically dry. "Um, it's chicken-fried steak."

He furrowed his brow. "A wha'? A chicken-fried steak? How can a chicken be a steak?"

I tried to think of an answer but I couldn't even remember what kind of meat was used. Why was it called chicken-fried steak, I wondered. I had been eating them so long I had never actually stopped to think about it before.

"Sam?" Rachel's sharp tone shattered my thoughts, making me realize that I was dumbly looking down at my steak.

And then it came to me. "It's steak, cube steak." I cut a square out of the side and asked, "Would you like a bite?"

He stared at it for a moment, considering it. Gravy dripped onto my hand, so I mopped the bite into the gravy once more and thrust it in his face, rambling, "You gotta have lots of gravy, otherwise you just get a fried piece of meat. My GamGam says the thicker the gravy the better, and I would trust her knowledge; she's from Texas - she would know."

Finally, he shrugged and accepted the protruded fork. The three of us - no five, including his friend and the bewildered server – waited and watched as he chewed. His expression was thoughtful.

"That's fucking excellent. I completely agree about the gravy."

He waved and continued walking, and the three of us were left looking at one another.

"Did you just tell a hot guy what your GamGam thinks about gravy? Wow," Rachel said, shaking her head as she turned back to her salad.

*

As we finished dinner I kept my ears trained on the conversation going on between the two guys. I became more intrigued with the gravelly voice of my chicken-fried-friend, and when they mentioned getting a drink at an Irish pub, I begged the girls to go with me. At first Rachel refused, saying how she was already embarrassed to be out, 'looking as she did', but I'm convinced she just didn't want to have to walk home.

There were only two pubs on Main Street, the closest of them being the livelier, more popular one, so we went there first. I kept my eyes glued on the door, ordering and sipping my beer as slow as possible, knowing it could take only one chance to miss them. After thirty minutes though, they didn't show. Rachel was getting grumpy and Crystal less stoned, but I pleaded for thirty more minutes of their time. "Can we just try the other one, please? Then we can go home."

"What has gotten into you, Sam? I've never seen you like this before," Crystal commented, readjusting her dreadlocked ponytail.

I didn't know what had gotten into me. I led the way out – and we found the crowd at the second pub was lethargic and sleepy, the bartender looking as though he hadn't moved in hours. I scanned the room, disappointed when I didn't see the two but I remained hopeful, ordered a drink and followed the girls out to the patio.

I was antsy as we chatted, my eyes darting between the interior of the pub and the street beside the patio, where a deep fog was starting to settle. Finally, my patience paid off when out of the mist the two appeared, looking as though they had showered and changed.

I knew they couldn't see us, so I stared at the familiar-looking one, trying to place where I knew him from because by then, I knew that I knew him from somewhere. He was tan in the way that only hours of daily sun could bring. Muscles revealed themselves beneath his shirt. When the other guy pointed at something to the left of them, he laughed, and a hearty, rumbling sound echoed in the night.

I lost sight of them when they entered the building. Rachel poked me in the shoulder, bringing my attention back to the table. "Sam, can you leave work early tomorrow?"

"Uh, probably not. I'm living in shitsville at work." A fluttery feeling filled my stomach, but rather than think about my responsibilities, I stood up. "Anyone want another beer?"

I walked to the bar and gave the bartender my order, pretending to be engrossed in my phone as he filled my order. I was too embarrassed to look up, feeling as though I was in high school again, wanting the guy's attention yet not wanting it to be obvious at the same time.

"Hello." A tan, muscled arm rested next to my own.

My heart started pounding. Butterflies batted wildly against the walls of my stomach and I felt encased in cold sweat. I looked out at the patio where I had left Rachel and Crystal, who had gotten up and were moving toward the bathroom, giving me thumbs-ups and silent cheers. This is what I had wanted, right? The bartender came back and set my drinks down, and my hand shook as I handed him my debit card.

"I've got those, mate. And another for me, please." The bartender nodded and picked up another pint glass.

"Thank you," I said, forcing myself to turn and face him.

"No problem. It's the least I could do. After all, you shared your dinner with me."

I tried to sound calm amidst my nerves. "What did you end up getting?"

"The chicken thing you suggested. It's fucking massive, isn't it?" He took a sip of his beer. "But, I still can't wrap me head around why it's called a chicken steak."

I couldn't help laughing. "Chicken-fried steak."

"Ah, yes, chicken-fried steak," he repeated. Holding out his hand, he said, "I'm Emmett."

I shook it. "Samantha. But everyone calls me Sam."

"Sam," he repeated, in his adorable sexy accent.

I cleared my throat, the butterflies resuming their flurry in my stomach. "Are you visiting us here in HB?" I asked, playing with a cocktail straw on the beer mat.

"Yeah, for a bit anyway."

Before I could ask what "a bit" meant, a glass shattered and we both looked around, searching for the source. Within seconds, Crystal was running out of the bathroom to the bar. "My friend cut herself," she said, to the bartender.

Abandoning the beers and leaving Emmett standing at the bar, I rushed after her. Rachel was kneeling on the floor, clearly in pain, her hand and arm bloody.

The bartender wrapped her finger with a wad of paper towels tightly, holding it to stem the blood flow. After a couple of seconds, he pulled it away and examined it. "You're going to need stitches, love. What happened?"

"The glass fell," Rachel said, her voice wobbling. "I tried to grab it."

"Is she okay, Sam?" Emmett called from outside the door.

"Hang on." I yelled back. "I can drive," I said, and Crystal helped Rachel up. I led the way out off the door where Emmett stood waiting.

"We're taking her to the hospital." I said, walking and talking at the same time.

"Do you need help?" He hurried to keep up with me.

"I don't think so. Sorry, but I gotta run, Emmett."

I hurried after the girls, thinking how cruel it was that I had to leave on a moment's notice. Just as I reached the door, Emmett's voice called out one last time.

"Can you meet me here, tomorrow night, at this time?"

I yelled a response over my shoulder, hoping he heard it as I rushed out of the door.

*

The hospital was packed, and there was a long wait before Rachel's name was called. A little boy ran around the room, yelling "zoom!" as he knocked magazines off of tables, with barely as much as an intermittent, "Zachary," from his tired-looking parents. He approached me with a taunting smile, threatening to swipe the magazines off the table next to me. I pulled them into my lap, leaned toward him and said just loudly enough for him to hear, "Don't fuck with me, you little shit," and just for good measure, gave him the finger. His face crumpled into a frown, and he ran back to his parents.

There wasn't much else to do but listen to an ancient video that played over and over stressing the importance of exercise. My thoughts started to drift, and I let myself think of the stranger from Australia I had just met. I thought of his full laugh, his crinkly eyes, and more superficially, those muscles...and, that accent. I played the conversation over in my head, thinking of how boring and plain I'd probably looked and sounded to him, nothing compared to the gorgeous and exotic Australian women he normally interacted with.

When the girls finally came out, Rachel's face was puffy from crying, her entire hand impossibly swaddled in a heavy dressing; Crystal still had her arm draped protectively around her shoulder. I rose and followed them toward the exit, making sure to turn my head and stick my tongue out at Zachary before wrapping my arm around Rachel's other shoulder, obligatorily.

I waited until we were in the car before I asked, "So?"

Rachel didn't seem to want to talk so Crystal answered for her. "She cut it pretty deep, right in the palm of her hand. About five stitches, right, Rach?"

Rachel shook her head. "Six."

I glanced at the clock. It was nearly two a.m. "Shit," I groaned. "Tomorrow is going to suck."

Once we were home, I quickly said good night to the girls and headed straight for my bed, not even caring enough to brush my teeth or change my clothes. I turned on the TV, pulled back the covers and crawled into bed - knee brace and all. My eyelids closed almost instantly.

*

I opened my eyes to glorious, uninterrupted, sunshine flowing through my bedroom windows. I stretched, feeling achy, remembering that I had fallen asleep with my knee brace on.

I suddenly bolted upright. There wasn't supposed to be a sun when I woke up. I grabbed my cell phone.

The battery was dead. Furiously, I plugged it in and jumped out of bed, landing right on my bad knee. "Shit!" I cried aloud, pain coursing through my leg. I pulled clothes from their hangers, my toothbrush, make-up bag and cell phone, and flew out of the front door, just to realize halfway down the stairs that I had left my keys in the house.

Traffic was horrendous. I kept asking myself over and over, what I was thinking taking a job in Beverly Hills when I lived in Huntington Beach. I called and left a message for Maria, making up an excuse about an accident and the freeway being closed but by the time I got to work, it was eight-thirty. I was an hour late.

She was sitting at my desk when I pushed through the doors. "I'm sorry, Maria. I…I…" I stopped. It was useless. Maria didn't listen to excuses.

She didn't say a word. Her scary eyebrows, risen higher than ever, said it all.

I knew that I was screwed.

The phone rang and I tried grabbing it first, fearing it would be Rachel who usually called around that time. But Maria was too fast for me.

"Good morning, Scarpulli's Flooring Systems."

Don't be Rachel. Don't be Rachel. Don't be Rachel.

"I'm sorry, ma'am, but she's a little tied up at the moment. May I take a message and have her call you back?" She looked over her shoulder at me, an evil smile plastered on her face. Her eyebrows, I noticed, had receded all the way into her hairline.

*

"Hello, Miss Samantha," trilled Eduardo, our DHL deliveryman as he sashshayed through the doors. Eduardo was the only reason I think I came to work, or at least seeing him was the only I thing I looked forward to at Scarpulli's, and he didn't even work there.

"Eduardo," I said quietly, disregarding his greeting and hastily motioning him toward me. "I think I'm going to get fired."

"Honey, you is so drama king. They is not going to fire you," he said, scoffing at me. He pulled out a pink pen with a fluffy pig on top and held out a clipboard for me to sign.

"I'm serious, Eduardo," I said, scribbling my signature. "Promise me you will go apply for that job at Sephora. You've been talking about it for months now, and I'm not going to be here to encourage you anymore."

"Oh, Sweetie, you know my brover would kill me if I left DHL so quick after he got me the job. Plus, the money is gud." He ripped off a receipt and handed it to me.

"But you are far too pretty for this job. And just look at those hangnails." I pointed at his fingers. (Honestly, I couldn't see a thing, but sure enough, he blushed).

"Stop it! How can you tell?" he examined his fingers closely while he muttered in Spanish. "Ay dios mio." Feeling my eyes on him, he quickly crossed his arms and hid his hands as he perched on the side of my desk. "Sweetie, what are you going to do?"

"I don't know," I said. I decided not to think about it until it actually happened and changed the subject, telling him about Emmett.

"What! No! Who is he?" Eduardo's hands flew up to his cheeks as he squealed with delight.

The sound of someone clearing their throat and the click-clack of high heels on hardwood floors interrupted us. Eduardo nearly dropped his clipboard as he slipped off my desk. He took one look at Maria and scurried out of the office.

"Samantha, could you follow me, please?" For the second time in two days, she motioned for me to follow her.

I felt panicky as we walked down the hall. What was I going to do if I was fired? My present state clearly didn't help in the job-hunting jungle.

"I have to grab something from my desk. You can meet me in the boardroom," she said, gesturing down the hall.

Upon reaching the boardroom, I realized my worst fears were confirmed. Three people sat at the table waiting to wipe their hands clean of me so that they could get on with their day: Martin, of course, and sitting opposite him, Cheryl, from Human Resources, her sausage-like fingers gripping her pen tightly, but the last person caught me by surprise; Nancy, vice president of the company and co-owner of Scarpulli's Flooring Systems. I had absolutely no fucking clue why she was there.

I walked in and timidly took the chair nearest the door. If they were talking before I came in, they had stopped when I arrived. I looked at Nancy and searched her face for some sign of recognition, but if she did, she didn't express it.

"Hello, sorry to keep everyone waiting," Maria called as she waltzed in. She carried a stack of papers under her arms and a smile upon her face. I couldn't believe it. She was actually enjoying it.

"Well, Samantha, I assume you know why you are here." She pressed her fingers together and formed a triangle with her two hands.

"Not really." I didn't want to give her any more satisfaction than she was already getting.

"You are being terminated, effective immediately," she said, launching right in. "We have taken the liberty of paying you through the end of the week." She handed me an envelope. "Rather generously, I might add." She looked at Nancy.

"I don't think we need to list the reasons for your termination. However, you have an official copy of your termination letter inside that envelope, as well."

It was like the motioning thing from the previous day. She kept saying "termination" slowly and deliberately, enunciating the syllables.

What a fucking idiot, I thought.

Nancy spoke up. "It is unfortunate that we have to do this. You realize though, this is a business."

I studied her face. She looked so tired. There were deep lines and dark circles under her eyes and her usually immaculate hair was flat and drab. Something was definitely up.

Maria took over again, cheerfully instructing me to pack my belongings and turn in my keys. It seemed the dourer the mood in the room got, the happier she became.

"Good luck, dear." Nancy said, as she passed my chair on the way out. She patted my shoulder lightly, and I felt the strongest urge to cry. But I would not cry in front of Maria, the Cruella DeVille of flooring systems.

I went back to my desk and numbly packed the few items I had kept there. Seeing the plant on the desk made me think of Maria's insouciant request not even twenty-four hours earlier, and a wide smile spread on my face. I knew there was one last thing I had to do.

Luckily, it was lunch and no one seemed to be around. I noted that Maria was still in the boardroom and darted to her office. I pulled out her desk chair, removed the plant from the pot and tipped the remnants of soil and watery sludge onto the course brown fabric. The stinky aroma infected the air immediately. I grabbed the gaudy little bear sitting on her desk and used it to brush the roots and potting soil onto the floor, shoved the chair under the desk and ran back to the box at my desk

I fixed a somber look onto my face and watched as Maria entered her office. I waited for a couple of seconds and upon hearing nothing out of the ordinary, I picked up my keys and the plant once more.

"Maria?" I said, standing in the doorway, fixing a somber look on my face.

"Yes, just leave the keys on your old desk." she said tersely, not bothering to look up.

I lingered, waiting for her to look up. Registering the plant in my hand, she said, "That plant belongs to Scarpulli's, Samantha," the familiar, condescending tone returning to her voice.

"I know. I just wanted to give it to you personally."

She raised one eyebrow, her patience clearly thinning. "Okay, you can leave it and your keys with me, as you absolutely seem to need to do."

Finally, she jumped up. "What the-" she said sharply, wiping at her flat, pancake-butt. I didn't wait another second- I pulled the plant out of the pot and threw it at the wall with all of my might. It smashed and separated immediately, sending soil everywhere and most impressively, onto her face.

She finally lost her composure and started toward me, bellowing for Martin "to remove the lunatic!" I turned and ran out as best as I could, wishing only that I could have stuck around long enough to hear everyone's reaction.

Chapter 3: Ear for the Ramblings

Though I had wanted to throw the plant at Maria's face, I couldn't have an assault arrest on my record, so I called Eduardo and merrily replayed the whole bit, including her dispatching poor old Martin, of all people, to stop me. But as soon as I hung up the phone it hit me that I no longer had a job. After my exit, combined with my injuries (and no college education), a lot of jobs would be immediately ruled out. The truth was, I could have used – okay, needed - the recommendation from Scarpulli's. I was left not knowing which direction in which to proceed.

As I drove on, deep in my thoughts, the pack of cigarettes in the passenger seat beckoned me. I gripped the steering wheel hard and pushed back into my seat. I am stronger than this. Then, traffic slowed. I looked at the speedometer. My speed approached 35, then 25. 15. 5. Stop. I waited. C'mon, traffic. My eyes moved from the speedometer to the thermostat. Slowly, as I feared, it started to rise.

Finally, we moved. I drove for a few minutes with speeds of around fifteen miles-per-hour. But the temperature wouldn't budge on the thermostat, and then smoke started to rise from the engine. I cursed aloud and changed lanes as quick as I could, turning on my heater to try and lower the engine temperature. I knew I would have to exit the freeway, and in one of the worst places possible for a girl like me: Watts.

I crept along, picturing rap videos and movies of drive-bys and gang-bangers lining their chain-linked lawns, pit-bulls in tow, ready to murder me. I clutched the steering wheel, trying to concentrate on clearing my head. A light turned red. I waited, pumping my foot impatiently, my head turning left to right in a state of sheer paranoia. The cigarettes beckoned once more. Finally, I succumbed.

Taking a smoke out, I stuck it between my teeth and bit down lightly, holding it in place while I searched for a lighter. The sweet, unlit tobacco tickled my senses and I hated the need I felt for it. I wanted to inhale that smoke, feel the first drag make me dizzy the way it always did after a few hours of not smoking.

The first puff made me dizzy, as expected. The light changed, and I dangled the cigarette out of the window. My mouth tasted like I had licked the inside of a dirty ash-tray. I took another drag, watching the traffic and the speedometer. I cruised at a steady speed of 40 mph for a full minute. Slowly, the thermostat lowered. And so did my mood.

I didn't want the cigarette. I didn't need it. So I threw it out the window. It felt good to make the right decision for once (even if I was littering). On impulse, I took the pack of cigarettes from the passenger seat and chucked them out of the window as well, followed by the lighter.

Immediately, someone honked at me. Nothing ever went unnoticed in LA.

*

Something had hit me as I drove home, and I realized there was only one thing I wanted to do right then. I parked my car and ascended the stairs, feeling strangely stronger and healthier. I changed into a bathing suit and shorts, grabbed a towel and some sunscreen and headed down to the garage to grab a board and a wetsuit.

I was going surfing.

Only problem was, there wasn't a board to be found. I had to think about where they could be. I hadn't used them in over two years, and it took me a minute to remember that I had taken them over to Pop's one Fourth of July to make room in the garage to actually use the garage for a car. I tried to think of any other place where I could get a board: there were trophy boards upstairs, but I wasn't going to put those in the water. Crystal and Rachel didn't surf and no one else would be home at that hour.

If I wanted to surf, there was only one place to get a board.

*

I parked my car in front of the place I had called home all of my life. The location - only a block's walk from the beach - was prime for us, as surfers. When I was young, Pop used to sneak out of the house and down to the beach for sunrise surf sessions while

I slept. As we both got older, it was I who snuck out for sunrise surf sessions, while Pop slept. It was ironic how things changed.

I walked up the steps, taking in our steel-blue, one-story bungalow. I looked fondly at the giant weeping willow that stood in the center of the yard, underneath which I had spent countless hours, as I knocked at the door.

"Pop?" I called. "Are you in there?" I waited to hear some sign of life: music, the dishwasher or Pop's parrot, Bertie. Almost instantly I was greeted by the familiar squawk, followed by, "Pop-Pop!"

"Hi, Bertie," I said to the bird.

Bertie had an impressive vocabulary and was nearly as old as I was. If she were familiar with the last word you said, she would squawk and repeat it. Although I wasn't particularly fond of birds, I was thankful for her presence in the home since I had moved out. She was good company for Pop, who oftentimes talked aloud. To my dead mom. I called it, 'ear for the ramblings.' He would say something like, "Wish you were here, Helen." or "She got an A, Helen!" Bertie, of course would squawk and say, "Hel-en!" Completely creepy.

Hearing no response from inside the house, I headed around back to the garage.

As I passed the old lemon tree, I heard the distinct music of Dick Dale. The "King of the Surf Guitar," was as much a part of my childhood as the beach itself. I smiled, remembering when Pop and I would jam on our miniature ukuleles, he pretending to drop into a tube, imitating the old surf videos and movies. Dick Dale was fine, good even, for him to listen to, it was just when he started listening to the slower songs that I needed to worry. That usually meant he would become depressed.

"Hey, Pop!" I yelled, finding him standing over a surfboard with a blow dryer, melting the old, hardened wax.

"Sammy!" He put down the blow dryer and turned down the music. "I wasn't expecting you!" He walked over, his arms outstretched. As he put his arms around me, I realized how much I missed him. I hugged him tightly.

He walked back to the stereo and switched it to a slower, quieter tune, "Esperanza." It was one of his favorites, one I knew reminded him of Mom. Before I could say anything, however, he went into Dad mode, asking "What are you doing home from work?"

I hesitated. Pop had enough to worry about. The last thing he needed was to be worrying about me. But I was tired of the lies. I wanted to start over again. Sitting down in the familiar large wicker armchair, I told him about my morning.

"And now," I finished, "I'm going for a surf."

I waited, expected some form of disapproval or warning, but it didn't come. Instead, he looked at me blankly and asked, "Why are you home so early from work?"

"I just told you." I squinted my eyes, studying him.

"Oh, yeah, sorry," he mumbled.

"Are you okay, Pop?"

He shrugged and continued scraping old wax off of the board.

"I think it'd be great if you got out of the house. Come watch the Grunion Run with me tonight. Please," I found myself begging again, adopting a tone from my childhood.

"I don't think so, honey."

I felt stung from his rejection and we were silent for what felt like minutes. I watched him gaze intently at a peeling picture on the refrigerator, the edges brown and yellow, like a fading bruise. The picture was of him and my mom on the beach in Dana Point. Both of them had long hair, and he had a surfboard propped under his arm. They were laughing at something, their mouths so big and wide you would think they could never ever experience pain, not with so much shared happiness between the two of them.

"I miss your mother so much," he said, softly.

"I know you do, Pop." As his words resonated, I felt his sadness. I didn't know this kind of love. I had never even experienced the fringes of a love like theirs. I also didn't know pain like his either, an eternal price he seemed to pay. I did the only thing I knew to do, and walked over and put my arms around him as he had done with me so many times before. I felt his body rock as he cried into my shoulder.

"Pop, should you be listening to this song?" I asked, gently.

Just as suddenly as he started to cry, he wordlessly wiped his face and stepped away from me, ignoring my question. The tune changed, and the trademark guitar riff broke out. Pop walked over to the stereo and turned the sound up, picked up the blow dryer and resumed melting the wax, turning his back on me.

I knew it was my cue to leave.

I grabbed a board and tucked it under my arm, feeling worse than I had in weeks. I limped down the drive, turning the conversation over in my head, coming up with no answers and feeling so helpless. If I could have, I would have done anything to cure his pain.

*

It was nice not having anywhere to be, and as I continued my slow onward pace toward the beach, the fresh sea air did its job and I started to feel better. I felt like a tourist as I took it all in, walking slowly along the path, looking up at the flags swinging lazily off the sides of the beautiful houses. The breeze was cool and the sun was warm. Laughter floated down the path. An airplane flew overhead advertising sunscreen.

It was hard to stay bummed out. Even schlepping along on my bum knee couldn't bring me down. Suddenly, I had a thought: was Pop even getting out of the house? I couldn't remember the last time I'd send him outside of his abode. Perhaps he was lacking in Vitamin D, and sun and surf was the cure for his new distant demeanor.

Descending the stairs and crossing the sand was no easy feat, and I needed to rest by the time I arrived at the edge of the sand where it's partially wet and becomes smooth from the tide going in and out. I raked my fingers through the sand, thoughts swirling around in my head.

I was ready to get into the water. I tried to stand up but my legs shook, warning me to take it easy. So I listened to my body, feeling the sun, staring out at the sea. The thin, flat waves weren't perfect - but neither were my knees - so instead, I imagined myself in a different scenario: an empty line-up; perfectly curved 6-8 footers, ideal for my small frame to move about and shred with ease; clear, crystalline crests with a high spray; a cloudless sky. I imagined my arms lithe and strong, powerfully propelling my body forward.

The wind blew coldly, bringing me back to reality. I looked toward the horizon, seeing a line-up of small, black dots. Low tide was approaching and the waves were becoming smaller and gentler.

It was time to get in the water.

Again I stood, and again, my legs shook their warning. But this time, I ignored them. I shrugged on my wetsuit, stamped into the surf and put my board down. After much effort, I was able to lie down in position. I started paddling.

Just as I had done a gazillion and a half times before, I paddled and paddled, only this time I didn't seem to get anywhere. The decent looking waves were still very far out, and when I turned my head around the beach was much too close. I stopped for a second and went still, resting my head on the foam and fiberglass wonder, feeling the cold water slap at my face as my board spun with the surf.

Suddenly, the waves became rough, and the water no longer slapped my face so much as drowned it. I started moving my arms again, but too late: a wave passed over me and my board and I were thrust under water. I kicked and thrashed about wildly, trying to get back above water but the chord was wrapped around my leg. For the first time in my life, I panicked, swallowing what must have been a pint of seawater.

Coughing and spluttering, I surfaced, my face white-hot from fear. I looked around, searching for a squall or the outskirts of an impending storm, something to explain why the water conditions had suddenly changed – but I saw nothing but a distant sea-trekker making its way into the port of Long Beach.

Angrily, I climbed back up on my board. Normally, a change in condition and larger waves were a good thing. Now, I was freaking out over a little water up my nose? I refused to let it get the best of me. I lay down and paddled hard, feeling my knees ache as they pressed into the board. But I pressed on. I found a spot and waited. And waited. But the waves were gone.

Finally, I gave up. All of a sudden the ocean was foreign to me, and I felt like a tourist trying to speak Spanish in a Portuguese-speaking country. I gave up and paddled back to shore.

*

I was peeling off my wetsuit when I heard my name. I jumped, the voice rattling me. I looked up and saw in the distance the familiar-looking, tall guy from the night before, Emmett, holding a surfboard, his wetsuit hung low around his hips. His tan was an even deeper golden brown in the sunlight and his muscles undulated across his chest and shoulders. It was nearly impossible for me not to stare to him. I forced my eyes to his face and, feeling self-conscious of my own body, wrapped the towel tightly around my shoulders.

"Hi," I called, shivering in the wind.

"Fancy seeing you down here," he called back, starting to cross the sand toward me.

I was edgy from my surf experience, and my insecurity grew as he got closer. I hurried to shrug the wetsuit off my arms while keeping the towel firmly around my shoulders, a difficult task in the most normal of circumstances.

"The same to you," I said, clipping my words and hurrying as I tried to pull the wetsuit around my hip, one-handed.

"I'm staying at the hostel, just back up the road there." He flicked his thumb behind him.

I looked over his shoulder, unsure of where he was referring to. "The hostel?"

"You, know, right back there." He turned and pointed.

The wind blew wildly and the towel tore from my grasp. I limped after it, the wet arms of my wetsuit slapping at my sides. I snatched it up, covering my blindingly-white skin as quickly as possible, feeling the sand grate my skin as I wrapped the towel tightly around myself once more.

"Are you alright?" he asked, giving me a sidelong glance.

"I'm fine," I said curtly, bending painfully to grab my belongings while clutching the towel tightly. By this point, I had given up on removing the wetsuit. "So how did you recognize me?" I asked, idly making conversation, hoping to distract him from the unattractive disaster that was becoming our second encounter.

He shrugged. "You're pretty recognizable."

For the second time, I wasn't sure what his cryptic words meant, but I didn't care to press it. I finally had my clothes together and wanted to get out of there. I had never felt so ugly, out of place or out of shape in my life. Surfing had always taken care of everything: I never had to worry about my weight or even try stay in shape – it burned and toned everything. I was tan (at least my face), year round. And though I had sworn that my hair was naturally blonde all those years, it turned out it was just from the sun bleaching it.

I was so ashamed. How did two-and-a-half years pass before it took a guy to get me re-think my lifestyle?

"You need a hand?" he asked, an exasperated tone inflecting his speech.

"Um," I hesitated, looking down at my board, my hand tied up from holding my towel in place.

He sighed, picked up my board and we set off. Both of us were quiet as we moved along. The wind continued to blow icily and combined with my wet wetsuit clinging to me, I was freezing.

"How's your mate?" he asked, breaking the silence after a couple of minutes.

"Oh, she's fine. Got some stitches." I was afraid if I talked any more my teeth would start chattering.

He nodded. "Good on 'er."

We reached the stairs. "I'll take it from here," I said, turning to him.

He set the board down. I shivered again and I felt panicky. "Okay, thanks." I said, dragging my words out, hoping he would get the hint.

He did. He didn't say another word, just turned around and walked off. For a second, I wondered if I should say something about our 'date', but he seemed like a smart person. He probably got that I was just uncomfortable and cold.

"Thanks again," I called after him, as he took off jogging toward the beach. I watched his perfectly sculpted form move effortlessly across the beach, and I wondered if I would ever move with that kind of ease again.

*

"Sam."

"Sa-man-tha."

I awoke violently. Rachel was standing at the foot of my bed yelling over the sound of some blaring infomercial. I grabbed the remote control and turned the volume down.

"How do you sleep like this?" she asked, incredulously.

I sat up and looked around. It was completely dark. "What time is it?"

"8:30."

"Shit! Seriously?" I rubbed at my eyes, willing them awake. "How's your finger?" I got out of the bed, feeling every muscle ache as I moved.

"Fine. C'mon, let's go out." She started toward the door, and then stopped. "Did you still want to go watch the Grommet Run?"

"You mean the Grunion?" I shrugged. "I don't know."

"Well, wake up some and come over. We can figure it out from there."

My knees hurt pretty bad as I moved around, so I swallowed half of a Vicodin before taking a much-needed shower, noting how much more swollen my most recently surgically repaired knee looked. I iced it down before walking next door, where I found Rachel attempting to pour a bottle of Jack Daniel's with her heavily gauzed hand. "Let me," I said, taking the bottle from her.

She nodded and lit a cigarette, sighing loudly. Ever the dramatic one, I knew this was a hint. "What happened?"

"Production on the film has been halted."

I raised my eyebrows. "You just found this out? At nine o'clock at night?"

She sighed. "Hollywood doesn't sleep, Sam." She had me there.

Crystal appeared, her face mirroring Rachel's, and I wondered if it was something in the air. "What's up with you?" I inquired.

She sat down and also lit a cigarette "I lost my medical marijuana license."

I almost laughed out loud, but tried to appear sympathetic in spite of how ridiculous Crystal sounded. I looked at my watch. It was nearly time for the Grunion Run. With a slight pang, I realized I had never heard from Pop, though I knew I shouldn't have expected to – he didn't call anymore, anyway.

Dixon appeared looking as glum as the rest of us. Normally he holed up in his room, but this time he opted to go out with us, and the four of us boarded a cab bound for Main Street.

"Wow, its super packed tonight," Rachel said, as we spilled out of the taxi behind a long line of cars. "And it's barely even ten."

The fog was starting to settle once more, reminding me instantly of Emmett. I was due to meet him. I could still make it, I thought, biting my fingernails as I thought. But I felt ridiculous pining after him, and had come to the conclusion that he was just being chivalrous after seeing me in my kinetic, moody, unattractive state, earlier. It seemed like the type of guy he would be.

I put him out of my mind, because I figured I must be out of my own.

We ended up at a favorite spot of ours (without having to wait in line, thanks to Rachel's merciless flirting) and were at the bar in mere minutes, with drinks in hand. We all had the same agenda:

get drunk as quick as possible – and so we did, spending the first hour doing shots, as people trying to avoid their problems often do. It wasn't surprising that we quickly became blurry-eyed and tipsy. Dixon, Rachel and Crystal moved over to the dance floor, and injury or no injury, I wasn't much of a dancer, so I found and settled on a TV in the back that was showing surfing. I watched semi interestedly for a few minutes, thinking of Emmett when Bondi Beach flashed across the bottom of the screen. I allowed myself to wallow in self-pity for a minute, wishing more than ever that I could re-wind history.

Rachel came up and yelled in my ear, startling me. "Babe, where have you been?" She drunkenly threw her arm around my shoulder.

"I've been right here," I said, staring at the TV screen.

Suddenly, I became sweaty and stone cold sober. In slow motion, the glass slipped right out of my hand, shattering on impact. Rachel screamed and backed away from me. I just stood staring, my mouth open wide in astonishment.

No. Way.

A busboy ran over with a broom and dustpan to clear up the broken glass. "Hey," I said, tapping him on the shoulder. "Do you have TiVo?"

" 'Scuse me," he asked in broken English, looking at me perplexedly.

But I didn't need TiVo. At the bottom, a name flashed across the screen. "Emmett Taylor," I read aloud.

A broad-shouldered, blue-eyed man with a shaved head was coming out of the water laughing at something, his surfboard tucked under his arm. I knew that confident laughter. I had gazed at those enormous, muscled arms.

My shock wore off as I realized why he had looked so familiar to me. I wondered if I had seen him in a surf documentary, or maybe even passed him on the beach at one of the competitions.

I needed air. I needed to think.

I found Rachel and told her, "Going down to watch the Grunion Run." She acknowledged me with a wave of her giant gauzed hand. I crossed the bar and stepped out into the night, leaving the beer smells and loud music behind.

I didn't feel drunk but I had to give it to the alcohol – or maybe the Vicodin – because either way, I was in virtually no pain as I walked down the crowded sidewalk toward the pier. I found a spot to lean on and stared at the black sea.

I observed the people dotting the beach, buckets and shovels in hand as the children ran amuck, squealing when the water inched toward them. Nostalgia coursed through me (something that seemed to be trending lately) and again I thought of my own childhood, about Pop. Normally over-protective, he had always loosened up around the water. We would stay out late - it was often near midnight before the run was over. Those days seemed light years away from then.

I looked at my watch. It was nearly eleven. I was tired, exhausted, really. It was time to go home. I walked in the direction of the taxi bay, which just so happened to be situated next to the pub I had met Emmett at. But it was way past the time we had agreed to meet; he wouldn't still be around.

I waited for the next cab. Within seconds, I heard the unmistakable accent and groaned. Emmett was jogging toward me.

"You've got a lot of nerve, showing up this late."

"I'm not-" And then I realized he thought I was there for him. It was cold, and I didn't want to hash it out with him around so many people.

"Why don't we go inside?" I suggested, pointing toward the pub.

"I don't think that's necessary."

"Okay," I said. I tried a different tactic. "So you didn't you tell me you're a pro-surfer." I relayed how I had seen him on FuelTV.

His face twisted "Okay, so now you're interested, now that you saw me on tele? That's why you're here?"

"I'm not- what?" I said, his words registering.

"You were rude at the beach today. Blimey, you couldn't have gotten out of there any quicker. But now you want me?" He crossed his arms, nearly spitting the words out.

"I'm not here because of you! I'm here for a taxi!"

He just shook his head. "Look, let's just call it a day, alright?"

I was so confused. And mad. I didn't know what was happening. Before I could say anything else, he was already turning and walking away.

"Wait," I said, but he was already ten feet away. I felt embarrassed as tears pricked my eyes. I didn't know where they came from, but I kept my head down and turned away. I didn't want him to see my face.

Chapter 4: Ambiguity

I spent the night in a cold sweat, tossing and turning. Alcohol seeped from my pores, making me cold, then hot, then cold again. And if I had been sore from the afternoon's surf when I had woken earlier, it was nothing compared to the stiffness I felt when I intermittently woke; every muscle ached like it hadn't been used in years. Truth be told, they hadn't really. At daybreak I finally gave up on sleep and turned the TV on, making sure to avoid FuelTV and all surf programs in general.

The weather remained overcast throughout the morning, and I indulged my dark mood by not getting out of bed. However, by ten a.m., I was restless, so I got up and made myself walk to get some coffee. I was slow moving as usual, but it felt good to be up and about and alone with my thoughts. At the coffee shop, I took a table by the window and called Pop.

"Hello?" he answered, gruffly.

It took me by surprise that he didn't answer with his standard, 'Yello.' He was usually jovial and friendly, especially welcoming when he answered the one. I figured he was just in a bad mood, so in a soothing manner I said, "Hey, Pop. How are you today? I missed you at the Grunion Run last night."

"Who is this?" he asked, warily.

I frowned. "It's me, Sam."

"I don't know any Sam's," he responded, and the phone cut off abruptly.

What the hell? I dialed the number again, carefully this time, in case I had previously misdialed.

"Yello?"

"Pop, it's me Sammy, your daughter," I blurted quickly, before he could hang up again.

"Duh," he said, mimicking my favorite word from high school. "How are you, honey?"

I smiled. That was more like it. I had probably just dialed wrong before. "I'm good, Pop. Are you up for some breakfast?"

"Sure, that sounds fine," he said, sounding like his old self.

I told him where I was, and he agreed to meet me in twenty minutes. For some reason, though, I couldn't get rid of the nagging feeling in the pit of my stomach, like something was wrong.

*

As I watched Pop walk through the door, it struck me how thin he was. Once again, I felt guilty for not taking notice, sooner. I squeezed my eyes shut, thinking that all the lies and guilt were going to consume me if something didn't change, soon.

"Hi, Pop," I said, standing to give him a hug. .

"Hey, pumpkin. How are your knees doing?"

"Getting better. I walked here." I said, semi-proudly.

He started to respond, but the waitress arrived. He was predictable as ever, ordering eggs sunny side up, one piece each of bacon and sausage, hash browns (extra crispy) and white toast. I ordered a muffin and some coffee.

"Pop, why didn't you come out last night?" I started, picking out a Splenda packet from the caddy as the waitress set my coffee down. It made me think of Emmett, so I shoved it back inside and opted for black coffee instead. I took a sip and nearly choked on the bitterness.

"Oh, you know…. That's a bunch of malarkey," he responded, avoiding my eyes.

"Really?" His words hurt, more than I wanted them to.

He didn't look up. "Things change, Sam. I've got too much going on these days to sit around and reminisce about the past on some beach."

It felt like he had shot a bullet through my chest. "So you can't go to the beach anymore, yet you can sit around and reminisce about the past in that dungeon you call a house? That 'beach' " I fiercely said, throwing up air quotes. "Is your second home, remember?"

He spat. "I don't even like it. It's cold, and the sand stays stuck to your feet. And it gets everywhere."

Who was this guy, and what had he done with my Pop?

"Are you okay?" I asked. "No bullshitting, this is so unlike you. You love the beach."

"Not since I had to fight them kooks in the war, in 'Nam." He set his cup down, his face sneering in disgust.

"Pop, what are you talking about?" I was genuinely dumbstruck.

"Hmmpf," was his response.

None of it was adding up, and it scared me. "Pop," I said slowly, "I think you need to see a doctor. Are you sleeping enough?"

"Why would I go see a doctor?" he snorted. "All's they do is poke you and scare you, with their 'diagnoses' and 'tests.' "

"What about Dr. Ewing?" I suggested, referring to my mother's old colleague.

"That clown?" He snorted again. "You mean the one who always wanted to sleep with your mother? I've known it all along. He's not fooling anyone!" He was agitated, nearly shouting.

"Pop!" I exclaimed. He had never, ever talked or acted toward Dr. Ewing like that before.

He didn't say anything more, and we were both silent as our food arrived shortly thereafter. Pop's order was all wrong. His eggs were scrambled and he had cottage cheese on his plate - Pop hated cottage cheese.

"Excuse me, I think there is a mistake," I said to the waitress, trying to catch her before she walked off. If he was in this bad of a mood, something as simple as messing up his breakfast could send him flying off the handle. But Pop didn't say anything. He was already digging into the cottage cheese.

I numbly chewed on my English muffin, not even bothering to butter it.

*

As soon as I left the restaurant I called Dr. Ewing's office. But he wasn't in; I had forgotten that he no longer worked Friday's. I made a mental note to call first thing Monday morning, though something told me I wouldn't have to worry about forgetting.

The June Gloom coated Huntington Beach in a dark, thick blanket of clouds. Part of me wanted to go home and hide under the covers, but I also felt restless; I needed to do something. I tried to get an appointment with Darren for PT, then remembered that the reason I didn't already have one was because he too was out for the weekend.

I slowly walked home. I realized that something in me had been shifting over the last few days, and that I was beginning to resent every aspect of my life. I had accomplished absolutely nothing, professionally or personally, in the two and a half years since my injury, and had become content to be the guinea pig for my doctors, letting them perform surgery after surgery without so much as a second opinion. Why had I accepted their diagnosis that I would never surf again? Why did I let my life come to a screeching halt with that accident? Where was that fire, that vigor, that zest, that I could do anything, that absolutely nothing stood in my way? Where was that girl?

Most importantly, where had my dreams gone?

Lost in my thoughts, I missed the turn to my apartment and was now several streets away. When I looked up, I saw a strange, unnamed building I had never noticed before. After a couple moments observation, I realized it was the hostel Emmett was staying at.

I wasn't angry at Emmett - even though he was kind of jerk the night before. If I had been in his position, I would have been mad at me, too. I hid myself from view and watched the entrance to see if maybe he would come out, then maybe I could explain myself, but the only person who seemed to be around was a tall, lanky guy with glasses who sat on the porch swing reading a book. After a couple more minutes, I approached him.

"Sorry to bother you," I said. "But do you know of a couple Australian guys who are staying here?"

"Zer are several Australian's staying here," he said, not bothering to look up.

"Ok, well, do you know Emmett Taylor?"

He ignored me, just turned the page of his stupid book.

"Do you know how to find out if someone is staying here?" I asked, changing tactics.

"You can ask ze front desk. Zer is someone working here who can help you with that," he said, still not looking up.

I felt like taking his book and throwing it into the bushes. Maybe then I'd have his attention. Instead, I said nicely, if not slightly sarcastically, "Thanks," and turned around to walk back down the stairs.

"Ze code is hash, nine. Just go in, zey can help you. I dun't know anyvon here."

"Hash nine. Okay, thanks." I moved toward the keypad and stared at it, trying to find the hash key he was referring to, but all I saw was a simple keypad. I pushed buttons, pretending like I knew what I was doing, when all I wanted to do was turn around and ask for his help once more. But judging from his demeanor, he had really gone out of his way to help me once, and I didn't think he would be willing to help me again. Thankfully, someone came out and I hurried inside before it shut.

I had been expecting a dirty, threadbare, frat-like atmosphere but the room was surprisingly welcoming. There were two large white wicker chairs with bright blue cushions facing out from either side of the bay windows. In the middle was a giant, widescreen TV, the projector type with the three colored lights at the front illuminating the screen. There were also a couple of comfy looking gingham couches and a big, antique coffee table scattered with various magazines.

I approached the desk to the left of the room. A young-looking guy was sitting behind it, laughing with a girl who stood to his side. I fixed a bright smile on my face and said, "Hi, I just have a quick question - I have a friend who is staying here, his name is Emmett, Emmett Taylor, and well, I'm not sure how to get in contact with him."

The guy asked in a thick Irish accent, "What does he look like, love?"

"He's tall, and muscular- with a brown shaved head. Oh, and he's Australian."

They both looked at me and started laughing. The girl said, "Darling, there are quite a lot of Ozzie's that come and go through here that match that exact description. You say your bloke's called Emmett?"

"Yes, Emmett. Emmett Taylor."

She flipped through the book and shook her head. "I don't see that name, but maybe the reso's under something different. You can leave him a message, if you fancy doing so."

The guy gave me a pen and paper and I scribbled my information out, adding:

Emmett, I'm sorry for yesterday. I would

*be grateful for the opportunity to explain exactly
what happened, if you could give me five minutes of
your time.
Sam*

*

I couldn't explain why, but suddenly, I was dying to hear from Emmett. The day passed from morning, to afternoon, to night, like any other day. With every second that passed I felt my chances of hearing from Emmett diminishing. I made up excuses in my head for him, than berated myself for thinking so desperately. It wasn't my best day ever.

I needed someone to talk to, but I didn't want to talk to Crystal or Rachel. The only other person I could think of that I could entrust to listen without judging was the mom of my best friend, Shane, who was off traveling the globe surfing.

The Baxter's knew me inside and out. They were Pop's neighbors and second parents to me. Like Pop, they were very open, youthful almost, and when Heidi answered I could hear loud music blaring in the background. She also sounded like she was a glass of Chardonnay deep, too, an added bonus when you needed someone to talk to.

I locked up the house and set off on foot, noting that Crystal and Rachel's house was also dark. The air was chilly once again, fall-like. But all of the walking I had been doing seemed to be paying off and helping with my recovery.

Though Pop's house was modest, many of the homes in downtown HB were anything but, and Heidi and Frank's home was no exception. It was something you might see in Architectural Digest: sprawling staircases, Viking kitchen fixtures, high ceilings, and expensive art. Shane's parents, though not pretentious, were quite wealthy, and when it came to their home money was no object. Looking back, it seemed as though the Baxter home had been under construction for 20 years, as there had always been a drop cloth, table saw or paint roller lying around, somewhere.

I knocked on the door and Matty immediately went to work barking. Heidi shushed the dog and called out, "Come in, Sam!"

"Down, Matty," I said as I walked in, fearful she might jump up and re-injure something. I patted her head obligingly and she answered me with a lick.

As I expected, the grand living room was lined with painter's tape. Heidi appeared with a bottle of wine in both hands. "Red or white?" she asked, holding each aloft.

"Um…Red. It's kind of chilly out." I followed her to the kitchen bar. "More work?"

She started uncorking the wine. "Yes, we decided to put in a fireplace. We've been entertaining more these days and the room just felt so cold and uninviting." She shivered, as if to help prove her point.

It made me a little sad to think that the room would be changing. I thought of all the years Shane and I had spent in the formal living room. Growing up, Heidi and Frank had never used it so we had made it our own, whether it be just for throwing our backpacks down in or practicing a speech for debate class. Like everything else in my life, it was one more thing changing.

I looked around the gorgeous kitchen as she opened the wine. It was my favorite room in the house; the gathering place of the home. Though it too had recently been updated, the enormous, barstool-lined island I now sat at in the center has remained a constant, the place where so many scenes of my life had been captured: snack time in elementary school, homework in high school, or just a place to sit and talk, as in the present.

Handing me a glass of wine, Heidi put her arm around my shoulder and squeezed me. "How are you feeling, honey?"

I don't know where it came from and I didn't expect to, but I immediately started crying. I hid my face in my hands, embarrassed and ashamed. She rubbed my shoulder sympathetically and said, "You've been through a lot. It's okay to cry."

I swiped my eyes with my sweatshirt, and took a deep breath and a sip of wine to calm myself.

"Do you want to talk about it?" she gently asked.

I caught her up to speed on everything; my job, injury and Emmett, ending with Pop. By then, Frank had also joined us. He quietly took a beer from the fridge and listened as I finished spilling my guts.

"I've noticed a difference in him, too," he commented. "He's definitely been more reclusive, and I don't think I've seen in him in the water in months."

I cocked my head. I had no idea Pop wasn't surfing. I knew he spent a lot of time alone, but not surfing to him was like not breathing for someone else. Once again, I wondered if that was the problem: that not getting into the water was making him-stir crazy, or just plain crazy for that matter. It offered a reason for the mood-swings and forgetfulness, and it could also explain why he was so thin – surfing puts on a lot of muscle.

We were still talking about Pop when the laptop on the counter made a weird sound. Being technically challenged (and still using the same monstrous computer I had owned since high school), I didn't pay much attention to it. But Heidi and Frank immediately crowded around it and Heidi motioned to me excitedly. "Sam, come over here."

I approached the computer and was astonished to see Shane smiling widely back at me. My hands flew to my mouth.

"Ohmygod, Shane," I said, reverting to my giddy high-school self at the sight of him.

"Welcome to Skype, Sam." I finally realized what he had been talking about all along. He had asked me to download the program ages before but technology scared me, and truthfully, I hadn't known what a Skype was.

"Mom, Dad, Sam, hello from Bali."

"Indonesia," I said, softly. Shane was in Indonesia. It seemed surreal that he could be talking to us, face to face, when he was thousands of miles away.

We got caught up for a couple of minutes before Shane looked over his shoulder. "I'm glad I have you all together." He motioned behind himself. "I have someone important that I want the most important people in my life to meet."

A beautiful blonde girl appeared. "Hiya," she said, waving at us, a sheepish smile on her face.

"Hi," we said collectively, waving back.

"This is Mags," he pulled her onto his lap. "She's from London," he said, feigning a British accent.

She rolled her eyes. "Has he always been this rubbish at accents?"

"Yes," Heidi and Frank said in unison. I laughed awkwardly, suddenly feeling very uncomfortable, like I was intruding on a family moment – something I had never felt with the Baxter's before. I started shuffling about trying to think up an excuse to leave. Without thinking of anything, I just said, "Shane, I gotta run. Nice to meet you," I waved at the computer screen and ducked out of sight.

I stepped into the night and started walking quickly, avoiding the direction of Pop's house. I wasn't ready to go home, and for a split second I considered stalking the grounds of the hostel once more and waiting in the bushes until Emmett returned. I pictured myself leaping out of the dark at the sight of him, and shook my head, wondering what the heck had gotten in to me. Was this what Pop felt like? I was starting to scare my own self.

*

The next morning, I dejectedly ate breakfast at the dining room table, staring out the window into the grey sky, my thoughts returning to Shane and 'Mags.' I wasn't sure what the lingering discomfort was attributed to but I chalked it up to his happiness. It wasn't that I didn't want Shane to be happy, but he had always gotten what he wanted, and not just monetarily but also in sports and with grades. Even now, all these years later, it seemed the silver spoon Shane had been born with was still tucked comfortably in his mouth.

I tried watching TV, but it did nothing to jog my restless thoughts.

I kept staring at my phone, willing it to ring. By lunchtime, it felt like a ticking time bomb that may or may not blow up. He's not going to call, I kept trying to tell myself.

Finally, I got up and drove over to Pop's. The music was blaring as usual as I headed around to the garage, and it immediately irritated me. I ground my teeth, wondering if visiting Pop was a good idea in my foul mood.

When I stepped inside, I screamed in shock. Pop was sitting in the familiar wicker chair, stark naked, holding a pair of jeans.

"Pop!" I yelled, shielding my eyes. "What the hell?"

He didn't say anything or didn't even move. I grabbed the nearest towel. "Cover yourself up," I said, tossing it into his lap.

He still didn't move. Exasperatedly, I said, "Pop? What the fuck?" I never cursed in front of him. But it wasn't a question – it was a statement.

"I don't know what's going on." Pop looked down at himself and then at me. "I have no idea what's going on. I have no idea what's going on." He was starting to mumble incoherently. Ineffable fear took hold of me.

"Wh-what do you mean, you don't know?" I stumbled over the words, dreading and needing his answer at the same time.

"I don't know what's going on."

Not knowing what else to do, I ran next door and straight into Frank and Heidi's house. "Please" was all I could manage to say. They didn't hesitate, and the three of us hurried to the garage where Pop still hadn't moved. By then, I was having trouble breathing.

"Pop," I said, starting to cry, "What's wrong with you?"

Heidi and Frank exchanged a look and Frank approached him. "Darrell? Are you okay?"

He was still unmoving. "I don't know." Finally, he looked up. "I can't move- some things can't move."

"What do you mean?"

"They won't move. Where am I?" he stared up at Frank with great big eyes, looking like a child lost in a shopping mall.

"Heidi, call 911."

Chapter 5: Waiting...

The next few hours were a blur of ambulances, bright lights, complicated machines and questions. No one seemed to know what was going on, namely Pop, and I felt myself losing control of my emotions as time passed without answers. The doctors and nurses tried asking me questions about Pop and his medical history, but I didn't have the answers anyone wanted or needed. I felt so helpless.

I could hardly speak, so Heidi took control of alerting the family - all two of them, everyone else was dead. When GamGam arrived we held onto one another like it was the end of the world. I felt like a piñata at a birthday party: beaten, haggard and broken, the crying and fear already taken over my body. As for GamGam, I had never seen her look so bad. Her normally impeccable appearance was disheveled, her eyes were red-rimmed from crying and she was wearing her gardening clothes. She took my hand, led me over to a hard couch and said, "Now it's time to wait.

*

Sometime in the evening, after they had performed a battery of tests, a doctor finally came out and talked to us. Heidi and Frank stepped aside and gave us our privacy.

He introduced himself and said, "I'm sure you're anxious for some answers."

We nodded obligatorily.

"Mr. Dane has suffered a stroke," he said. "This would explain the memory loss, confusion and paralysis. Judging from the scans, I suspect there may have been a series of minor strokes leading up to the one earlier today. As strange as it may sound, they can occur without the patient's knowledge; unfortunately, a series of them can cause serious damage."

The doctor continued, going into greater detail. Finally, he looked at GamGam and said, "There is something else I need to ask, before I go." He shifted a bit. "You're his mother - is there a history of any dementing diseases in you or your husband's family?"

Her face went white. "I- I can't think of anything on his side, and I'm not aware of anything in my own family."

He nodded, scribbling on a clipboard. Finally, after another silence, he stood up. "Mr. Dane is coherent, but seems to have trouble remembering a lot. We don't want to jump to conclusions, but there are many questions we will continue to ask you - the people who know him best. But you may see him now." We stood, and he added, "You must remember that his body has been through a lot. Be gentle. And prepare yourself."

Neither of us spoke, both of us individually absorbing his words as we followed him through a maze of gleaming corridors. The air stank of disinfectant, and I made myself focus on the scent, hoping it would keep my head from going to dark places. It was already taking everything I had not to scream aloud.

When we saw Pop, he was unrecognizable in his white gown, lying still on the hospital bed. Gone were his standard issue Hawaiian shirts and contagious smile. Instead, there lay a pale, weak man I didn't recognize and instantly, my chest swelled. I felt like I had inhaled those nasty chemicals from the hallway and now I couldn't breathe. Great sobs came out and I rushed to his side crying, the unfathomable unfolding before my eyes. "I can't lose you, I love you too much," I said, my body convulsing.

He tried to move to hold me. It only made me cry harder. GamGam came over to the bed and steered me away, and I clutched on to her as though my life depended on it.

*

GamGam was going to sleep at Pop's, but I refused to leave his side. While I was exhausted and needed sleep, I wanted to be there in case anything else happened. I only left his side to call Rachel and Crystal, who had separately and together left me three messages, and Heidi and Frank, who had done more than their share of helping our family. And in spite of everything going on, I found myself disappointed when there was no message from Emmett. I hated myself a little bit for feeling like that.

Sleep eventually came, but it was broken. The nighttime hours passed without end. I would wake up every so often and check on Pop, relieved that he was breathing and sleeping. Then I would imagine myself doing anything and being anywhere else in the world and drift back to sleep, before the cycle would start all over again.

When I awoke in the morning it was daylight and GamGam had returned. I opened my eyes as she sat a cup of coffee down on the hospital table. This time she was dressed impeccably, her blondish-grey hair perfectly styled and make-up set. "Here baby," she said, holding out a couple of pills. "Take these."

I wondered how she knew my head hurt. As if in answer to my unspoken question she said, "I've been through this before, with your grandfather. Feels like a nasty hangover, doesn't it?"

I nodded, barely able to remember anything surrounding my grandfather's illness.

She sat down on Pop's hospital bed and took his hand. "I've been up thinkin' all night."

I nodded again. I felt shaky and unable to speak.

"Uncle Chuck's flyin' in," she reported in her Texan drawl. "He'll stay until we figure out what exactly is going on."

I smiled feebly, hoping it could express my gratitude for me.

In the afternoon, Pop was summoned for physical therapy, so GamGam and I took the opportunity to eat lunch outside of the hospital. When we returned, the nurses had a good status report for Pop: he had the use of his left hand and was able to feed himself; he knew who we were; he knew he was in the hospital. But he didn't know why he was there, and his whole right side was paralyzed - the doctor said that was common with his type of stroke – and he could barely hold onto a walker. He needed help using the restroom. I had a hard time celebrating the small victories when it seemed there was so much he couldn't do.

The tests continued. So did the questions. I told them everything I knew of Pop's daily life. By the end of the day, I was beyond exhausted, so I let GamGam persuade me to go home to sleep in my own bed that night. As I fell asleep, my thoughts drifted to Emmett, and though I felt guilty, I yielded. There was no fight left in me.

*

On the third day in the hospital, the lead doctor in charge of Pop's care finally had some news. He put some scans up against the neon board, and GamGam and I crowded around to survey them.

Pop didn't speak.

"This is an MRI scan of the brain. Here we have some areas where stroke damage has occurred," he pointed to a spot, and then another, both looking the same as every other area; grayish-green and brainy, for lack of a better word. "As I originally suspected, there have been a series of minor strokes that have led up to the eventual larger one, this time triggered from a brain hemorrhage. High blood pressure, one of the ailments affecting Mr. Dane, can cause a brain hemorrhage, which we suspect is the culprit in this case. It can also cause diabetes, heart attack and even death." He turned toward Pop. "We've been treating you with a blood pressure medication that you're responding well to. Do you understand me, Mr. Dane?"

"Yes," he said in a scratchy voice.

He turned back to us. "There is something else," he said, looking down at his papers. "We've discovered extensive damage to Mr. Dane's liver and kidneys. We've put him on a medication to counter the effects, though it will take some time for us to see how effective this medication is. I'm confident we're on the right path."

I pinched the area above the bridge of my nose, something I only did when I was extremely stressed. With resignation, I asked, "How long is he going to be like this?"

"It could be a few days, a couple of weeks or even months before his memory starts to return. In some cases, it never does. He's going to need a full Neuropsychological Evaluation, something that will be handled outside of the hospital." His beeper went off and he excused himself abruptly.

GamGam sighed, and took a seat on one side of Pop. I took the other. I sat facing him, watching as he fell back to sleep and tried to imagine my life without him. No more breakfasts. No more paddling out together. No more Dick Dale. No father to give me away, if or when I got married. I tried to imagine him in a nursing home. Torturing myself further, I tried to imagine attending his funeral.

I couldn't do it. Failure just wasn't an option.

*

By the end of the third day, I couldn't sit around in the hospital any longer. The first night I had stayed with him, I think I had been impervious to pain thanks to the adrenaline that had been coursing through me. The second day I think I had felt the pain, but it was like hurting yourself in a pool; you feel the injury initially, but the pain is delayed thanks to the drag of the water. But by the third day things had calmed down, and I became more acutely aware of my sore knees and aching back. It was time to start exercising again, and not just at PT. I drove to the gym, hitting the Elliptical for thirty-minutes of agony.

On the drive home, I thought of his prognosis, the "what ifs," the "how comes," the "why us? 's. As I drove, I wondered - had my mom still been around, would he have gotten sick? And if he had, would he have had access to better care, because of her? Perhaps she might have known a colleague who specialized in this field?

I thought once more of how selfish I had been. I really hadn't stopped to think of Pop – outside of how it affected me, anyway. I wondered if this was karma, and forced myself to step outside of myself and recognize my greater responsibilities – I owed it to Pop.

As the questions surrounding his illnesses deepened, I needed more than the grey answers the doctor was giving us. Though I wanted to sleep in my own bed, I thought of GamGam alone and decided to stay with her at Pop's. I stopped by my house, picked up a couple of icepacks and my portable tens machine (for the muscle stimulation), and spent the night on the computer looking up and researching what I could on strokes, depression and dementing diseases. Every word the doctor had used, I Google'd. I researched physicians. I looked at holistic health. The internet was a buffet, and I was insatiable.

*

I awoke early and crept quietly out of the house. It was still dark and the fog had returned, shrouding me as I walked the short blocks to my apartment. It was cleansing, and as I climbed the old staircase that led to my apartment the first rays of sunshine peeked on the horizon. It was so beautiful; I couldn't remember the last time I had slowed down enough to enjoy a sunrise. So instead of entering the apartment right away, I took a seat on the patio and watched the sun make its way across the sky.

Once inside, I plugged my dead cell phone in to charge while I showered and got dressed. I packed a backpack with the necessities and slipped quietly back out of the apartment. I didn't have a destination but breakfast seemed like a good idea, so I set out for Main Street. I remembered my dead cell phone and pressed the power button. After a couple of seconds, it alerted me of a message. Sighing, I knew I had to check it. These days it could mean anything.

There was only one message. I gasped when I heard the deep, gravelly voice.

"Sam, its Emmett. I just got your note here, been in Mexico all weekend. If you would like to give me a bell, you can reach me on-"

Abruptly, the phone cut off.

"No, no, no!" I said, frantically replaying the message.

But there was no more. The rest of it was gone.

My heart sank. I couldn't help the tear that ran down my cheek, but I swiped at it anyway, angrily.

Then the unthinkable happened. The phone actually rang, coming up with an unrecognizable number. I stopped walking and answered, keeping my eyes shut.

"Sam?"

"Yeah?" I held my breath.

"It's Emmett. Did I wake you?"

I breathed out. "No, I'm already awake."

"I wasn't sure you would be. Care to join me for a bit of brekky?"

There was no fight left in me. I couldn't play hard to get. "Breakfast would be great." I recommended a popular place and we agreed to meet in twenty minutes.

*

I got to the restaurant before him. My hand shook as I sipped the water I had been offered and I realized how nervous I was. I tried rolling my shoulders, tapping my foot, but nothing seemed to work and before I was ready, he was walking toward me, his face fixed with that grin I had missed the last time I saw him. It was contagious, and my own face turned upward with a smile.

"Morning," he said, taking a seat across from me, his long legs barely fitting under the plastic table.

"Morning," I responded, preparing myself to spout off the mini-speech I had quickly assembled.

"I owe you an apology," he said.

Surprised, I said, "You owe me an apology?"

"Yes, for how I treated you, just before I left."

I pictured him once again walking off into the night. "Can I ask what made you change your mind?"

He took a big gulp of water. "Your note. Took me by surprise."

I nodded, digesting his words.

"To be honest, I didn't come here to buggerize around and I defo didn't expect to meet someone. Things have been stressful enough back home- I simply wanted to get away and shred some waves. The plan had been to go straight to Mexico," he stopped, repositioned himself and started again. "But since we had to deplane in L.A. anyway, Kev and I thought we'd stay a couple of nights before continuing on to Mex. Then I met you, and you were just so bloody beautiful - especially when you were struggling with your wetsuit and all that."

He took another drink of water and continued. "Then you just sort of took off, and never mentioned meeting me, like I had asked. So I was cheesed off – and then you started going on about seeing me on tele. I was like, what the fuck? To be fair, I treated you a bit rough in return but back home you see a lot of sheila's mucking about who'll do anything for a little fame."

He stopped and laughed, seeing my confused face. "I'm speaking a bit too much Australian, I see. What I'm trying to say is when you surf competitively you get these fuckin' whores that will do anything. It sounds great, but it's-" he stopped, searching for a word. "Disheartening. I'm not like that."

It was my turn to raise an eyebrow.

"Anymore," he conceded. "When I first started ripping, sure."

"So you still haven't said why you came back." I tried to follow where it was all going.

"I'm getting there, don't get your knickers twisted. So, Kev and I left for Todos Santos the morning after I saw you last. When I got to the carpark and opened my board bag I realized I left one of my favorite boards here, at the hostel. I had to fly back out of L.A. anyway, so I extended my layover and drove down here to pick it up from the hostel - that's when I got your note." He shrugged. "I don't fly out until tonight, so I thought I would see about meeting you again."

He wrapped it all up so nicely. "So where's Kev?"

"He's moved on to the North Shore. I've got to get back home, to Oz."

I felt it was my turn to speak. "I also would like to apologize. Things have been a little crazy for me. As you can see, I'm injured, but before that I too was a surfer, and a pretty good one at that. So when I saw your face on FuelTV, I recognized it. My life has always been about surfing- my own, not someone else's. I'm not a groupie or one of your nancy's."

"Sheila's," he corrected.

I raised my hand in acknowledgement. "Sheila's. Anyway, the day after I met you I lost my job, which might help explain why I was acting sort of weird." I took a deep breath and continued. "But, most importantly, I have a very sick father right now. I don't know if it's right for me to be here or not," I paused, thinking of Pop and the years he had spent wallowing in my mother's memory. "But know that I can't consume myself with it, either."

He surprised me by reaching across the table and squeezing my hand. "I'm sorry about your da."

I felt overloaded and needed a change of subject. "So- you mentioned you're Australian- what else are you? Tell me about Emmett."

We talked about his home in Australia and I told him about growing up in Huntington Beach. We both had wanted to become professional surfers. We had grown up in similar towns with similar lifestyles, yet in opposite hemispheres. And only one of us had made our dream happen, thus far.

"Do you want to come out for a surf with me this arvo?" he asked, seeming to read my mind.

I rubbed my forehead, feeling stressed once again about Pop. "I don't' think I can. My sick father that I told you about – he's in the hospital. He had a stroke this weekend."

"Seriously? Babe, what are you doing here?" Seeing the look on my face, he amended his words. "I didn't mean it like that. But shit, you must be really upset."

"It's fine. I mean- he's getting better. I was coming for breakfast, anyway, before I return to the hospital. Which, speaking of…" I let my voice trail off.

"Can I walk you back?" he asked, tentatively.

"Yes." I gave him a reassuring smile.

We stood up and walked out and he surprised me again by taking my hand. It was large and warm, and my cold one felt tiny in his. "Do you mind?" he asked.

I smiled, liking that he asked. "Not at all."

"So, who's with your dad? Your mum?"

His words freaked me out. Should one of us – GamGam or myself - be staying with him all the time?

"Um, no, he's by himself. My mom- she's no longer with us."

He stopped. "God, I'm such an arsehole."

"No, no, you couldn't know." I wrapped my other hand around his, both of my small hands encasing his larger one. It felt very intimate – but also very natural.

We continued on in silence. After a couple of minutes, he spoke up. "I sort of know how you feel. I… I lost me own bro. Surf accident. I don't really talk about it, but I just wanted to let you know I can relate."

I cast him a sideways glance. He caught my eye, and we held each other's gaze. There was a moment that passed between us that felt deeper than the present, than just two near-strangers having a breakfast date. We walked along quietly, again. The fog had lifted and it looked like it was going to shape up to be a beautiful day. As I had feared at the breakfast table, I found myself not wanting my time with Emmett to end, and Pop's house appeared all too soon.

"Well, this is me." I said, motioning to the house.

He turned to face me. "What are you doing tonight? I mean, after you leave the hospital."

"Um…" I wasn't sure what the day entailed with Pop. "I'm really not sure."

He pushed a stray piece of hair behind my ear. "Have dinner with me."

I screwed up my face, thinking. "What time is your flight?"

He waved his hand. "I can post-pone it 'til tomorrow."

"I thought you said you had to get home?"

"One more day won't hurt."

I hesitated, unsure if it was such a good idea. We had shared a nice morning together, but I was dangerously emotional. More time with Emmett would make it that much harder to let him go.

"I can come to the hospital, you know, eat cafeteria food. You have to eat."

It didn't take much to break through my weak resolve. "Okay."

"Excellent." He smiled widely, and kissed my cheek. "How's about I call you later this arvo?"

"Okay," I said again.

He squeezed my hand one last time and walked back in the other direction. I watched him for a few seconds, then turned and climbed the steps to the house.

GamGam was sitting at the kitchen table drinking coffee. I dropped my backpack next to the refrigerator like I was fourteen again and said, "Good morning. I got up early and didn't want to wake you. Ready to go see Pop?"

Before she could answer, I saw a movement in the doorway and looked up.

"Uncle Chuck!" I ran over and hugged him tight, feeling grateful for his presence.

"Hey, kiddo."

We caught up for a couple of minutes and then left right for the hospital. It was starting to become a routine and I began to feel strangely comfortable in it.

Pop was awake when we arrived. He recognized Uncle Chuck immediately. Even more surprising, he was talking a lot. He stayed awake all morning and was even able to get out of bed and push his walker around some more. By the time he came back from his PT the therapists were raving about his progress. I didn't want to leave, but I had my own PT to attend to and I needed to phone H.S.S., the surf shop I had worked at in high school, about a job.

Once in the car, I dialed the familiar numbers. It took a little time to be transferred around but when my old boss, Greg, picked up the phone, I knew immediately that I was taking a step in the right direction.

"Sam!" he answered. "What a surprise! How are you?"

I brought him up to speed on everything. Embarrassed from my injury and unable to face the world I had been shut out from, I had stayed away from the shop since I got injured, so there was a lot to tell him. I told him about the extent of my injuries, getting fired (or, losing my job, as I called it), and about Pop, before ending with," Things are crazy, Greg, but I need a job."

"They made a mistake getting rid of you, but you don't belong in a flooring shop, anyway."

His words made me feel guilty, especially when I thought back on just how irresponsible I had been.

He continued. "We've actually got something opening up here in the offices, part-time, if you don't mind keeping up with the reception work. Pays better, too, but I can always keep you downstairs like you used to be, if you prefer."

I groaned inwardly, thinking of my challenges with Scarpulli's, but I was going to have to grow up someday. I told him yes, I'd love to, and he instructed me to come in on Wednesday to fill out some papers and to work out a schedule. I thanked him and hung up the phone.

I arrived at ECM for PT early. Brian came out right away and said, "I want to try some pool work with you. Do you have a bathing suit with you?"

He knew me too well. "Of course I do."

He smiled widely. "Then come on back."

I walked into ECM feeling fresher and more prepared than I think I ever had before. Brian noticed, too. "Look at you," he said, watching me as I walked down the hall toward the back of the clinic. "You're barely even limping."

I smiled, pleased he noticed my progress.

"Let's do a quick massage and then we'll get you in the water."

*

I felt butterflies as I changed into my bathing suit, the kind I felt back in high school before a tough water polo match. When I walked out, Brian was crouching by the side of the pool, a slew of Styrofoam weights and noodles at his side.

"Give me a quick lap across the pool," he instructed, once I was in the water.

I kicked off, feeling some minimal pain as my quadriceps muscles clenched, but that was normal. I continued kicking my legs and moving my arms, making my way across the breadth of the pool. Brian was waiting on the other side, holding a Styrofoam noodle with a smile.

"I'm going to give you a series of exercises I want you to do, using this. Three sets of ten, on each leg."

An hour and a half later, Brian was helping me out of the pool. I grabbed my towel and dried off. "Let's get you some ice and stem," he said, leading me back into the clinic.

Once I was hooked up to the wires and the ice packs were in place on my knees, I asked, "How do you think it went today?"

"Really well. I had a feeling you would respond well to water therapy. You're a fish," he said, fondly, "And your mindset has changed. Mental commitment is a huge part of recovery."

"Am I okay to do workouts on my own?" I asked, thinking of my time on the Elliptical the night before.

He nodded. I could tell he was surprised and impressed. I hadn't been excited about working out since right after the first surgery, when I still had hope. "Just stick to the basics- elliptical, biking, resistance bands. Don't over-do it."

While I was driving home, Emmett called as promised and we agreed to meet in front of Pop's house at 7:00. It was becoming something of a 'spot' for us, like the quad when you were in high school, or a coffee shop in college. After I steered my car onto Pacific Coast Highway, I opened up my sunroof and windows, turned the music up and sang along loudly, letting the cool ocean air and music infect me.

*

After I had climbed the stairs of my apartment, I could see, through her open window, Rachel laying on her couch in the dark. Until then, I didn't realize how much I missed her, even though it had only been a couple of days.

"Hi," I said, into the darkness.

She started, her hand flying to her chest. "You scared the bejesus out of me, Sam." She sat up as I walked in. "How are you doing?"

"Pretty good, considering," I said, plopping on the couch. "Pop's doing better and better. How about you? Still no work?

"Actually, production has resumed again. I just finished a sixteen-hour day on set," she said, lying back down.

"How's your finger?" I asked, wriggling my own.

"It's fine. Hey, did you hear from that guy?"

"Actually, I'm having dinner with him tonight." I said, slightly sheepishly, feeing weird saying it out loud like I was doing something wrong. "How's the film?" I asked, changing the subject. Is it everything you expected it to be?

She went into detail, and this time I listened attentively. It was important to keep the few people in my life close to me, as I was learning quickly how things can change in a snap.

When she finished, I said, "I'm so proud of you, babe. I know how much being in an independent film has meant to you. Who knows, maybe next time you'll be starring in one." I reached over and squeezed her hand.

She squeezed mine back. "Thanks. Pop will get better, and soon you'll be able to surf again," she said, sitting up and yawning.

I stood up. "Well, get some rest. I'll be coming and going a lot but I'm only a phone call away." I waved good-bye and walked over to my own apartment.

I was nervous as I showered and selected an outfit. Should I dress sexy? Conservative? I wasn't sure what the right choice was and went with a long, flowy sundress, figuring I could wear flip-flops and dress it down and bring a pair of heels if I needed to dress it up. I did my hair and make-up with much more care than usual, and when I stopped and surveyed myself I figured I actually looked kind of nice. It felt good to clean up and make an effort.

I had given myself extra time so that I could stop by the hospital before meeting Emmett. GamGam was knitting, and Uncle Chuck and Pop were snoozing. I smiled at GamGam, walking over to Pop's bedside and clasping his warm hand. I looked down at him, noting how much healthier he looked. It made me grateful for the simple things. A good family. A new job. My father's improving health. It was funny how it took a near-tragedy for you to cherish things.

"Has he been sleeping all day?" I asked.

She looked up. "No, he was awake all afternoon. He just fell back asleep," she set down her knitting. "My, you sure look beautiful, darlin'."

I looked away. "It's just dinner," I said, trying to downplay it.

"Don't apologize. Darrell's doing just fine. He would want you to go out and have some fun."

I didn't want to disturb his peaceful sleep, and disentangled my hand from his. But he woke up, surprising me by keeping my hand in place. I sat down on the side of his bed. "Hey there," I said.

"Sammy," he said, happily.

"Hi Daddy," I said, smiling widely at him.

He tried sitting up, but I patted him gently. "It's okay, Pop. Don't push yourself too much."

He nodded and smiled at me. "You look beautiful."

"Thanks." I kissed his cheek. "I'll be back first thing in the morning, okay?"

"I love you," he said, holding out his good arm for a hug.

"I love you, too," I said, relishing the moment, hugging him tightly.

Chapter 6: No Reason, Other Than the Obvious

Emmett stood waiting in front of Pop's house as planned, in jeans, a short-sleeved, button-down white shirt and Rainbow sandals, his ever-present smile fixed in place. "You look gorgeous," he said, embracing me.

"Thank you. You look great yourself," I said, noticing something on the ground next to his feet.

"I got you a gift," he said, picking up a small, shrub-like plant. "I didn't want to be just any other bloke and get you flowers, so I did a bit of research – all bloody day, to be fair - and found a place where I could get plants from Oz. This is a wattle plant. You see them all over the place back home – big with me landscapers. Nothing special, just something different."

"Wow." I was genuinely impressed. Not only did he think to get me a gift, he put thought into it and gave me something that would uniquely remind me of him. "Emmett, this is so thoughtful. I love plants. Thank you so much." I hugged him again.

I placed the plant in the backseat of my car and we set off on foot for Main Street. Once again, he took my hand.

"Hey, you mentioned something about landscapers, when you were giving me the plant. What's that about?" I asked.

"Ah. Me da's had a construction bizo for years. He likes to work with specific people, whether they be landscapers, plumbers or so on. When I'm not competing on the circuit I work with him."

"So, you build houses?"

"Mainly, yea."

There were so many things I wanted to know about him. "This might be a personal question, but why do you call your dad 'da'?"

He let go of my hand to let a family by on the tight sidewalk. Once they passed, he picked it back up again. "Kyle- that's me bro - had a bit of speech problem when he was a little bugger and couldn't say 'dada,' as I could, so he just said, 'da.' I guess it sort of took in our home, because we all call him that, even mum. They're both Pommie's, so we say things you won't hear other Ozzy's say."

"Pommies?" I questioned.

He laughed. "It means, 'Prisoner of Mother England.' That's what Ozzie's often call the ex-pats. They're British, by birth, anyway. Been in Oz for decades now, though."

I was intrigued. "And you were born in Australia?"

"Yea."

"I don't know a lot about Australia," I conceded. "Where do you live? I mean, in relation to like, Sydney?" I laughed. "Shamefully, I must say that's all I know about your geography."

"Sydney isn't far – maybe about a hundred kilometers away from me home. It's a lot like here, really. I live right on the coast, so it's beautiful weather, fantastic beaches and good surf pretty much year round. Actually, it's bloody amazing. I wouldn't live anywhere else in the world."

We arrived at Main Street just as the sun was setting, and agreed on a new sushi restaurant that looked relatively quiet. It was compact like most sushi restaurants, and even more so due to its touristy location. Thankfully though, it was Monday night, so we were able to get a cozy booth.

Emmett and I shared similar taste in foods, and over-ordered sushi rolls and sashimi. We drank beer and laughed as we compared our different cultures. I felt good with him, and comfortable in his presence. He was not only good-looking and easy-going, but we seemed to share so much in common, and he and I had grown up doing a lot of the same things - just on different continents. I ended up drinking more than I probably should have, but thought, screw it. Why not? When was the next time I would meet a guy as cool and fun as Emmett? I tried not to think of his leaving, longing to stay in the moment.

After dinner, feeling warm and happy thanks to my beer buzz, I invited him back to my place to have a glass of wine on my rooftop deck. I didn't want to say good-bye just yet.

The rooftop deck I shared with my neighbors wasn't anything special. Ugly pipes protruded out of the ground, and there was hardly enough room save for a few lawn chairs and an old bench. But what lacked in the dumpy complex was made up for by the location. The view was priceless - on a clear day you could see

Catalina Island, several miles off-shore, in the distance. If you were really lucky, the views swept from Long Beach in the north to Laguna Beach in the south, an expanse of at least twenty miles.

We stopped at a liquor store and picked up a bottle of wine on the walk back to my car. Emmett commented on my recovery. "You're doing heaps better than you were just last week."

"It's amazing how quick the body can recover," I said, in agreement.

Back at my apartment, I was thankful that Rachel and Crystal's blinds were pulled shut and Dixon wasn't anywhere to be seen. I wanted to keep what little time I had left with Emmett to myself.

"This is a really nice place," Emmett commented, as I moved around the kitchen.

"It's not half bad. I mean, the place itself is a shithole, but the location is worth every penny," I said, my voice muffled from deep within the cabinet as I searched for wine glasses.

I came back into the living room and saw him admiring the three surfboards that were leaning next to the front door. "You're boards are beautiful."

"Thanks. My dad made those," I said, proudly.

He raised his eyebrows. "Is he a shaper?"

"Kind of. It started as a hobby back when I was in high school. He shaped all of my boards, and as I became more and more well known locally, people started noticing my boards, and his talent. He probably could have done it professionally."

He ran his hand along the smooth edges before moving to the photos on the bookcase. "Is this you in school?" he asked, pointing at a photo of myself, Shane and the rest of the guys from our group.

"Yep, that's me." I leaned in closer, noting my ponytail and lack of make-up. "God, I was such a tomboy."

"And this must be your Pop."

I looked at the photo his was pointing at. It was Pop and I on a family vacation in Catalina. I picked up the photo with a sigh. "Yeah, this was just before my accident, before things started to get bad for the both of us." I set it back down softly and turned away, but Emmett caught my arm.

"You have nothing to be ashamed of." He looked straight into my eyes.

It unnerved me, and I cast my own downward. "I'm not."

Of course I was, and obviously he saw through it.

"It must be really tough to see someone you love get sick like this."

An unexpected tear rolled down my cheek, but I didn't bother brushing it away. I kept my eyes trained on the ground. Emmett moved closer to me, raising my chin up so I had to meet his eyes. He moved his thumb gently across my cheek and swept the tear away.

"I'm sorry," he whispered, and he leaned in and gently met my lips. It was tender and filled with understanding, something that only he who had lost a loved one could express. He pulled away slowly, and I wished that I had met him in a different time and a different place.

*

Up on the deck, it was pitch black. I uncorked the wine and idly commented on the lack of moonlight as we waited for our eyes to adjust, my mind still replaying the scene in the living room.

We took a seat side-by-side on the bench, quietly staring out at the dark expanse of ocean. Emmett put his arm around me, and my skin ached for his touch as we rested against one another. It had been a long time since I had been so close to a guy, like that.

"This is the best night I've had in ages," he said into the darkness.

I turned toward his dark shape. "Really?"

He nodded. "Yea, it is."

I felt the same way, and wanted to be the one to kiss him this time, but I was afraid to let myself want him more than I already did. The wind blew, and I shivered.

"You're cold. It's been a long day for you, and I should be getting on."

I didn't want him to go but I was afraid of what might happen next, feeling prudish like I was in high school again. He removed his arm from my shoulder and stood up.

"This has been a lovely evening."

I walked him to the top of the stairs and said good night. He hugged me again, but this time we didn't kiss.

"Can I call you in the morning?" he asked.

For a brief moment, I thought, why? Where is this even going? What is the purpose of this?

But my heart spoke for me. "Sure, I'd like that."

*

It was still dark when my phone rang the next morning. I picked it up and pressed it to my face, barely conscious.

"Sam, its Emmett."

"Hi," I said, sleepily.

"Sorry to wake you love, but I've got bad news. I've got to get a flight back home this morning."

I sat up, suddenly no longer tired. "To Australia?"

"It's an emergency." He sounded exhausted.

"Well then of course you have to go." I said, politely, but I felt deflated. "Do you need a ride or anything?"

"I'm already at the airport, babe. I didn't want to call any sooner and wake you up, but I wanted to say good-bye."

I nodded into the darkness. It was probably better this way. "Well, good-bye, Emmett."

"Can I call you when I land?"

It seemed like every time I prepared to say good-bye, he would find some way to keep things going. But I was just as guilty, letting him lead me on, and said, "Sure."

"Speak to you in approximately fourteen hours."

I clicked the phone shut and looked at the clock. I had to be up in two hours. Back to reality.

*

I was the first to arrive at the hospital. Pop was awake, trying to spoon some applesauce into his mouth but was only successful in making a mess of himself. I wanted to laugh – under any other circumstances, I might have. Instead, I wiped his chin and helped him with the cup.

As we sat watching a re-run of the Andy Griffith Show, I realized that not once had he complained about being in the hospital. This was a problem. Normally, Pop hated anybody fussing over him. He was independent and strong in mind, believing in mind over matter; I don't think I had seen him take much more than an Advil over the years. So when GamGam and Uncle Chuck arrived, I asked GamGam to join me for a cup of coffee in the cafeteria and voiced my concern.

"I've thought about that, too," she shared, stirring her coffee. "But we have to remember that he is sick. I think until he stops showing improvement - which he is by the way, improving every day- do we let ourselves worry."

I supposed she was right, but I couldn't quite shake my doubts once they were in my head. We went back up to Pop's room, took our seats in the chairs next to the bed and waited- for some news from the doctor, for the therapists to arrive, for Pop to do something out of the ordinary. I thought of Emmett, but then felt guilty about Pop, and worried about him once more. We were all so anxious, afraid to move – it was like there were wall-to-wall dominos in that room, so scared we were of our peace falling apart at any moment. It was exhausting.

Finally, our patience was rewarded. Sometime mid-afternoon, the doctor knocked on the door. Pop was thrilled, but in the way that a three year old is thrilled over a lollipop. That bothered me.

I tried to pay attention to the doctor's words, but they sort of fazed in and out. I kept grasping words like, "Medication, rest, therapy," words that were familiar- but only in regards to myself. I realized that they were releasing Pop and that it was our problem now - that it was up to us to take care of him. I felt even more exhausted just thinking about it, and likened to how new parents feel when they prepare to leave the hospital for the first time; overwhelmed, scared and unsure of exactly what to expect.

The doctor must have known what I was thinking. He patted my shoulder lightly. "Ms. Dane, you have to realize how well your father is doing, considering. Most patients are here at least five days. He's responding well to his medication and he's making great progress. Don't worry too much until you have to."

It angered me that everyone seemed not to want to worry yet. I was having trouble not freaking out – worrying was just the beginning. The man that lay in that hospital bed was not my father, Darrell Dane, I wanted to say to him. But of course, to a doctor he was just another patient.

I was silent as we wheeled Pop out of the hospital and helped him into GamGam's sedan. On the way home, I stared out of the window. All of my newfound optimism was gone – I felt so hopeless.

At Pop's, things had to be moved around to accommodate him and his walker. A special dinner needed to be prepared for him. We had to line his bed in plastic, in case he had an accident. I felt like a noose was tightening around my neck suffocating me.

I didn't expect it to happen then, but I was walking to Pop's room from the kitchen when I finally lost it. I shouted out to no one in particular, "I'll be back!" bolted out of the house and ran with the wind. I ran and ran and ran, pain ripping through my knee but I didn't care. Pain felt good. Pain made me feel alive. My hamstrings and calves and quads kept moving me, so I kept going. Snot and tears streamed across my face in the cold wind. Yet, I still kept running. Somewhere, around the wetland area on the outskirts of Huntington Beach, my legs and knees finally stopped working and I fell to the ground.

The physical pain was nothing compared to what I felt inside.

I forgot that I had my phone, and it surprised me when it rang. An unrecognizable number scrolled across the screen. I knew it was Emmett. I composed myself and answered.

"Sam, it's me, Shane."

My heart fell. It was too much, hearing my best friend's voice when I needed it most. I started to cry again. "Shane," I sobbed into the phone.

"Oh God, babe, you sound awful. I just talked to my parents and heard about your dad."

I sniffed loudly. "Yeah."

"Are you okay? Stupid me, of course you're not. Jesus, why am I even asking? I'm on my way home, kid."

"K," was all I could manage.

"Hang in there, Sammy. I'll be home soon."

*

I had made a decision as I limped the mile or so back to my apartment. I couldn't take the helplessness, the fear, the unknown. I needed to do something.

Effective immediately, I was going to follow in my mother's footsteps. I was going to be a doctor.

I went straight to my room, turned on the computer, typed in the webpage for the local community college and started the process of registering for fall classes. I had to take my future into my own hands, and every step closer I got to becoming a doctor was a step closer Pop got to getting better and us never, ever having to feel like that again.

The computer informed me I needed placement testing. I scheduled an appointment for the following morning, the first available. I kept working, researching, doing what it took to get my records together, making calls and poring over the internet. By the time I realized how late it was, it was almost time for Emmett's call.

I didn't care what the right and the wrong thing was to do anymore, in regards to him – he made me feel good and I would take whatever made me happy.

I continued waiting, and when it had been well over twenty hours since he'd left (it hadn't gone unnoticed that he had said, 'speak to you in 14 hours') I finally gave up and went to bed.

I didn't sleep well and was exhausted when I woke up for my eight o'clock a.m. placement testing. Nothing, not even coffee could get me going that morning. The tests were long and arduous and I couldn't focus- I knew I was probably not in the right mindset for solving algebraic equations. But my test results came back almost instantly, and I was surprised to find that I had placed well. I spent the morning filling out the necessary paperwork and applying for financial aid. Most of the fall classes were already filled up, so registration could be put off. I would have to petition when classes resumed or wait for spring. Either way, at least I didn't have to make any more important decisions right then.

But my responsibilities didn't stop there. I still had to go to H.S.S. to fill out paperwork. I parked in the familiar parking structure, taking the elevator to the corporate office.

"Hi, I'm here to see Greg," I relayed to the receptionist.

"Oh, sure, you must be Samantha. His office is the last door at the end of the hall."

Beyond the giant, assuming desk she sat at the office was pretty casual. Beautiful photographs of neat barrels and idyllic ocean scenes lined the walls. It was so much more welcoming than Scarpulli's, with its grey cubicles and scary safari scenes, and I felt my stress abate some.

Greg's office door was open. His back was turned as he examined something on a side table. I knocked gently, taking in the view that some people would pay millions of bucks for.

He swiveled around and got up when he saw me. He walked over and hugged me. "Come on in." He gestured to a deep-brown leather chair, taking his own seat behind the desk, facing me.

He studied my face for a second. "Jesus, Sam. You look terrible."

On any other day I might have been offended, but I knew then he was just saying it out of concern.

"How is your dad doing?"

I answered his questions, and when I had finished he said, "If he's cool to get visitors, I'd love to come by and see him. It's been way too long."

I thought about it and figured it couldn't do any more harm to Pop. We talked a little more about him and then moved on to the reason I was there.

"Are you cool with a Monday thru Friday schedule? You're not in school are you?"

"Not until September." I said, feeling proud. I had definitely taken a step in the right direction.

He clapped his hands. "Perfect." He called Lila at the reception desk and had her bring in a W-2 form and take photocopies of my Social Security Card and Driver's License. He gave me a new parking pass and within minutes, I was out of the door.

I stopped and got a coffee, hoping it would perk me up. I sipped the sweet, milky concoction, trying once again to focus on all of the great things that were happening: Pop was out of the hospital, I had a job at H.S.S., and now, I was a student. The title gave me a little thrill, and I wanted to share it with someone.

I wanted to share it with Emmett.

I felt like he had awoken something in my soul. Even if it was destined just to turn into a friendship, this was a person I wanted in my life. So I decided to take matters into my own hands. I went to the liquor store, bought a calling card, found the piece of paper with his number on it in my backpack and dialed his number.

The phone rang unfamiliarly. It rang and rang, and finally, his gravelly voice was on the line.

"Yeah?"

"Hey, it's Sam. Sorry to wake you."

He cleared his throat. "That's alright, love. How's your da?"

It cheered me that he cared enough to ask me about my family. "Pop's doing better. He's home now."

"Excellent, babes. And how about you? How are your knees?"

I took a seat on the dirty bench outside the liquor store. "My knees are fine. Everything is fine. I just wanted to make sure you got home okay. You know, since I hadn't heard from you." I tried to come out sounding concerned, but feared I just sounded desperate.

"Didn't you get my text?"

"No, I didn't."

"I wondered, since I hadn't heard from you. I was going to call you when I woke up." He yawned. "This time change is bullshit."

"How long is it?"

"Fifteen hours. Just fuckin' inconvenient enough that you're asleep when I'm awake, and vice versa."

"Now that I know you are safe, you may go back to sleep." I laughed, hoping he grasped my teasing tone.

"I'm glad you called, Sam. I'll call you when I wake up properly."

We hung up, and I felt much, much better.

*

At the apartments, Crystal was the only one around, so I made lunch and ate it with her. It was nice to have someone's company that wouldn't bombard me with questions or beg me to reveal my thoughts. I just didn't want to have to think or feel for a few minutes.

Chapter 7: Reunited

After a grueling three-hour PT session that afternoon, I left feeling sore and tired. I knew the pain was a good sign - it meant I was making progress- but it took some getting used to feeling physically exhausted all the time again.

I had left my phone at home during PT and had several messages waiting for me when I got to my apartment: one from Rachel, one from Emmett and one from Shane, who had landed. I called Rachel back first, who not surprisingly, didn't answer – she kept an odd schedule. Next, I called Emmett, who didn't answer either.

I didn't bother calling Shane back. I knew exactly where he would be. I parked excitedly and walked straight into the Baxter's home. Predictably, Heidi was shoveling large spoonfuls of pasta into a bowl and more predictably, Shane was wolfing it down like he was still growing.

"Sam!" Heidi exclaimed when I walked in. She took another bowl out of the cabinet and spooned more pasta into it.

Shane swiveled around on his bar stool and grinned at me. He was deeply tanned, his iridescent green eyes brighter than ever and his hair was longer than usual, almost bleached-blonde from the sun. As for his arms, they were a man's arms: all rippled and sculpted. I hardly recognized him.

I threw my arms around his neck. I couldn't believe how long he had been gone. I felt so grateful to have him there. He knew me better than anyone - and knew how much Pop's illness would affect me, knowing when it was serious enough to get his butt on a plane and be there in person.

"How are you hanging in there, kid?" He patted the stool next to him.

I answered by blowing out my breath and shaking my head. I brought him up to speed as we ate, and he asked to see Pop right after we finished.

We walked over, finding the house unusually quiet. I searched all the rooms, the garage and the back patio but GamGam, Uncle Chuck and Pop were nowhere to be found. I joined Shane in the kitchen and shrugged. "They must have gone for a walk or something."

I took out two glasses and poured some water. "So, tell me about Mags."

He laughed. "Dude, she's awesome. I met her in Australia. She's a nurse from England. Apparently, those people travel way more than we do, because there was shit tons of Brits in Australia, and it's like way further for them to fly than for us."

"Where is she now?"

"She's still in Oz. She could only get a week off to go to Indo with me, although I still tried to get her to come home with me."

I wondered how different things would have been if Mags were there with us. Would I have to call her 'Mags?' Selfishly, I was glad she wasn't. I didn't want to be reminded that I was no longer the most important woman in his life.

"Mom tells me you met someone, too," he said, kicking me playfully under the table.

I blushed. "Um, yeah, kind of. I don't know what you would call it though. He had to go back to Australia, too. Wait, how weird is this whole Australia thing?" I motioned back and forth between the two of us. I proceeded to tell him how I had met Emmett and about his abrupt departure.

Shane raised his eyebrow. "Be careful, Sam. Those Aussie surfers, they're major players. I would know. They've been my competition with the ladies." He wiggled his eyebrows up and down. "Holy shit, dude, I almost forgot. Happy early birthday!"

It took a second to register. I couldn't even think of the date.

He took in my face. "You totally forgot, didn't you? Ah, Sam, when are you going to realize that it's okay to be selfish on your birthday?"

I was prepared to relay just how selfish I had been before Pop got sick, but I didn't get a chance. The front door squeaked open, and Pop's voice sang out, "Ber-tie!" and Bertie started squawking, "Pop, Pop, Pop!"

Shane and I met them at the door. Pop's face lit up when he saw Shane. "Shane!"

"Hey, Darrell," Shane said. I studied his face. His tone was light, but I could tell he was shocked by Pop's appearance. They clasped one another awkwardly around Pop's walker. We all shuffled into the living room, which was dark and smelled musty. I walked around and opened the windows, grateful for something to do.

"Sam," GamGam said, patting the couch. "Come sit."

I obeyed her and settled onto the comfy old couch.

"We have some rather extraordinary news," she started, looking at Pop.

He nodded. "My memory – it's back."

My eyes widened. "What?"

Pop's face changed. "We've been talking, the three of us," he gestured to GamGam and Uncle Chuck. "About what has to happen next. To me. It's possible – it's almost certain," he amended, painfully, "That this lucidity will falter."

I cocked my head.

"I'm going to need help, honey," he said, softly. I read his face, his posture and his tone. It seemed like it was the first time he had said it aloud. "Not just for this," he gestured to himself. "But, with everything. I almost died. Your mother's memories are killing me, literally."

"I don't follow." I looked at Shane, and he too didn't seem to understand.

Pop sighed. "I'm depressed. I have been, for a long time. I can't live like this anymore."

Suddenly, it dawned on me. "Like, 'The Notebook,' " I said aloud, but no one seemed to understand. "You know, the lady has Alzheimer's and she can't remember anything, and then suddenly she does, and then she doesn't again." I was babbling, but I was beginning to understand. "It means that you're going to forget again."

Uncle Chuck nodded gravely. "That's what we suspect."

"What about here, our home? What about the house? What about me?" I hated how needy I sounded, but it was my father, my Pop, perhaps one of the few times I could or would have to talk to him like that again. I felt like I deserved the right to be selfish, this time. But those days seemed to be gone.

"I don't know, honey." Pop said, his eyes imploring me.

I didn't say anything else. I was thinking of the ending to The Notebook, when the old lady dies.

*

Shane and I left Pop's and grabbed a much-needed drink. We didn't go to Main Street like we normally would have; instead, we went to Newport Beach. Once we had settled on a place and sat, Shane said, "Dude, this shit with your dad..." he trailed off. "It's hardcore."

I nodded. "I know." We were both quiet, thinking our own thoughts.

"So guess what?" I took a deep breath, and said aloud for the first time, "I signed up for classes. For college. I'm gonna follow in my mom's footsteps."

He took a hearty swig of beer. "You want to be a doctor?"

I nodded.

He grinned and high-fived me. Classic Sam and Shane, I thought. We had been apart for months I guessed, I couldn't remember how long it had been, but between the trailed off broken sentences, the high fives and the camaraderie we just seemed to pick up where we left off, no matter how long we had been apart.

"I'm heading back to Oz on Saturday. Mags only has a few more weeks left before her visa ends, and my parents are making me do something with my life at the end of the summer." He rolled his eyes.

We sat in silence, both of our minds reeling. It had been one week to the day since I had been fired from Scarpulli's. In that week I had shed my crutches, met Emmett, become a student and possibly lost the father I had known forever.

We didn't stay out much longer. I dropped Shane off at home and headed to my apartment. I was so sleepy - more than ready for bed, but when Emmett called again I shrugged off the fatigue.

We talked for a long time. Again, he asked how Pop was doing and how I was feeling, and I asked him how he felt being home, and how the construction business was. He lamented, telling me more about his home, his 'flatmate' Natalie and their dog. He still didn't mention anything about why he left so abruptly, but neither did I. Talking with Emmett took my mind off everything else, and it was the one escape from reality I had left. After a half hour or so he had to leave for work, so we hung up. I went to bed content and dreamt of surfing with Emmett.

*

I woke up early and went to the gym. Less than fifteen minutes passed before GamGam called and told me they were able to obtain a last-minute appointment with Dr. Ewing. I wanted to be there, so I headed straight to Pop's, sweaty-workout clothes and all.

Pop, Uncle Chuck, GamGam and I all piled in GamGam's sedan for the doctor's appointment. We had always been such an independent family, and I marveled at how we had all rallied around Pop.

We shuffled into Dr. Ewing's office one by one. I signed Pop in, not recognizing any of the front office staff since my last visit several years past. I took a seat in the waiting area next to GamGam, clutching my purse tightly as we waited for Pop's name to be called.

The office unnerved me. It was the very place that my mom had practiced medicine. I could picture her walking around the office, requisite stethoscope around her neck, marking charts and asking questions.

I observed Pop while we waited. He was quiet, looking through a magazine as he hummed lightly to himself. He hadn't said much that morning, and I wondered if last night's sudden lucidity had been just what we feared most, a fluke and then suddenly, gone again.

"Darrell Dane?" An unrecognizable nurse called Pop's name from across the waiting room, propping the door to the back offices open with her generous behind. GamGam and I stood and flanked Pop's sides, accompanying him to the back.

We helped him first onto the scale, where I was proud to note he had gained a little weight. Next, they checked his vitals before the nurse announced that Dr. Ewing would be in shortly, and closed the door shut as she left.

"It's been a long time since we were here, huh kiddo?" Pop remarked, looking around the room.

I nodded, not sure what or what not to say. I was terrified anything could trigger him, but Pop appeared cognizant and aware of his surroundings.

Within minutes, Dr. Ewing was swinging open the door, shaking GamGam's hand and giving me a big hug. Looking Pop over, he asked, "Good morning, Darrell. How are you feeling?" clasping his shoulder.

"I've been better," Pop answered, his head sagging slightly. I studied his face, wondering if he recognized the doctor, one of my mother's oldest friend's.

GamGam handed Dr. Ewing a file that she had comprised of Pop's labs, scans and paperwork. He looked them over quietly, and my heart pounded as we waited.

"Darrell, can you remember when the last time you saw a doctor was?"

Pop squirmed a little. "No."

"How is the depression?"

"Uh, still there." They exchanged a look – and I knew then that the regular Pop, the one that I knew, was fully aware of everything going on.

"Your blood pressure had lowered and his currently in the normal range, Darrell. It appears that you are responding well to the medication they prescribed you in the hospital." He continued asking questions, and between the three of us we answered them as knowledgeably as possible.

"You're doing very good, Darrell, making wonderful, progressive strides." Turning to me, he asked, "Samantha, can I have a word in my office?"

Though outwardly he appeared cheerful, his enigmatic tone alarmed me. I followed him obediently, feeling like a child again as I sat in the straight-backed chair in front of his desk.

"Do you know why your father stopped coming to see me?" he asked.

I guessed it had to be about my mom, and told him about Pop's outburst at breakfast. He nodded. "Yes, the last time I saw him he voiced the same suspicions about me and your mother."

He leaned forward, continuing. "I'm not sure if you are aware of this, Samantha, but Darrell has suffered from depression for a long time. I tried to persuade him to seek counseling, but he refused. I offered a low-dosed anti-depressant, and he refused that as well. Eventually, as you already know, he stopped coming to his appointments altogether. Obviously, we can see now that he didn't seek secondary medical advice."

He sighed, stopping himself from elaborating further. "You've been through too much already. You don't deserve this."

I shrugged. I knew he had more to say, and wanted him to get it over with already.

He leaned back. "It's imperative to get the Neuropsychological Evaluation completed as soon as possible. You're going to need to know how much damage has been done, and where he stands mentally. What you're seeing now may be temporary," he paused and cleared his throat, continuing, "It's a real possibility he may regress again. I would need to make some calls, but I could probably get you an appointment with a Neuropsychologist, sooner rather than later. And with Neuropsychologist's, it's usually later." He offered a wan smile, scribbling on a pad in front of him before standing up. Together, we returned to the treatment room.

He wrote some more prescriptions and GamGam put everything in the file. I thanked Dr. Ewing for his time, noting how depressed I felt as we were leaving.

No wonder Pop had stopped coming.

*

That afternoon, I stuck around Pop's house for his PT. Though he was stronger, I could tell how frustrated he was that he hadn't regained the use of his right arm. His mood soured as the hour passed, and by the end of his session he was downright angry. He ate his lunch without abandon, slopping soup down his shirt as he tried to bring the spoon to his mouth with his untrained left hand. When the spoon inevitably shook and he spilled again, he threw it down angrily.

"Pop, maybe soup's a bad idea," I said, and handed him a sandwich.

He glowered as he accepted it, but appeased me by eating it.

"Whaddya say we go for a walk, just you and me?" I asked.

He perked up some. "Okay."

I informed GamGam and Uncle Chuck of our plans. "That's a wonderful idea," she said, consulting her watch. "In fact, could you stick around for a few hours? I really need to get down to my house in La Jolla and could use Chuck's help, if possible."

"Of course, Mom," Uncle Chuck said.

Pop refused the wheel chair I offered to push him in for our walk, opting instead for his walker, and we moved at a snail's pace down the sidewalk. He was downright stubborn, a trait I had definitely inherited from him. Pride swelled in me as I watched his laborious gait.

We walked the length of the block and turned around again. What might have previously taken only five minutes, now took thirty. When we made it back to the house Pop sagged against the sofa and fell asleep almost instantly. I sat down next to him and felt my own eyelids close.

When I awoke, Pop was sitting up, holding a photograph of he and my mom, his eyes shiny. I was terrified that something was about to happen.

"Honey, we need to talk."

Here it comes, I thought, bracing myself. But for a moment, the room was silent.

"It's time to sell the house, Sammy. If I go to Maui with Chuck, we both know I won't be coming back."

A lump formed in my throat. I looked around, trying to imagine my life in Huntington Beach without this house, my home. Moreover, I couldn't imagine living in HB without Pop.

"You could come with us, to Maui," he said, taking my right hand in his left.

I tried to picture myself in Hawaii. "When would you want to go?"

"Sooner, rather than later."

For once, I didn't have anything to say.

*

The more I thought of Pop being gone, the more I didn't like it. As beautiful and amazing as Hawaii was, I couldn't imagine him anywhere other than in HB.

But I had to think of what was best for Pop. The quieter lifestyle would suit him. He would have the world's best beaches at his front door. He'd have a comrade in Uncle Chuck, someone to look out for him.

But if we did sell the house, what did we do with all of the stuff in it? All of the boards in the garage, the countless pictures and memorabilia Pop had collected.

I felt like I was growing up in fast forward. There were too many changes happening, all of them out of my control.

Chapter 8: Surprises Abound

The time change between Huntington Beach and Australia was dramatic. It was either late-night or early morning for one of us when Emmett and I talked. It took some getting used to but eventually we found a good schedule that worked for us both and took turns calling one another.

That night, it was my turn to call him, so when I saw his number show up on the caller ID I was surprised

"I have some excellent news," he said, excitedly.

"What's that?" I asked.

"There's a huge competition next week and I'm going to be in it."

"That's awesome, Emmett," I said, peering into the refrigerator for some food.

"Sam, the competition is in HB!"

"Oh!" I raised my head excitedly, bumping it in the process. "Ouch."

"Yep, heaps of my mates were already heading out for it, so I just entered at the last minute. I'll be there on Tuesday."

"This is fantastic!" I rubbed my aching head.

"Yeah, I'm fucking stoked. I got a flight, just need to get a hotel sorted. The hostel is already booked up."

"Shut up, you stay with me. Duh."

He hesitated. "Are you sure? I mean, with everything going on with your da and all…"

It was an impulsive gesture, but it felt right. There was no denying how crazy I was about him. "I'm very sure. You're staying with me."

"Excellent! I'd much rather stay with a beautiful woman than a bunch of smelling, farting blokes." He laughed. "So what have you got going on today? Tomorrow, I mean, for you. This time thing is fucking with me head."

It was inevitable that he would find out, though given everything going on I couldn't care less. Casually, I said, "Actually, it's my birthday. I'm sure I'll have to do something."

"What!" he exclaimed. "Why didn't you tell me?"

I put the phone on speaker and set it on the counter as I opened a can of soup. "I don't care about birthdays. They do nothing for me. And right now, there is so much more important stuff to think about."

"Well, you have to do something for your birthday!"

"Well, I don't have any plans." Remembering, my time on the computer and my revelation, I told him about school.

"And what do you want to study?" he asked, loudly. I could hear hammering in the background.

"I, uh, want to be a doctor." I felt silly saying it aloud.

"That's fucking brilliant," he said. "Me mum's a nurse."

"Really? My mom was a doctor. That's part of the reason why, obviously."

"Ah, babe, that's great. She would be really proud, I'm sure."

I wanted to tell him how much his support meant to me, even if they were just words. But I knew he was busy. "Emmett, let's talk later."

I heard him cover the phone as he spoke to someone else. "Yep, that's a grand idea. Speak to you first thing in the morn, babe."

"Okay. Have a good rest of the day."

I hung up, realizing how much I liked being called babe. I didn't know I was one of those girls.

*

"Good MORNING!" Rachel and Crystal chimed in unison as they pounced on my bed and woke me up. "Happy Birthday!" Rachel said, throwing her arms around my neck.

"Thanks, Rach."

"Happy birthday, Sam," Crystal said, also hugging me.

"What do you want to do first?" Rachel asked.

"Uh, brush my teeth," I said, laughing. I rubbed my eyes. "What time is it?"

"Nine," Rachel answered, bouncing up and down on my bed like she was seven-years-old.

She stopped bouncing and I heard my phone ringing. "Hello?" I said, answering?

"Happy Birthday, babe!" Emmett said.

"Thanks, Emmett." I felt my cheeks go instantly red. I swatted them off my bed. "What are you doing?"

"I'm out with Kev and some other mates, in Sydney."

"Oh that's right, it's Friday night there, huh?"

"Yea. I just wanted to wish you a Happy birthday, proper. Enjoy your day, babe, do lots of really selfish things. Seriously."

"Okay, I'll try," I said, laughing.

I threw back the covers, opened my blinds and stretched. Sunlight filtered into my room, and I knew it was going to be a good day.

*

I showered and walked into the living room, surprised to find Shane sitting on the couch with Dixon. I also found it surprising that Dixon was still awake.

"He-ey, kiddo," Shane said excitedly and picked me up, swinging me around. "Shane," I laughed, feeling dizzy. "Put me down."

"I'm going to swing you…around…for every year…you've had a birthday. Don't puke, Sammy."

After two more times, he stopped. We stumbled around and fell onto each other. I doubled over, laughing. "Whoa."

I realized how much I needed that laugh. I looked around my living room which was decorated with streamers. "Who did this?" I asked, my eyes wide.

"The girls," Dixon said.

"C'mon, kid." Shane plopped onto the couch and patted the seat next to him.

"Dixon, why are you awake?"

"Didn't go to sleep yet," he said, nonchalantly.

"Sam, you didn't tell me how cool your friends are," Shane said, picking up a bowl from the table. "I'm bummed I'm leaving tomorrow."

"So am I." I sighed. "But we have today!" Looking in his bowl, I instantly recognized the round, colorful balls. " Where'd did you get the Trix?"

"I stopped at the market on the way over and got all of our favorites: Lucky Charms, Fruity Pebbles. They're on the counter." He took an enormous bite and chewed noisily. "So I was thinking we could get out today. Maybe head down to San O?"

I reached for his bowl, taking a heaping spoonful. "What about 54th street, in Newps instead?"

He high-fived me. "Fuck yeah."

Rachel returned and demanded to know what I was doing for the day. I informed her of my surf plans, and upon reading her face, I knew she was disappointed that I was spending it with Shane. "I promise, we'll do something tonight."

She didn't say anything, just gave Shane a dirty look. He looked at me and shook his head. "American girls."

I slugged him in the arm.

*

Shane and I stood in front of the ocean surveying the waves, my heart thumping wild in anticipation. After my disastrous session last week, I was much more nervous this time.

Shane gave me a sideways glance. "You look ridiculous."

"What?" I had left the wetsuit at home, opting instead for a rashguard and boardshorts this time, thanks to the warmer temperatures.

"You know, those knee braces."

He was right, I probably did look ridiculous but I was going for safety. "You didn't see me try to surf the other day."

He shook his head bemusedly. "C'mon."

We walked to the water and set our boards down. I laid on mine gingerly, feeling the hardness of the board underneath my knees and was thankful I had worn the braces. We started paddling out, and like the last time my arms burned within minutes. I didn't care though, and continued paddling, rising and falling with the waves. The farther out we went, the bigger they became and eventually we had to duck under to pass them. At least this time I wasn't nearly drowning.

Finally, we came upon a small line-up of surfers. We stopped paddling and straddled our boards as we waited for our turn to catch a wave.

"How do you feel?" Shane asked.

"Tired, but good."

We had a lot of waiting to do. Shane caught a small wave but ended up wiping out quickly. I tried dropping in on one, but my legs were weak and I couldn't hold myself up; I wiped out quickly, too.

It had been years since Shane and I had surfed together. I relished the time we spent in the line-up, talking and laughing like we didn't have a care in the world. With my injury, I wiped out a lot and eventually, it became tiresome ending upside-down with salt water in my nose and throat. I left Shane and paddled back toward the beach. Halfway, however, I was so exhausted I just let the surf carry me back in. I peeled off my rashguard and lay out on my towel, letting the sun warm me.

Shane stayed out for a long time. He was a lot better than he used to be and even caught a few airs. It was fun to watch.

When he had surfed himself out, he paddled back in, stating immediately, "I'm starving."

I rolled my eyes. "What a surprise."

We packed our boards into the back of Shane's truck and stopped for lunch at In-N-Out Burger. The day was very warm, feeling like summer for the first time in weeks. PCH was packed as we made our way back home.

"To your dad's?" Shane asked, as we approached the city limits.

"Yep."

Arriving at Pop's, I was shocked to see Greg and Tim, from H.S.S., also getting out of a truck. Greg had said he wanted to come by and see Pop at some point, but it really surprised me to see Tim, the big-wig of H.S.S. and the legend behind the Tim Howard Leukemia Foundation Open, the very open that Emmett would be competing in the following week.

"Hey guys," I said, greeting them and introducing Shane.

"We didn't mean to come by unannounced," Greg said. "Tim and I had a meeting yesterday about the Open, and when I mentioned that you were coming back to work for us Darrell's hospitalization came up."

"Why don't we go inside?" I suggested.

The four of us walked into the house together. But as soon as we got into the kitchen I knew something was wrong.

GamGam and Uncle Chuck were sitting at the kitchen table, looking depressed and somber. For a second, I feared the worst. "What is it?" I immediately asked, eschewing introductions and formalities.

Uncle Chuck ran his hand through his hair. "His memory is gone again."

I breathed a sigh of relief. "I was afraid it would be something worse. Thank God."

"Well," GamGam said, looking extremely tired. "He still knows who we are and where he is. But he doesn't understand why he is paralyzed and what the medication is for. He's very, very angry."

The doctors had said nothing was predictable but I hadn't expected so much of a setback. Shane put his arm around me and squeezed my shoulders.

Uncle Chuck was the first to register our guests. "How rude of us," he said, standing up. "Chuck Dane." He shook the hands of Tim and Greg, and gave a hug (that man-hug, fist-clap, chest bump thing) to Shane. GamGam did the same thing, except she gave Shane an actual hug.

"Maybe we should come back another time," Tim said, exchanging a look with Greg.

GamGam stood up. "There really is no good time, gentlemen. Who knows, maybe it'll be good for him. He's just restin' right now." She led the way to his room and we all trailed after her, eventually crowding around Pop's bed where he was lying awake.

"Hi, Pop." I leaned down and gave him a hug. "How are you feeling?"

"I'm really tired," he said, holding onto my hand.

"Do you remember Tim and Greg?" I gestured to the two of them.

He scrutinized them for a moment. "Sure, I do."

Suddenly GamGam gasped. "Oh my word! Samantha, darlin', we completely forgot your birthday!"

I looked up at her, embarrassed. Everyone chimed in, and I thanked them as politely as possible, turning back to Pop. "So Pop..." I started again.

"Eighteen today," Pop said, looking at me fondly.

"Er, thanks, Pop." I didn't have the heart to correct him.

"So Tim, when are you going to hurry up and sponsor my daughter?"

He laughed. "Just as soon as we can, Darrell." His tone was light, but his face was grey. It seemed everyone who saw Pop was shocked by his appearance, and I wondered how it had gone unnoticed by me for so long.

"How's the shaping going, Darrell?" Greg spoke up.

Pop snapped his fingers. "That's right, I've been meaning to talk to you guys over at the shop. I'm working on some new stuff right now and need to clear out the old boards. I was thinking about selling them. Do you want to see them?"

Tim's wheels seemed to be turning, because he was slow with his response. "I'm sure we could work something out, Darrell."

Pop hopped out of bed excitedly. I tried to help him, shocked by his litheness, but he appeared just as springy as ever, minus the still-paralyzed right arm. We all followed him to the garage, Shane and I bringing up the rear.

"This is all so freaking weird," I said to Shane, walking slowly. "I never know what to expect anymore."

He nodded, but remained tight-lipped.

Pop showed them a couple of boards in the garage. "This is just a couple. I've got hundreds of them."

Tim humored him by asking questions, Greg chiming in here and there. After a few minutes, GamGam put her arm around Pop's shoulders. "Honey, you haven't got any shoes on. Let's go get you back in bed."

Pop nodded. "Okay, Mom."

After Pop was back in bed, Greg and Tim announced their departure. Greg reached out and patted Pop's foot. "Darrell, looking forward to seeing you out in the water again." But his words sounded much lighter than his face appeared.

GamGam stayed with Pop while the rest of us spilled into the living room, which I started pacing. "I wonder what he's talking about."

"What do you mean? I mean, specifically?" Uncle Chuck asked, laughing wryly.

"These boards. I don't know what he's on about. He's obviously stuck in time seven years ago, but I can't remember him having hundreds of boards sitting around."

"Could be something fictional in his head," Shane suggested.

"What about his storage unit?" Uncle Chuck asked.

I looked at him. "What storage unit?"

"He was talking about a storage unit earlier today."

I thought about it and turned to Tim. "We're going to need to look into this, Tim."

He nodded. "We should be going, but there was a reason for our unannounced arrival. As you know, I am a leukemia survivor, and discovering answers and finding cures to these horrible diseases is the reason why we hold the Open, to raise money for funding for research. I'd like to have Darrell as a special guest this year at the auction, if you think he is up to it. Though after seeing him, I'm not so sure..." he trailed off. "Of course, if he can make it you are all welcome."

Uncle Chuck and I looked at each other, and Tim and Greg rose. "Thank you both for coming. This means so much to us," Uncle Chuck said.

Once they were gone, I said, "I want to go to this storage unit, ASAP."

Shane gave me a look. "Sam, I know you're anxious, but that storage unit will be there tomorrow. Why not enjoy your birthday?"

Uncle Chuck agreed. Snapping his fingers, he said, "Hey, why don't we get dressed up and do dinner tonight, all of us. Your parents too, Shane. I think it would be good for Darrell to get out."

I didn't want to go to dinner, I didn't want to party, I didn't want to celebrate. No one seemed to get it. "Look, I appreciate it guys, but this is just another day to me. How can I be celebratory when all of this is going on with Pop?"

Shane shrugged his shoulders. "You gotta eat, though."

With Shane, it was always about food.

"What if we did both, went to this storage unit and did dinner. Would you feel better then?" Uncle Chuck asked.

I could do dinner. Maybe then everyone would be appeased. "That I can agree with."

I returned to Pop's bedside and sat down. "Pop, how do you feel about going to dinner tonight? Somewhere nice, maybe like, Captain Jack's in the harbor?"

His face broke into a big smile. He reached out to me and rubbed my cheek. "My little girl's an adult now."

I realized he was using his right hand. I pulled it from my face and looked at it. "Pop, you're using your right hand!" I looked at GamGam, who had looked up from her knitting.

He looked at me strangely. "So?"

It was impossible to keep up with where his mind was at any given moment but I hugged him anyway, happy at least for the small victories. "Hey, do you have a storage unit I don't know about? I, uh, have some extra stuff that I don't have space for."

He looked at me. "I do, honey. I'll get you the keys." He threw back the covers and got out of bed, again, with much more ease than I expected. My first instinct was to stop him, but then I made a decision. Unless it was physically harming Pop, I guessed it wasn't necessary to baby him. I just needed to get used to him like that. But I wasn't sure if that could ever happen.

I followed him to the office, where he rifled around in some drawers. The room was immaculate, like most of the home. Books lined the walls (mostly my Mom's medical books) and there was one lone two-drawer file cabinet next to the big desk.

"Aha!" He held up a key.

The doorbell rang. GamGam left to answer it, returning with Pop's physical therapist. Though she was impressed that Pop had regained mobility of his hand, she was unimpressed that his memory had regressed. "It happens," she responded simply, before averting her attention to Pop and beginning their session.

GamGam agreed to stay with Pop during PT, so Uncle Chuck, Shane and I set off for the storage unit. It wasn't hard to find, and once we arrived and unlocked the door, we prepared ourselves for what could lie behind the closed door.

"On three?" Uncle Chuck said.

In unison, we said, "One, two, three!" and Uncle Chuck threw open the door.

Pop had been correct. Indeed, there appeared to be hundreds of boards in the small space. There were shortboards and longboards of various lengths and sizes, fins disassembled, stacked gently upon one another.

"Holy shit," Shane said.

There was also a grouping of large Tupperware containers in a corner. I moved carefully between the boards and opened the first one, which contained 8-track tapes and records. It was heavy, so Shane lifted it up for me. I opened the next one, which housed a bunch of old, brown photographs. I rifled through the ones on top but didn't recognize anyone. "Uncle Chuck, you might like to look through these," I said, and Shane took the container over to him.

The last one was full of papers. "Ho-ly shit," I said aloud. On top was my mother's death certificate.

My eyes scanned the document. It was slightly disturbing to be reading it but I couldn't stop myself. "I hereby certify…blah blah blah…I went to and took charge of the dead body….eewww," I pushed on, running over the graphic wording. "You think they could candy coat it a little." I continued reading. " 'Causes of death: Multiple Blunt Force Trauma; Crushed Chest and Abdomen."

I set the paper aside. I couldn't read any more. It felt too sadistic.

"Sorry, kid," Shane said.

I kept looking through the papers, but there wasn't much else besides a bevy of newspaper clippings. Pop had obviously been obsessed.

Finally, I stood up, my knees and back aching from sitting on the cold cement floor. "Happy Birthday to me. What a day."

I walked out of the unit breathing deeply. Reality sure was a motherfucker.

Chapter 9: The Thing With Tragedy Is...

If it was really necessary for everyone to "celebrate" my birthday, I would have much rather preferred to grab a pizza and stay home, but I seemed to be the only one interested. Everyone else wanted to celebrate in a fancy way. Perhaps it was because it was the first time I'd had everyone important to me together in one place, but either way, the planning became infectious. I decided to go out and buy myself a new outfit for my birthday dinner.

I didn't go anywhere special, just to one of the small shops on Main Street, which I preferred to the giant, sprawling malls such as South Coast Plaza. I selected a dainty gold blouse and a pair of navy blue trousers, a necklace and a pair of wedge sandals, an outfit I felt was modest and respectful. I tried the outfit on in the dressing room and was both pleased and surprised by how much older I looked - I had always looked way younger than my actual age.

I went home, poured myself a glass of wine, threw on some mellow tunes and took a hot bubble bath. I felt a million times better as I blew out my hair, carefully applied my make-up and got dressed. As I was leaving, I noticed Crystal in her living room. I poked my head in the door and said, "Heading to dinner with the fam. Drinks later?"

She looked at me apologetically. "I told Rach I'd meet her up in Hollywood."

I was taken aback, surprised that they would be so far away, after the fuss they made over my birthday that morning. "Oh. Well, that's cool. We can hang out another time." As I turned to leave, Crystal added, "You know Rachel. She made other plans because you didn't call her all day."

It hadn't occurred to me that the planning had been purposeful, that Rachel had organized something she knew I wouldn't be able to go to. Or, that someone I called one of my best friends could be so malicious and cunning. "She was bothered that I didn't call her?" I repeated, sarcastically. "Does she ever stop thinking about herself? This isn't about her, or Shane," I added, because I knew she was jealous that I had made time for him and not her, "Or me, for that matter. My father has had a life-threatening event, has been in the hospital and possibly could have died. Maybe, just maybe, I'm choosing to spend some time with him and my family - my family I never see - instead of sitting around gossiping, smoking and drinking all day. I mean, fuck," I said, angrily.

"Sam, I didn't mean it like that," she came up to the window. "I get it, really I do. No one blames you for wanting to be with your family."

I started to head down the stairs. "Really? Because that sounds exactly like what Rachel is doing."

She walked out of the house and leaned over the railing. "She's just being dramatic."

I scoffed. "Well, it's a good thing she's getting paid for it." I waved good-bye and opened my car door."

"Happy Birthday, Sam," she said.

I stopped, my words reverberating. Crystal was the other person I used to sit around and gossip, smoke and drink with all day. I didn't want to hurt her feelings, too. "Sorry, Crystal. I like hanging out with you. I'm just... really sensitive. You know," I added helplessly, hoping she did know.

*

I tried my best to push away my anger when I got to Pop's, and started to get excited about the prospect of my family and the Baxter's, all out for dinner, together.

Not surprisingly, though, Pop was in no shape to go out of the house. Though he was out of bed and watching TV, to my consternation he still thought it was my eighteenth birthday. I wanted to cancel it all but GamGam wouldn't hear of it. She was staying with Pop no matter what, so I sat on the couch with the two of them while I waited for Uncle Chuck.

When he appeared, he was wearing a pair of khaki pants and a Hawaiian shirt, the exact same thing Pop liked to wear. It killed me to realize how much the two of them looked alike, or rather, what Pop used to look like.

We said good-bye and walked over to the Baxter's. Heidi had a couple of bottles of wine opened on the counter and offered me a glass as soon as I walked in. Normally, I didn't use alcohol as a crutch, but that night I was very thankful for it.

Heidi was beaming as she handed me a gift. "Happy Birthday, sweetie."

"Heidi," I admonished, looking at her and Frank. "Not necessary."

She shooed me. "Open it."

I opened the edges delicately. "God, Sam, just open it," Shane said, rolling his eyes.

"The paper is beautiful. I don't want to ruin it." I stuck my tongue out at him. It was a brand new laptop, very light, very modern and very expensive looking. I looked up astonished. "You guys."

Heidi clapped her hands excitedly. "Shane told us how you've had the same computer for years, and now that you are going back to school you're going to need a new one. And now the two of you can Skype with one another."

I hugged them both tightly. I didn't have a mother, and my father may have been sick, but these people around me - they were my family, too.

I pulled back and saw Heidi wiping her eyes.

"Mom, don't start crying." Shane said. "You'll get Sam going, too."

I laughed, thankful for Shane's crassness, for once.

*

At the last minute I asked to change restaurants. I didn't think I could eat at Captain Jack's without Pop, so we drove to Newport Beach to one of Heidi's favorite restaurants, The Cannery.

Dinner was a surprisingly raucous affair, considering there were two 25-year-olds and three people pushing 50 together in one group. It seemed we all needed to let our hair down, for we consumed four bottles of wine between the five of us. The theme was 'embarrassing Sam', and everyone had a story to tell. I was in stitches by the time dessert arrived.

"Wait, wait, wait," Shane said, wiping his eyes. "Sam, remember that time when we were 10, and you had that sleepover… around the time one of the Halloween movies came out?"

"Oh God," I groaned, knowing exactly what story he was going to tell.

"Brady, Q and I snuck in through Sam's bedroom window – she always left it open - and hid behind the couch while we waited for a really scary scene. The girls were all lying in sleeping bags on the ground, and Sam got up to do something. She was about to discover us, so the three of us jumped out from behind the couch and yelled as loud as we could. She was so scared she peed her pants. I mean, we could actually see it."

"It's true," I conceded. "I didn't want to get up – we were totally freaked – but I had to pee so badly. When they jumped out, it literally scared the pee out of me. I was mortified at first, but then I just got pissed off and chased after Shane and tackled him. I think I was actually bigger than you, wasn't I?" I giggled, remembering. "So I tackled him, and sat on his back and punched him, pee in my pants and all."

Everyone was laughing. "You guys never told this story!" Heidi said.

"Well, Mom, it's not one of our better moments. Pretty embarrassing for us both, really."

The waitress arrived and asked, "Would anyone like anything else?"

The adults declined but Shane looked at me and said, "We're not driving – what do you say, Dane?"

"Yep." I turned to the waitress. "Two shots of your bartender's most disgusting concoction."

I was drunk and happy, and neither Shane nor I were ready to go home, so we stayed in Newport and bar-hopped. It was great, just the two of us hanging out, and I don't think we'd ever been able to legally drink in a bar together before. When Emmett called, I didn't answer. I wanted to cherish every second with Shane. We reminisced and laughed, and the next thing I knew it was two am - closing time.

We took a cab back to HB. In typical fashion, I fell asleep on Shane's shoulder. The next thing I knew he was shaking me awake, saying, "Sam, we're at your apartment."

I sat up and said, "Don't leave me."

I wasn't ready to say good-bye.

"Okay, kiddo." We scooted out of the van and stumbled up the stairs to my place. I kicked off my shoes and went straight to the DVD's. "What do you want to watch?"

He didn't even look up from untying his own. "Perfect Summer."

I should have known he would choose the classic surf film.

We went to my room and fell on my bed. I managed to stay awake for about five seconds before I passed out. When I awoke again, Shane was reaching across me for the remote on my nightstand. "Do you care if I sleep here?"

"Like you need to ask."

It was quiet for a while, save for the sounds of the cars and in the distance, the crashing of waves. I closed my eyes and was almost back asleep when suddenly he was right next to me.

"Sam, can I ask you something?" he whispered.

"Hm?"

"Do you ever…wonder?"

"About what?" I asked, sleepily.

"About… you and me? What might have happened. You know, if we let it?"

It wasn't the question I was expecting. I thought about it though, maybe even truthfully for the first time, and I supposed that there was a time back in high school when I had let myself crush on him. But that was back then. "Yeah, I guess I have."

He was quiet for a moment. "And?"

I rolled toward him. "And, I think you are the most amazing person ever and I can't live without you…but you're you."

He moved even closer. "But…"

It scared me, Shane acting like he was. I was definitely unsure of where things were going. "This had better not be one of your sick jokes, Shane."

He didn't say anything. Instead, he surprised me by kissing me, and my initial reaction was to push him away. "Wait, what about Mags?"

"Sorry." He rolled over and stared at the ceiling. "Mags is great, but these last few days I've been…I don't know, wondering, having these feelings. I think I've always had them, you know. I mean, you're like, any guys' dream woman and you've always been here. Right in front of my face." He turned back toward me, resting his head on his hand. "When I heard something had happened to your dad, all I did was think of you. I was so worried. I knew I had to do everything in my power to get home, to be here for you."

I knew it was the full range of his emotions. I replayed the last few days in my head: Shane and I grinning at one another over bowls of spaghetti at his parent's house; swinging around in my living room and crashing into one another; falling asleep in the cab with my head on his shoulder. Remembering my thoughts when I saw him the other day - how different he had looked, how much older, I wondered if he was right. Maybe we were ready to step into the next part of our lives, possibly together.

So I pressed my lips to his and kissed him back. We held it for a moment. Though I didn't feel anything sexual like I had with Emmett, there was something special there. But I felt incredibly guilty.

He placed his hand on my cheek. "My sweet Sammy."

I smiled into the darkness. "I'm glad you are here. I don't know what I would have done without you."

"Me too, kid."

We laid there looking at one another for a few moments before I turned and shifted. I didn't want to mess up the beautiful friendship we had and I sensed he was leaning that way too. He wrapped his arms around me and said, "Maybe we call it a night? Blame it on the booze?"

I squeezed him tight, relishing the moment. I was sure it would never happen again.

*

Before I even opened my eyes, I knew Shane was gone. I lay in my bed and replayed the events that were already starting to fog over and fade away, like a dream does the longer you are awake. I knew we had done the right thing by stopping things from happening. Life had been intense the last few days and it was easy to get emotional. Alcohol only intensifies it.

When I stood up, my head started pounding so badly I felt like I was in Chuck E. Cheese with a bunch of screaming kids. I took some Advil and a strong cup of coffee to the rooftop deck and sat for a long time, enjoying the sunshine and staring out at the ocean, wondering if I really did have feelings for Shane. But the more I thought about Shane, the more I thought about Emmett. Though I had only known him a handful of days, it was he who electrified me, not Shane. But I still didn't regret the kiss. It was good to have explored the curiosity that may have lived on dormant.

*

Shane called while I was in the shower and left a message that simply said, "Get your butt over here." His tone was light and playful as it had always been and I hoped that meant things wouldn't be awkward.

His bags were by the door when I got there, ready for his departure. It made me sad – it was too soon. While I didn't want anything with him romantically, I didn't want the only person who 'got me,' my best friend, to leave.

"Walk with me," he said, meeting me in the formal living room.

He led the way down the path toward the ocean. We crossed PCH and took a bench next to the railing that faced the water.

He turned to face me. "I meant what I said last night," he started. "About me and you. I do wonder sometimes about what would - could," he amended, "...be. But, like you, I don't think it's worth the risk."

I nodded, and he continued. "Mags is amazing. I'd really like to give it a shot with her. And it sounds like you have something going with your guy. But let's keep in better contact, okay Sam? Use the computer. I took the liberty of installing Skype. I even wrote you step-by-step instructions on how to use it." He laughed. "You're so retarded with that stuff."

"Does this mean you aren't coming home at the end of the summer, like your parents want you to?"

He cocked his head and scratched his chin. "It means I'm going to try and do what it takes to stay with her. Heck, maybe we'll see each other in Oz."

I tried to imagine: Shane, Mags, Emmett and myself having a drink together in Australia. I couldn't.

He looked me in the eye. "You keep your head up, kid. I know what this thing with your dad is doing to you. Anytime you want to come visit me, just say the words, whenever or wherever that may be. I'll make sure you get a ticket."

We hugged one another tightly. I wondered when or where I would see him again. I hoped that it could be under better circumstances.

Like the afternoon sun, I felt my youth slipping away.

*

I spent the rest of the evening and the following day at Pop's. He was in and out of his weird time warps; one minute he was in the present, the next somewhere else. It was tiring to keep up with.

I was definitely avoiding Rachel and Crystal. I hadn't called them and they hadn't called me, and that bugged me when I thought about it, even though I tried not to. I knew I should have been the bigger person, but it was hard because I didn't feel like I had done anything wrong. Besides, there were bigger things I had to worry about.

By Sunday night, Pop had been home for almost a week and we hadn't had a proper talk about the future. GamGam asked the Baxter's to stay with Pop and she, Uncle Chuck and I went to dinner.

GamGam spoke first. "I know Darrell hasn't had the Neuropsychological Evaluation, but with his ups and downs this week I reckon it's high time we made some permanent decisions concerning his daily life."

She continued. "We're goin' to need the ability to make informed medical decisions for him, at least for now. First thing in the mornin', I'm calling my lawyer and drawing up a Power of Attorney for all three of us."

Uncle Chuck and I nodded. I was glad she was taking charge.

"Now here's the tricky part: where does Darrell go? Where do we think is the best place for him to be right now, and with whom? I don't mind staying with him here but I would need to make permanent arrangements pertaining to my own home, my cats, so forth."

"What about Hawaii?" I asked.

They both looked at me. "Pop said he was thinking about going to Hawaii with Uncle Chuck. Did he say anything to you?"

"He hasn't mentioned anything." Uncle Chuck said. "But that could be a good idea. I could take care of him."

GamGam shook her head. "Chuck, you know how much work that would be. You are still young, darlin', and maybe," she hinted, "You might still meet a nice girl."

He laughed. "Mom, I'm almost sixty years old. I don't think that's a deciding factor in my life decisions anymore."

"Okay, so hypothetically Pop goes to Hawaii." I continued. "What about the house? What about all the stuff?"

GamGam pursed her lips. "We would have to sell both of our houses, no doubt about it."

I stared at my mashed potatoes. Huntington Beach had been my home all of my life – could it still be my home without Pop and Shane in it?

GamGam patted my hand. "For now, we'll get the Power of Attorney and we'll get the evaluation completed. Somewhere in there, we'll figure out where Darrell goes."

I scowled. *Where Darrell goes*, like he was a pair of shoes being put away.

*

The next morning at PT while Brian was examining my knee, I finally told him that I had been surfing.

"How did your knees do?" he asked, moving my kneecap in a circular motion.

"I couldn't stay up very well. But it was amazing being out there. It's my home out there, I mean what else can I say?" I shrugged, having no intelligent words to offer up.

"Good," he patted my leg. "It's important to stay motivated. Just don't overdo it. How's your dad doing?"

Again I shrugged, not really wanting to talk about it.

"Okay, we're going to do floor exercises and the elliptical today."

Normally, I would have protested. But I felt like I had finally turned a new leaf in my recovery process. More work meant I was closer to getting better - and that meant closer to surfing again.

I had a good session. On the way out, Brian commented on the decrease in swelling. "Keep doing what you're doing. It's working."

*

I changed at the clinic and drove straight to H.S.S for my first day back at work. I was early, but didn't go straight up to the offices. The store had recently been expanded to include a coffee shop and a specialty board shop, so I took a couple of minutes and wandered through the boards, observing their various dimensions. I let my hands graze their shiny, silky surfaces as I passed through, thinking of Pop's boards in the storage unit.

"Morning. Did you need some help with a board?"

I turned around and nearly ran into a guy. "Oh! Sorry! No, I'm Sam, I'm sort of new. I'm working the reception desk in the offices upstairs."

"I've never seen you before. I'm Garrett." He held his hand out.

I shook it. "I actually used to work here in high school, but I've been gone for a few years."

Garrett and I idly chatted as we wandered back toward the entrance, where I found Greg buying a cup of coffee. "Well, it was nice to meet you, Garrett. I'll see you around."

Greg politely asked about Pop as we took the elevator up. He introduced me to Lila once again and had her take over my training. There wasn't a whole lot to cover that I didn't already know, and within minutes I was alone behind the mighty desk.

The work was interesting, as I expected it to be. Mostly, everything was related to the forthcoming surf competition. The papers circulating the office were all marketing materials, logo's and drafts for press releases. I found myself lingering on them as they were handed to me to distribute.

However, the best part of it all had to be the famous surfers that were in and out of the office all day. Tim was well known, respected and liked in the world of surfing, and his competition had become a big So-Cal surf competition, bringing in surfers from all over the globe. Tim was also Australian by birth, and there were floods of Aussie's in particular that were expected to be arriving the next day.

Five o'clock arrived faster than I expected, and I actually found myself not wanting to leave. I wasn't avoiding anything and I wasn't bored. I was finally interested in the work I was doing.

Chapter 10: Some Answers are Better not Knowing

The next morning I awoke early. I was picking Emmett and a few of his buddies up from the airport later that evening, but most importantly, the day had finally arrived for Pop's Neuropsychological evaluation. There was much to do, and I wouldn't be coming home until late that night.

The Neurosurgeon came off of Dr. Ewing's recommendation, a Dr. Pham based out of Laguna Beach. Dr. Ewing informed us he was on track to become one of the most sought-after Neurosurgeon's in Southern California and that his practices were cutting edge. Being none the wiser we accepted his referral, though I wasn't sure I liked the words 'cutting' and 'practices' when referring to my father and his doctor.

We opted for the scenic drive down PCH rather than the quicker freeway. Pop was placated by the world outside his window and at one point looked at me and said, "I may call Bobby this week and see if he wants to go surfing. He lives here now."

I was getting used to Pop's randomness, but I didn't have a clue as to whom he was referring to this time. "Who's Bobby?"

"You know, Bobby Sanchez. We went to high school with him."

"We?" Who did he think I was today? My mom? GamGam?

He rolled his eyes. "Like you don't know who I'm talking about."

Uncle Chucked looked over his shoulder and winked at me.

Dr. Pham's office was grandiose, like most other doctor's offices in Orange County. Big marble columns supported an expensive-looking building, and perfectly manicured flowerbeds bordered the sidewalk as we pulled into the drive. In another day in another time, I might have thought it pretty, but right then I just found it all ostentatious and tacky.

GamGam parked the car and Uncle Chuck hopped out and opened Pop's door. He didn't move, just sat there with a slight smile on his face. We waited for him to move, my patience fizzling by the second. Finally, I said, "Pop do you need a wheelchair?"

He looked at me and said, "Why do you keep calling me 'Pop'? He looked around him. "Are we at the dentist?"

I rubbed my forehead in exasperation. I was so tired of it all, already. Uncle Chuck gently grabbed his arm, saying, "C'mon, Darrell. Let's go."

"Okay. But only if I get a sucker."

Uncle Chuck appeased him and we walked up the ramp and through the sliding doors. The office was packed, and the interior again reeked of money. Several mounted plasma-screen TV's showed morning programs and nature shows, and expensive art adorned walls so white, they looked bleached - they were that blinding in their newness. It was a complete 180 from Dr. Ewing's offices.

I went to the counter. "I'm here to check in my father, Darrell Dane. We have a nine o'clock appointment." I wrote his name down and waited, watching Pop as he sidled over to get a cup of coffee.

The receptionist took copies of Pop's insurance card and asked me to take a seat. I took one close to the coffee station, where Pop was attempting to fix himself a cup.

Suddenly, Pop's mood changed again and he got angry, throwing a cup at the wall. Uncle Chuck and I ran over to him, putting our arms around his shoulders to calm him down, like he was toddler throwing a temper tantrum.

"It's okay." I said, nearly saying 'Pop' again.

"What the hell is this, Samantha?" He looked at me with a scowl.

"What do you need?" I asked, adopting a soothing voice, thankful he knew me again.

"I just want a fucking cup of coffee!" He slammed his fist on the table, and several people looked over at us. I tried not to show my embarrassment. Uncle Chuck steered Pop away from the coffee station and back toward GamGam.

"I'll make you a cup, Pop," I said to him over my shoulder, mentally noting to make it decaf. I picked up the 'pod', a little plastic cup that looked like cream for coffee. I followed the instructions listed on the wall, but the blue light just keep blinking and no coffee came out.

I was just as lost. Pop had every right to be upset.

After a few more frustrating minutes, I walked away with a cup of steaming liquid. He took the cup and sipped his coffee without further incident during the hour-long wait for the doctor. I watched the other people, wondering what brought them to the facility. There were old and young people, none of them showing any outward signs of trauma like Pop. It made me even more worrisome.

Eventually Pop's name was called and we were escorted back by a tight-lipped, nonplussed nurse. She took Pop's vitals, and when she reported Pop's weight, I noted proudly that he had put on even more weight. She then showed us to a room where we would wait for the doctor, just as the nurse had done at Dr. Ewing's office.

When the doctor arrived, he was as curt and efficient as his nurse, not even bothering to look up from his laptop as he walked in and greeted us. "Mr. Dane, I'm Dr. Pham. It's nice to meet you," he said.

"Well, do you have it?" Pop asked.

The doctor looked at him. "Have what, Mr. Dane?"

"He wants to know if you have a lollipop." I said, feeling the need to answer for him.

"We'll get you one after we finish some tests."

Pop didn't say anything else, and we all sat quietly as the doctor read over the notes sent by Dr. Ewing. I fidgeted with Pop's hair, feeling anxious as he sat there oblivious to the world around him.

"Alright, Mr. Dane, do you know where you are?"

"I'm at the dentist, STILL waiting for a sucker," he said with a scowl.

Dr. Pham nodded, typing.

He did the usual eyes, ears and throat check, tapped his knee with that silly tool meant for checking reflexes and flashed a light in his eye. Next, he had him take a math test you might see a seventh grader take, and played a question and answer game using small objects, something meant for a toddler. I felt humiliated – for Pop, for my family, for myself. I kept telling myself these were standard testing procedures.

The doctor continued asking him questions about where he was born, where his parents lived, if he had any siblings. Pop answered, "yes," but he didn't indicate that his brother was in the room with him.

"Do you have any children, Mr. Dane?"

We all held our breath. But Pop didn't skip a beat.

"No."

Dr. Pham stopped typing and everybody looked at me. A lone tear streamed down my face and I looked away, not wanting this cold doctor to see me cry.

"I'd like to run some further tests. Do you have the time to attend to these now?"

GamGam answered yes, and a nurse escorted us through a maze of hallways to another wing of the building. They drew more of Pop's blood (to rule out systemic illnesses, we were told) and had him take a PET Scan, something I'd never even heard of before. It was approaching 11:00 by then, and I knew I had to call Greg and explain that I wasn't sure what time I would be in. He was understanding and told me to come in when we were through.

Two hours later, we were ushered into Dr. Pham's office, and I was positive it wasn't a good sign. On the fluorescent boards were Pop's scans, and I braced myself for the worst.

"I believe Mr. Dane is suffering from Frontotemporal Dementia," he began, eschewing any formalities. "It is a form of dementia that causes degeneration of the frontal lobe of the brain. It typically affects younger patients, as opposed to Alzheimer's, which tends strike an older age group. Frontotemporal Dementia can be genetic, but in Mr. Dane's case I believe it has been triggered by a series of silent strokes."

GamGam and I looked at one another, fearful again, like we had been in the hospital. This was concurrent with what the doctor had said there, too.

"Furthermore, I would like to look at his heart. There can be other complications, such as atrial fibrillation, hypertension, blood clots. We need to find and isolate what is causing these silent strokes."

"So what happens next?" I asked.

"There aren't a whole lot of long term treatment options, unfortunately," he said. "There are medications he can take that will help with some of the symptoms, and we will switch them around until we find one that suits him best. I would like him to continue physical therapy, stay in a steady routine surrounded with the things he loves. Keeping a positive state of mind is very important."

I had a thought. "Is it possible that it's his surroundings that could actually be causing this? My mother died a long time ago, and he sits around all day looking at photos of her, talking out loud to her, basically acting like she is still alive."

"Depression is very common in patients with dementia. Anxiety can cause changes in the nervous system, which regulates the contraction of blood vessels."

I pursed my lips. "So maybe in his case regularity wouldn't be such a good idea?"

"It is hard to say. Different people react in different ways. Dementia is a very complicated disease, Ms. Dane."

I sat back, digesting everything.

"You're head is in the right place, though. Maybe you should think about being a doctor," Dr. Pham said, giving me the first smile he had offered all morning.

*

It was after two o'clock by the time I reported to the offices at H.S.S., and I didn't like it. I knew that Greg understood it was because of Pop, but I wanted to turn over a new leaf in my professional life; being late on my second day wasn't how I wanted to start. At five o'clock I switched off the phones like I normally would, but instead of leaving I asked Greg if I could stick around and help out. With the competition less than three days away I knew there would be plenty of work to do.

And I was right, there was. Greg kept me busy until nearly 8:00, when I looked at my watch and gasped. "Shit, I've got to get to the airport!"

He waved me off. "Go, go. Thanks for sticking around."

I walked out of his office quickly and grabbed my purse and keys from my desk. I was pushing the down button when Greg yelled, "Hey, Sam?"

"Yeah?" I yelled back.

He poked his head out of his office. "I forgot to ask you something. Tim wanted to know if you could work the VIP booth down at the competition. You know, handing out passes and all that stuff."

Work at the competition?

Like I had to think twice. "I would love to."

The doors opened just as I remembered something else. "Hey Greg? Pop was right about the boards. You guys can use them for the auction."

He clapped his hands. "Excellent. Tim will be very pleased."

I left feeling very, very happy - and excited. Emmett was coming.

*

Airports everywhere had become a pain in the ass in the post 9/11 era, and LAX had to be one of the worst. Picking someone up was nearly impossible: you could barely stop long enough to load your passenger and their bags into your vehicle before airport police would be on your ass, ready to fine you. Emmett's flight had been delayed and not knowing how long it could be, I was forced to loop and loop until he called – I wasn't paying for parking.

When I saw him, my heart started beating and my hands felt shaky as I steered toward curbside. I parked the car, put on the emergency flashers and took my keys from the ignition to open the trunk for him and his friends, he were filing behind him.

He set his bag down and gave me a huge hug. "You look bloody gorgeous."

I barely had time to respond before sure enough, the airport police cruiser had paused next to my own. "We've got to get going."

We piled into my old car and I navigated out of the airport. I looked into the backseat, where the other three Aussie's were squished in and introduced myself. Turning to Emmett, who was sitting in the front seat, I said, "Emmett, you must be exhausted from all of this travel. It's barely been a week since you left."

He shrugged. "It's a small price to pay to do what you love."

"So how was the flight?"

"Uneventful," Kevin said, from the back. He didn't offer much, just like the first few times I had met him.

"If you guys aren't too tired, I was thinking maybe we could grab some drinks tonight on Main Street?" I said, into the rearview mirror.

"Abso," CJ said, who looked exactly like Riley. Turning to him, he asked, "Mate, did you find out when the rugby is going to be on?"

Riley leaned toward me and asked, "Is there an Irish pub near Main Street?"

Emmett and I looked at one another, laughing. "A couple, actually." I said.

"Brilliant," CJ said, enthusiastically. "We can watch it there."

It took less than forty-five minutes to get back to HB. I remembered that there was absolutely nothing to eat and drink in my house, so Emmett offered to freshen up at the hostel with the guys while I went to the store.

Thirty minutes later, I picked the four of them up once more and drove us all back to my apartment. The Aussie's argued over their iPods, while I mixed up some cocktails. It was sort of exhilarating, entertaining a group of gorgeous Australian guys at my beachside apartment (even if they weren't exactly in town for my benefit, and my beachside apartment was a complete dive).

Just before we were getting ready to leave, Crystal wandered over randomly, like always. But her appearance was shocking, and I gasped when I saw her.

"Crystal! Your hair!" Gone were her trademark dreads, replaced with a pixie-style haircut. It even looked like she was wearing make-up. She looked gorgeous, and it was apparent the guys thought so too, because they all stared as she walked in.

She flushed. I don't think she was used to being the one that got the attention. "Where's Rachel?" I asked, trying to mask the lingering iciness I felt.

"She met some guy in Hollywood and has been staying with him the last few days." She gave me a hug. "Sorry about your birthday," she said, lowering her voice.

I shrugged. It still bothered me, but what was done was done. I introduced Crystal to the guys, and asked her if she wanted to come out with us to Main Street. Riley and CJ chimed in, and that was all it took; she agreed. Kevin remained quiet most of the time, but now that I'd had some time with CJ and Riley, I could see why: it was hard to get a word in edgewise with their enthusiastic banter.

The six of us walked to Main Street. I noticed that Emmett had also been quieter than usual, and I didn't think it had anything to do with the two guys.

The first Irish pub we went to was showing their rugby match, and we commandeered an area of tables and chairs in a corner. Though Emmett was quiet, he was attentive and affectionate, rubbing my back here or holding my hand there. Again, there was undeniable sexual chemistry between us.

It was late by the time the game finished and most everyone had an early start in the morning. So Emmett, Crystal and I said good-bye to the three guys at Sixth Street, before parting ways with one another at the apartments. Once Emmett and I were in my room, I shut the door and leaned against it with a sigh. "Finally, I get to spend some time alone with you."

He didn't say anything, just cornered me against my door and kissed me deeply. It was our first 'real' kiss, and it was charged with unleashed sexual energy. I pulled away, feeling breathless.

"Shit," he said, looking into my eyes, and we kissed again, but this time moved to my bed. The sexual tension was palpable, and the thought that Shane had been in my bed a few days earlier didn't occur to me until much later, when my head was resting on Emmett's chest and I was gasping for air.

*

We woke up at daybreak and met the guys at the pier, having agreed the night before on a location to surf. The conditions were pretty clean, with small, 2-3 footers that would suit me - and my hampered knees - just fine.

I still couldn't stay up on the board very long, and spent more time upside down in the surf again, but I had a great time; Emmett and his buddies were infectious.

Afterward, I left the four of them to go visit Pop. It was more of the same though, his moods and remarks all over the place. GamGam and Uncle Chuck were visibly tired, and I felt guilty not doing my part around Pop's house.

"We were wondering something," Uncle Chuck said, yawning. "Do you think there's a way we can get Darrell behind the scenes at the competition? It would be really good for him to get out of the house and around some surf action."

I thought about it. The Open drew thousands from all over, and I wondered if it was a good idea to have Pop around so many people. "Well, I don't have a lot of pull with the competition itself, but I'm sure it'd be okay for you guys to hang out at the VIP booth with me."

"What's the worst that could happen?" Uncle Chuck said wryly.

*

When I got into the office I found Lila wide-eyed and gabby. "Guess. What."

"What?" I asked, placing my purse in a drawer next to the desk.

"Well, guess who is the real question." She took off the headset and handed it to me. "Reggie Macintosh is here." She pointed down the hall toward Tim's office.

Reggie Macintosh was one of the biggest names in surfing, and one of H.S.S.'s most coveted surfers. I accepted the headset from her and put it on. "He's probably here to do something for the foundation," I answered practically.

She shook her head. "I've seen the press release - he's not supposed to be there. She snapped her gum, looking longingly at Tim's closed door.

I shrugged. I didn't get giddy around the pros the way the other girls did, like Lila. The phone rang and I answered, waving goodbye at Lila. As I was transferring the call, Tim's door opened and he and Reggie walked out.

"Alright, Reg, you can just go on downstairs and pick out what you like. Sam here can help you with that. Sam?"

I took off the headset and stood up. "What's that, Greg?"

"Can you escort Reggie downstairs to the boardshop and set him up with Garrett? I've got some last minute stuff to do for the event tonight and can't help 'im meself."

I came out from behind the desk. "Of course. Shall I put the voicemail on?"

"Oh, Greg can answer it for once. Won't hurt him. Reg, mate, I'll see you tonight. Sam here will take good care of you. Oh and Sam, stop by my office on your way back up."

"Of course, Tim."

Tim walked back to his office, and I escorted Reggie to the elevator. Though I didn't hyperventilate like the other girls I did respect a good surfer and there I was, standing with one of the best who was just a couple of years older than I.

"So, how's your trip been to HB so far?" I asked, as we entered the elevator.

"Oh, I just got in this morn, but good, I spose." he responded, sounding exactly like Emmett.

I nodded. "It's been kind of cold for this time of year, but it's all about the waves, isn't it?"

He leaned against the wall of the elevator. "Its winter back in Oz, and freezing fucking balls," he said. "I'll take what youse have here."

I noticed how much the Aussie's seemed to curse. It didn't offend me at all, but it was funny how they used it as an adjective.

We exited the elevator and I introduced him to Garrett, who seemed just as star struck as Lila.

"Alright, Sam. Thanks. Will I see you tonight?" Reggie asked, just as I was turning back to the elevator.

"Yep, I'll be there." I said, and waved good-bye.

I went straight to Tim's office once I was back upstairs.

"Will you be able to attend the auction tonight, after all?" he asked.

I slapped my forehead, remembering that I had completely forgotten to give him an answer. "I'm not sure."

He shook his head. "Well, it's no big deal, really. Unfortunately, I can't integrate Darrell's boards into the auction tonight; it's just too short of notice. But I would like to put them up on the Foundation's website where people can bid on them. All the proceeds will go to your father's care, of course."

"That's not necessary," I said, wondering if I was the right person to be having this talk with him.

"Well then youse can pick out an organization you want to support, if you like. Either way, think about it, we can introduce Darrell tonight, let people know about the website and maybe have him down at the competition? I don't know if he can handle all that physically, but I remember what it was like for me when I still had leukemia. I would have done anything to be around surfing. I know how much he loved the sport."

The past tense wasn't lost on me. Loved.

He leaned in. "You hanging in there, love?"

I answered with a shrug. I just didn't know how to answer that question anymore.

"Alright, think about it. If you decide to come, you know where to find me."

I thanked him and returned to my desk, my head spinning from everything.

Chapter 12: The Shore was Awash with Aussie's

I let Emmett and the Aussie's borrow my car to drive down and surf Trestle's in San Onofre, a beach about an hour south, so I had to walk to Pop's house when I finished work that night. I didn't mind, for I was really beginning to relish the time alone that walking brought.

I found Pop in the garage sanding down a board. He didn't greet me when I walked in, but he didn't appear upset either, so I took a seat in the big wicker chair and watched him for a while.

Finally, after about five minutes of pure silence, I spoke up. "Pop?"

He didn't respond.

"Pop? Can I talk to you?"

"Yeah, go ahead," he said, without looking up.

I got up and walked over to him, gently taking the sandpaper from his hand and putting it down. I led him to the chair I had been sitting in and had him sit. I leaned against the wall and crossed my arms, gathering the right words to say.

"So, you know Tim, from H.S.S."

He rubbed his hands together and nodded.

"Well, Tim would like us to be his guests tonight at the foundation dinner. You know, the one that he does every year?" I said, reminding him of the very event he attended up until three years ago.

"He'd like us to be his special guests, Pop. Sit at the table with him and all. Would you like to go?"

He got up and started pacing. It made me nervous.

"I've been working on a couple of boards today, for you." He went over and motioned to the board on the table.

I furrowed my brow, but said, "Oh, uh…thanks."

"We can go to the dinner," he said, returning to where I stood. "But we've got to get in early. You don't want to be tired for your first heat. And besides, I'll be up all night finishing these new boards if we don't get home at a decent hour."

Once again we were lost in time, and this time he thought I was still healthy and aspiring to compete professionally. The night he was referring to we had attended Tim's foundation dinner and we had stayed out late but I wasn't entered into the Open, then.

"Sure thing, Pop." I agreed, appeasing him. "Hey, where are GamGam and Uncle Chuck?"

He returned to his sanding. "They're both sleeping."

I wandered out of the garage and back into the house. I sat on the couch and waited for one of them to wake up. After twenty minutes or so, Uncle Chuck stumbled in bleary-eyed, his hair a mess.

"Jesus, Uncle Chuck."

He yawned. "Yeah, I know. Where's Darrell?" His eyes suddenly widened with worry.

"Pop's fine, he's in the garage sanding. Hey, so, are you guys still up for attending the foundation dinner tonight?" I gave him the information and relayed Pop's reaction when I had told him about it.

He continued to shake his head as I talked, and when I finished he said, "We've got to figure something out. He... he hasn't had a tangible thought in days, and his memory is all over the board. I can't sleep, and I know Mom isn't either."

I looked down. "I should be helping out more."

He shook his head vehemently. "You need to get your shit together dear, pardon my French. What I mean is we need to figure out a permanent solution for your father now, not before or after we get a lawyer, and that solution just may have to include daycare or hiring a nurse."

GamGam came in then, looking as worse for wear as I had ever seen her before, and I knew that Uncle Chuck was right: we did need help.

GamGam agreed that it was worth trying to get Pop out of the house. It would be the first social event he had been to since the stroke.

They agreed to pick me up at seven o'clock, just an hour from then. It wasn't much time to get ready, and I still needed to find out where Emmett was, so I bade them good-bye and walked home.

I was just about to get in the shower when Emmett appeared in my room.

"Hello, love," he said, greeting me with a kiss.

"Hi," I said, adopting my shy voice once more, because that's how I seemed to feel when I hadn't seen him in awhile.

"So what's your plan tonight?" he asked, stretching out on my bed.

It dawned on me that I would have to leave Emmett while I attended the dinner, and I didn't want to. "I completely forgot about this dinner thing," I started.

"Me too," he said, laughing.

I looked at him curiously. "And what are your plans?"

He stopped laughing and frowned slightly. "Well, I'm not sure, actually, but apparently you have to have an invitation, and Kev got me one at the last minute. Obviously, I would have got you one if I could."

"Where is it?" I asked, my curiosity piquing.

"Dunno," he said, simply.

I looked through my closet for some clothes, talking about my day and meeting Reggie.

"Fuck Reggie Macintosh," Emmett said, cutting me off.

I peered around the door at his face and realized he wasn't joking. "Do you know him?"

" 'Course I know him."

"I thought he was okay," I said, not wanting to upset Emmett but curious nonetheless as to why he hated him.

"Yeah, well that's because you're a sheila. That's his specialty."

I didn't have time to find out more. I leaned across the bed, kissed him and said, "I'm really, really glad you're here," I said, changing the subject, but noting to get to the bottom of it all later, when I had more time.

*

The dinner was at a restaurant in nearby Sunset Beach, a small community between Huntington Beach and Seal Beach. We disembarked at the valet stand and I grabbed Pop's hand, who looked sort-of normal in his regulatory Hawaiian shirt and chinos. It was comforting seeing him like he used to be, and on impulse, I said, "I love you, Pop."

He squeezed my hand. "I love you too, honey."

We filed into the restaurant and were led to a private room at the back. It was packed, filled with a who's-who of locals involved in the surf community. I held on tightly to Pop's hand, something I normally wouldn't have done, and I couldn't help wondering if it was for my benefit or for Pop's. I was nervous for us both.

Tim saw us right away and greeted us warmly, introducing GamGam and Uncle Chuck to his family. It seemed Tim had briefed them on Pop's accident, because they were overly nice to him, almost to the point where they treated him like a child. I knew that they hadn't treated him like that in the past, and had to remind myself that it was hard for everyone to get used to seeing the new Pop.

"Sam, come with me," Tim said, leading me to a makeshift bar at the back of the room. As we got closer, I recognized some of the guys; notably, Reggie, CJ, and Riley. I laughed upon seeing them.

Tim looked at all of us. "Don't tell me youse know each other?"

"She's with 'im," Riley said, pointing at Emmett, who was with Kev and a girl on the other side of the room, "And so are we, so now we know her."

"And you met Reggie today," Tim said. Reggie smiled, showing at least fifteen perfectly capped teeth.

"Hello again," Reggie said, this time, flirtatiously.

I laughed uneasily, not taking my eyes off of Emmett - who still had not seen me yet.

"Well then," Tim said, turning to the bartender. "What'll it be, Sam?"

I asked for a light beer, not wanting to drink too much in front of my bosses and family. "So how was San O?" I asked, Riley and CJ.

"Fucking excellent," CJ said. "Much better this arvo, thanks to a northwestern swell. Got some good sets in before heading back here."

Reggie flashed another expensively-perfect smile. "Do you surf too, Sam?"

A pair of arms snaked around my waist, making me jump. I turned around and saw Emmett, who smiled and kissed my cheek. "Hello, babe."

"Oh fuck, Taylor, already?" Reggie said, dropping pleasantries.

Emmett's arms tightened around my waist. I anxiously looked around for a distraction and saw my family at the other end of the room, pulling out chairs as they prepared to sit down. "Excuse us," I said, pulling Emmett with me.

I normally wouldn't have introduced a guy to my family so quickly, but it seemed nothing I did with Emmett was concurrent with my usual methods. I didn't want Emmett to get in a fight, and I didn't want my family to be alone, so I pulled out a chair next to Pop and patted the empty one next to it for Emmett to sit on.

"Pop," I said, taking a deep breath. "This is my friend, Emmett. He's visiting from Australia"

Emmett extended his hand. " 'Ello."

Pop eyes widened in amazement, but he didn't say anything.

"Pop, can you say hello?"

"Occy!" he said, excitedly.

We all looked at him.

"You're Occy!" Pop said, again.

"Pop, what are you talking about?"

"Are you here for the Open?" he asked Emmett, ignoring me. Nothing but pure delight showed on his face.

Emmett's face reflected my own. "Er, yes, yes I am."

Pop elbowed me in the ribs. "Some dinner, huh? Tim's pulling out all the stops this time, getting Mark Occhilupo to come."

I looked at Emmett, wondering where Pop was getting the reference to the famous surfer. In turn, GamGam and Uncle Chuck looked at me, but I just shrugged.

Pop took a sip of the water the waitress put before him. "I've been a fan for years, you know."

"Is that right?" Emmett said, humoring him.

Pop started rambling about the seventies and growing up in La Jolla, but his words didn't register. Luckily, the music stopped and Tim's voice boomed over the loudspeakers.

" 'Ello, everyone," he greeted us. "Can you take a seat please? We're about to get dinner started."

Thankfully, Pop shut up and Emmett squeezed my hand under the table.

*

After the dinner, Tim came over and took a seat with us. "How's he doing?"

"He's doing pretty good," I said, watching Pop as he hummed to himself.

"Do you think he's up to being introduced to the audience?" Tim asked, also watching Pop.

I looked at GamGam and Uncle Chuck. "I don't know."

"What if I just brought the mike down 'ere?"

I shrugged. "Sure."

Tim ran up to the stage, grabbed the microphone, and ran back to us. " 'ello again everyone, I hope you enjoyed your dinner. I'd like to introduce a special guest tonight. Some of you may know the Dane's as Sam here has been active with the organization for a few years now." He introduced GamGam and Uncle Chuck, before finally clapping Pop on the shoulder.

"This is Darrell Dane, Sam's father. Darrell used to be quite active in the community before he got sick, which I'm going to let Sam tell you all about. Sam?"

My eyes widened. I hadn't expected to have to talk. I cleared my throat and accepted the extended microphone. "Hello, I'm Sam Dane."

I felt my face go hot as someone (probably CJ or Riley) let out an ear-splitting whistle. It gave me some courage, so I fixed a smile on my face and continued.

"Many of you know me and my dad, Darrell Dane. We both used to surf a lot, before I got injured and he got sick." I cleared my throat again, trying to gather my thoughts. Pop grabbed onto my hand and I looked at him, memories flooding into my head. I felt myself choke up, and had to turn my face for a moment before I could continue.

"Sorry," I said. "My dad had a stroke last week, so this is all really new. Anyway, before he got sick he was a surfer and a shaper. A really good shaper. We will be donating some of Pop's one-of-a-kind boards to be auctioned off. All proceeds will benefit Tim's foundation, of course, and I know it would be such an honor to see Pop's handiwork put to a good cause."

Pop squeezed my hand and started clapping wildly. The audience followed suit. I smiled and thanked Tim for having us, before passing the mike to him once more.

I looked out at the audience and caught the eyes of Reggie, who was staring straight at me. His gaze was unnerving.

*

Pop and insisted on sitting next to 'Occy', and was currently snoozing on the other side of Emmett. He had fallen asleep midway through another speech Tim was giving and I caught GamGam's eye, knowing we needed to get him out of there. I was just unsure of how to do so without drawing more attention to ourselves than we already had.

I leaned into Emmett and whispered, "When there's a moment, we're going to bolt, okay?"

He nodded. "I'm ready to go anyway."

"You don't have to leave," I said.

"I'm not leaving you."

Ten minutes later, the speeches were finished and there was an intermission. I made a beeline for Tim, thanking him quickly and explaining that we needed to get Pop home. He was very understanding, and bade us all good night.

It was a good thing Emmett didn't mind leaving with us, because Pop refused to leave without him. Emmett assumed his new character and coaxed Pop out and into the night. He fell asleep once more in the car, and for the duration of the car ride home we were all silent, lost in our own thoughts.

Back at my apartment, Emmett and I went up to the rooftop and sat quietly on the bench, staring into the night. He was respectful of my silence, but I worried about what his own meant.

There was so much to worry about. Having Emmett stay with me had seemed like such a good idea at first, but with everything going on with Pop I was starting to worry that it might be too much too fast. We stayed on the roof until we couldn't hold our eyes open any longer. We went to bed together, but this time nothing happened – the evening had just been too emotionally draining, at least for me.

*

I was due on the beach at 6 am to help out with the competition. It was hard getting up and leaving Emmett in bed, especially when it was still dark out. Garrett, the guy from the board shop who was working the booth with me, met me at the coffee shop, looking just as bleary-eyed as I. We bought cups of coffee and walked down to the quiet, empty beach, the beach that would be jammed packed within just a few short hours.

We found Greg, who was studying a clipboard. He looked just as tired as Garrett and I, and I wondered what time he had left the restaurant.

"Sam, I'm so glad you're going to be helping out. You know more about this competition than any of the juniors - no offense, Garrett."

It felt nice, being needed for something. I put on my professional face and asked him where he wanted me first.

There was no shortage of work, and we worked tirelessly through the morning. By the time Garrett tapped me on the shoulder it was nearly eleven a.m. "Let's grab some grub."

We went to the closest place, Taco Bell. We talked while we waited in the long line, and the more I learned about him, the more I liked him. Though he was young, his mellow demeanor made him feel like an old soul.

"So where all have you surfed, Garrett?" I asked, as we squeezed into a corner table.

"I haven't really been anywhere, but I've never had that itch to see the world." He took a bite and continued. "I love this place. I was born here and I'm sure I'll die here. What about you? What's your plan?"

I finished chewing and thought about it. "I don't know, anymore. I'm the opposite of you, I guess. I'm dying to see the world - I want to wake up on some beach far away, grab my board and paddle out with the sunrise. Surf all day, stopping just to eat. I want to drink beer by moonlight and fall asleep in the comfort of someone's arms." I laughed. "God, it sounds cheesy saying it all aloud."

The alarm I had set on my watch ding-ed: we were due back.

The beach had begun filling up, and the sun was hotter than any day I could remember thus far that summer. Greg had me running all over the place, and I did so happily. I couldn't remember a time I had loved my job more - or thought of my knee any less.

I had given Emmett vague directions on where to find me, and I could hear his laughter before he came into view. Catching sight of him, my heart thudded wildly. His massive, bronzed form was in sharp contrast to the smaller, much whiter bodies around him. Without any sunglasses on, his eyes scrunched up the way I loved, with the wrinkles appearing in the corners. I loved looking at him.

I had to admit it. I was falling in love with him.

Emmett's friends were far from chopped liver themselves, and between the three of them they were turning a few other female heads. I instantly felt territorial. I walked around the table and hugged them all, pulling them into the shade of the VIP tent.

"So what time are your heats?"

"We haven't found out yet. We came to you first," Emmett said, putting his arm around me.

"Are you guys all in the same bracket?" I asked, clasping his hand.

"They're all seniors, except me," Riley answered. "I'm in the Men's group."

"So you'll be competing before them."

It felt weird calling them 'seniors,' but that was the nomenclature of the surf industry. I instructed them on where to find the booth with the information for their times, and also where to be for their heats.

Emmett didn't wander off very far, affording me a chance to catch a glimpse of his pre-surf routine. Whether it was stretching, doing pushups or just standing and watching the shore as the surfers competed, Emmett looked natural and at home on the beach.

I was just about to join him when a large gust of wind shot sand in my direction, stinging my bare legs as it flew at me. The wind continued to pick up, and I wondered if the weather was about to change. Sure enough, the sky darkened and the shoreline turned into a whitewashed mess before a massive downpour occurred.

The competition was placed on hold.

Chapter 12: More Than Just One Good-Bye

The weather didn't improve. In fact, it got worse, the mid-afternoon downpour continuing into the evening. I still had work to do at the office, and Emmett needed to do some computer work for his business back in Australia; we agreed to meet back at my place later that evening.

I had been so busy with my new job, Pop and Emmett's arrival that I had been forced to cancel my PT appointment the day before. I didn't want to fall behind again, so I called Brian and he squeezed me in for a quick appointment. Due to the lack of time we had he worked me even harder, but I was beginning to like the pain. I was still making remarkable progress every day

I avoided going to Pop's house like I had planned. It was so emotionally exhausting to be in his presence, and it was becoming harder and harder to bounce back to my chipper, positive self when I left him. I made up a lame excuse about needing to stick around at work and promised GamGam I would come by the following evening.

Emmett greeted me with a smile and a kiss, and asked for a full report of my afternoon since I had left him. I wondered if this was what it felt like to come home to someone. If so, I liked it. A lot.

To date, I hadn't given Emmett the full lowdown on Pop's deteriorating health. He was a smart, perceptive man, and I was sure that he had some idea of what was going on. But given the direction things were heading in, I felt it was necessary to inform him on what may lie ahead in my future.

"So you know how I told you that my mom died when I was a baby," I began.

He nodded.

"Well, her death was an accident. She was hit by a train going full speed and was killed instantly."

He cringed. "Jesus."

"The accident wasn't her fault, though: it was the railroad company's error. She had no warning that a train was coming toward her. Anyway," I said, hurrying through the story that I rarely told, "Pop and she were like, high school sweethearts. Like, really, really in love. First everything's and all that. Pop has never been the same since she died."

I continued. "The thing is, Pop's now got dementia. The doctor's think he was depressed for so long that it started causing these silent strokes."

He nodded.

I prepared to say the words I had been afraid to think. "I don't think Pop is ever going to be the same again."

He shook his head solemnly.

"When do you start university?"

I scratched my head. "Sometime in mid-August, I think?"

"Well, I've been wanting to ask you something."

It was his turn to shift a little. "Would you like to come visit me, in Oz? There are excellent waves near my home. It could be--" he scratched his chin. "It could be therapeutic for you."

"You want me to come visit you?"

"Well, I think given our situations, we could make this work. If you wanted to, that is." He looked at me unblinkingly. "I'm crazy about you, Sam."

I knew that I was crazy about him too, but I wasn't sure I could invest myself into something more than what it was at the moment, just yet.

He seemed to read my thoughts. "Don't over-think it. Just know that there is an invitation for you to come to Noraville, anytime you fancy."

*

Apparently every person Emmett had ever known was a surfer and was in HB for the Open, because his phone kept going off with texts and phone calls. I wondered what kind of life these Australian's led. They all seemed to be professional surfers, one day in France, the next in Rio, partying, surfing and traveling. Did they slip something in the water there, that afforded them boundless income and natural talent?

The social atmosphere during the competition was electric. Though I had to be back at the booth at six am the next morning, I still went out with Emmett and his friends on Main Street that night. Crystal tagged along again, and it occurred to me that I hadn't seen or talked to Rachel in almost a week. It was an unprecedented amount of time that had passed in mutual silence, and it seemed that neither of us was going to budge. I felt guilty on some levels and worthy of an apology on others, but I tried not to think about it and tucked it away into the back of my mind.

The sidewalks of Main Street were brimming over with people. Every bar had a long line, and this time we didn't have Rachel to save us.

So we picked a rooftop bar with a view of the ocean. It was a good thirty minutes of waiting before we even saw the entrance of the bar. We were getting grumpy, and I was nearly ready to call it a night. Then, who other than Reggie MacIntosh should pass right by us in the VIP line. He stopped when he saw us.

"Hello again, Sam," he said, reaching out to me.

I stood frozen by Emmett's side, remembering both of his reactions to Reggie.

"I purchased one of your pop's boards. Can't wait to take it out. Maybe I'll use it tomoz, during my heat?"

Emmett flinched by my side. "Reggie, you're pathetic. Get the fack away from me girl."

Reggie shrugged and waved. "See ya, Sam."

Everyone was silent as he moved inside. I was officially done, ready to go home. "Emmett, maybe we should--"

Suddenly the bouncer came for us. "All of you, let's go. Get your ID's out."

We procured our driver's licenses' and passport's and moved inside, thankful to be out of the cold night. But it was more waiting for the busy bartenders to take our order. When it finally was our turn, we doubled up on drinks.

I got hammered, blacking out for the rest of the night.

*

I woke up to Emmett shaking me. The sun was barely rising, but that meant it was time to get up. My head spun and I felt sick, but I had to take responsibility for my actions. There was no calling in sick during the Tim Canton Leukemia Foundation Open.

There was barely enough time to shower and throw on some clothes. When I went to say good-bye to Emmett, he was very quiet, cold even.

"What's wrong?" I asked.

"We'll talk about it later."

It definitely didn't set my day off on the right foot. At the beach, Garrett looked as groggy as he did the day before. "You're not much of a morning person, are you?" I asked.

"Fuck," he said, coughing. "After all the shots we did and cigs we smoked? No, I'm not feeling particularly awesome."

"We?"

He raised his eyebrow. "You don't remember seeing me last night?" He laughed. "Oh God, that just makes so much sense now."

"What do you mean?"

He sat down on a chair. "Well, you were talking to Reggie Macintosh when I saw you and you were all, "Garrett, ohmygod!" he said, adopting a valley girl-like voice. "And you were like, 'Shhhh, don't let the other guy see me!' Whatever his name was. I had no clue what you were talking about."

"Wait, I was talking to Reggie Macintosh?" I asked.

"Haha, more like flirting with Reggie Macintosh." He scratched his head, ruffling his curly hair.

I groaned. No wonder Emmett had been so pissed.

"Yeah, much as you tried to hide talking to Reggie Mac, which by the way was about as well as I could hide an elephant on this beach here, Case in point, that other guy you were with wasn't very happy. Especially when he had to carry you out of the bar."

I didn't have time to ask more. Tim showed up, so Garrett and I had to get to work. The morning passed quickly and slowly my hangover wore off. It was a Friday, and it seemed like more people were okay with taking the day off. I recognized folks I hadn't seen in years, knowing them either through H.S.S. or Pop. More people came, seeking me out. I guessed that the word had gotten out after our appearance at the foundation dinner and they were curious about what exactly was going on with him, unabashedly asking questions that were occasionally offensive.

The competition itself was slow going. They always started out with the youngest group first, and since the waves were choppy and sporadic it took nearly all day to make it through the Groms. Then, it was Riley's group, the Mens, and by the time they had finished, the waves were flat and washed out. It was going to be interesting to watch Emmett's group try to do something with them.

Contrary to the day before, I hadn't seen Emmett all morning. But as soon as they announced the lineup, Emmett appeared, standing just a few feet from Reggie. They were both sporting their rash guards and official numbers. Emmett's look was complimented by a fierce scowl, Reggie's with a Cheshire cat-like grin.

I recognized the board immediately. Indeed, it was one of Pop's.

It was going to be a very competitive heat.

Reggie was set to go first, then Emmett, and so on. The announcer called out Reggie's name and honked a horn. Reggie took off, paddling quickly into the surf. Due to the flat waves, it was a couple of minutes before he attempted to catch anything. When he saw finally saw something worth going for he charged it, paddling ferociously. Just as the lip started to curl, he stood up and took off.

The tube went on and on, and you could see Reggie crouched low inside of it. When he came out, he nearly lost his balance but caught himself, tearing up the lip for a couple more seconds before the wave washed out. He faded into the white foam, and that quickly, his run was over.

He paddled back in to cheers and applause. It was a good run, affording him pretty solid scores from the judges. I looked at Emmett who was doing shoulder-rolls to relax himself. They announced his name and he got in position. They blew the horn and he took off, just like Reggie had. I held my breath in anticipation.

He paddled out faster and stronger than Reggie, and didn't have to wait as long for a good wave. Within a minute, he was crouching low on his board, cruising comfortably inside a barrel. As he finished, he popped a wicked air and I exhaled, clapping excitedly for him.

He came in amid applause and I waved at him, trying to get his attention. But he didn't even look over at me.

I felt a pang of fear. I really hoped I hadn't ruined things with him.

*

When I was finally able to get away and talk to Emmett, the forces weren't in my favor. Ultimately, he had lost to Reggie and was in a piss-poor mood, and completely cold when I asked him to talk. Under different circumstances, I might have waited, but we didn't have time on our side. I couldn't let the tension between us drag on.

I had been formulating what I would say to him throughout the morning. I didn't want to concede that I had been blackout drunk, but I was ashamed I had been flirting with Reggie, as Garrett had said I was. So I told a little white lie.

"I'm sorry," I said, when I had him alone. "If I upset you, it wasn't my intention to do so."

He crossed his arms in defiance. "You embarrassed me."

I nodded my head. "I know you don't like Reggie, but you see," I started rambling, something I did when I was lying, "I was talking to Reggie because he knows Tim, the owner of H.S.S. He's uh--" I racked my brain for something, "Collaborating on a new clothing line, and I had a question for him that I had been meaning to ask all day."

He cocked an eyebrow suspiciously.

"I knew how crazy today it was going to be today, and I needed to get these papers done. I also knew how much you disliked him, and I didn't want you to think the wrong thing by my talking to him which looking back was the wrong way to go about it.

I gulped. "Seriously." I put my arms around him and leaned my head back to look into his face. "I've been thinking about what you said, and you're right, we can make this work."

His face softened.

I continued. "What if I came out to Australia before school starts, like you mentioned before?"

He gave me a small smile and I felt immense relief. We talked casually about times and travel logistics; he also mentioned some places he would like to take me, and I eagerly agreed.

But in mind, I questioned why I had sought out Reggie, and suspiciously so. They say your truest self comes out with alcohol – was there something there that I was ignoring? But it didn't matter. I firmly ignored it and made a note to stay away from Reggie Macintosh.

*

Just before I was set to leave the beach for the day, Riley took me aside.

"Your mate," he said, rubbing his tanned arm, "Is she taken?"

"Who, Crystal?" I asked, with some surprise.

"Yea." He nodded his head emphatically.

"No, she's not." I said.

He shuffled. "Do youse think she might come to dinner tonight?"

"I'm not sure, Riley. Would you like to come home with me and ask her yourself?"

"Eh..."

I took his arm and led him toward the steps with me. "Come on. Let's find Emmett."

The three of us walked to my apartment. Passing by Pop's, I felt guilty - it had been nearly two days since I had seen him. I made a promise to myself that I would go first thing in the morning.

We walked up the stairs, and to my chagrin I saw that Rachel was home too. I was glad that the guys were with me because I knew that had they not been, there would have been some kind of stand-off between the two of us. As soon as she saw me, she walked into her room and closed the door.

"Crystal, you remember Riley."

She smiled. "Hey."

He shuffled his feet. "Hiya,"

I sighed. "Crystal, Riley would like you to come to dinner with us tonight."

She shrugged her shoulders. "Sure." She took a box from under the table and addressed Riley. "Care for a smoke?"

He sat on the opposite couch. "Fuck yea."

Emmett grabbed my arm. "I need to talk to you."

We walked next door to my apartment. I was nervous, wondering if Emmett had a change of heart.

He stood in front of me and grabbed my hands. "I've got to get back home," he said.

"So soon, again?"

He nodded. "There are some things going on...that, I really can't talk about, yet."

I was curious, but I didn't probe. "When?"

He sighed. "Now."

My heart fall. "Can I at least be the one to take you to the airport, this time?"

"Please."

*

I didn't care about the $5 parking at the airport this time, and walked with Emmett as far as I could into the terminal. He set his board bag down and turned to face me.

"Figure out the dates to come and see me. I'll buy your ticket. I need to have something to look forward to," he said, hugging me.

"I'll do it tonight," I promised.

We didn't say anything more, just hugged for as long as we could. As he was about to leave, he leaned down to kiss me gently. "I'll give you a bell as soon as I land." He then grabbed his board bag and duffle and hurried off.

*

I didn't go to the dinner with everyone else that night as planned. Instead, I went straight to Pop's.

Uncle Chuck was the only one there with Pop. "Where's GamGam?"

He looked up from a book he was reading. "She went back to La Jolla."

I grabbed some Iced Tea from the refrigerator and sat down with him. "How long will she be gone?"

He closed the book. "Well, sweetheart, probably throughout the weekend. She's going to put it on the market."

I was taken aback.

"We got the call from the Neurosurgeon this morning," he said. "Darrell's prognosis isn't good, Sammy."

I feared the worst. "Is he...going to die?"

"No, I don't think so. But dementia is irreversible. There seems to be a lot of damage done already."

That, I had suspected. But there was more, I knew it. "Uncle Chuck, what are you not telling me?"

He rubbed his beard. "Mom and I, we think he may need to go into a facility. We don't think we can cope with the range of his needs between just the two of us."

I pictured Pop's thin frame, lying in a hospital bed in a smelly nursing home. I shook my head emphatically. "No." My vision blurred with tears. "I can help, I'll move in with you guys. He can't go there." I broke down, realizing for the first time that I would never have my wonderful, strong father back, ever again.

"Hey hey hey," he said, hugging me. "We're going to do everything we can to help him. No one is giving up on Darrell. That's why the facility could be a very good option for him.

But I couldn't focus on what he was saying. All I heard was that Pop was basically being put away.

*

After I calmed down, I went to Pop's room and found him sleeping. I lay down on the bed with him, wanting now to savor every second I had with him.

He awoke and looked over. "Sammy?"

I was so relieved. Of any time I needed Pop to recognize me, it was then.

"Hi Pop," I said, softly.

"Where have you been?"

Guiltily, I lied, "I've been working, Pop."

He surprised me by taking my hand. "I'm really sick, aren't I?"

I moved his arm and rested my head on his chest, like I did when I was a child. "Yeah. Yeah, you are."

"I can't remember anything, Sammy. I can't remember how to take a bath or eat, sometimes."

"It's okay." I patted his chest.

I felt his chest catch beneath me. "I've let you down."

I sat up and looked at him. He was crying. I threw my arms around his neck. "No, you haven't, Pop." I started crying with him.

"I'm so proud of you, honey," he said, into my shoulder. "You're so beautiful and smart, like your mother." He pulled back and tucked a piece of hair behind my ear, regarding me with shiny eyes. "You're the best thing that ever happened to me."

*

When I woke up the next morning, I knew immediately that I needed an outlet for my fears and negative energy. It would be too early to go into the office, the competition was over and I would be heading to Pop's later that afternoon. Plus, I needed some exercise, so I decided to take my first yoga class ever. It was exactly what I needed. The deep breathing, meditation and stretching did wonders for my body and my mood. Afterward, I decided to pop into H.S.S. to do some light work. There was always so much post-competition paper-pushing to do, and I knew Monday would be hectic enough with my normal workload.

I was the only one there, and it was nice and quiet – inside, anyway. It was another beautiful day in HB and it seemed the crowds had lingered post-competition. You could hear children screaming and laughter, but it was like white noise to me and helped me get my work done. When the elevators opened, I didn't even hear them.

"Sam?"

I looked up and nearly shot out of my seat, so surprised I was to look into the face of Reggie MacIntosh.

"What are youse doing here on a Saturday morn?" he asked, propping himself up on his elbows and staring at me.

"Ah, um, lots of work to do." I laughed nervously.

"So where's that whacker? Emmett?"

I cleared my throat. "He had to return to Australia."

"Sounds like Emmett, running off like that. Well, be careful with him. He's got quite a reputation you know, with the ladies." He ran his hand through his hair.

I wanted to ask him what he meant, but then I figured he was probably just trying to rile me up. I didn't say anything.

"So are you coming to Oz anytime soon?" he picked up a pen on the desk and started doodling on a piece of scratch paper.

"Actually, yeah, I'll be there in a few weeks."

"But you'll be there to see Emmett, eh?" he said, putting the pen down.

I finally looked up. "Yes." He had a smattering of light freckles across his nose and his strawberry blonde hair was long and unruly. Emmett definitely beat him in the looks department.

"Okay, well, here's a coupla numbers you can ring me on. I'm always gone, but give me a fair days warning and I'll be sure to be around."

What made him think I was interested? His confidence was starting to irritate me.

Handing me the paper, he said, "I'm not trying to fuck you. I'm just saying, come to Bondi when youse get in town. I've heard about how you used to rip. I'd like to see you in the water. I know a lot of people, and I could probably get you noticed by some sponsors. You're welcome to stay at me flat also, if you like." He winked at me.

I was about to say something when Tim came walking down the hall. "Sam? I had no idea you were in the office."

Glad for the distraction from Reggie, I said, "I was just about to leave."

Reggie started to move away, and then came back to me. "Just give me a bell. I promise you, it's an amazing scene in Bondi. Way different than pissing the time away in Noraville."

He walked off, following Tim to office.

Though Reggie's pushiness irritated me, the thought of being sponsored, of surfing in Bondi Beach, of doing what I loved most professionally made me wonder if there was a way that I could get to Bondi without hurting Emmett. As I grabbed my keys and left, my thoughts wandered between Emmett's world and into Reggie's.

That was it. It was time. I pulled out my cell phone and called Emmett.

I was ready to go to Australia.

Six Weeks later

Chapter 14: It's a Good Day for G'day

While I never would have wished Pop's illness on anyone, I was grateful for the moments we had shared in recent months as I began to accept my changed life. Starting from the day Emmett left, I did everything I could do to maximize my time with Pop. We took a lot walks, we talked about surfing; sometimes, we just lay together in his bed, listening to Dick Dale. And I read to him, a lot. He had a thing for Moby Dick. Maybe it was the sea, or Herman Melville's prose, but he loved that story. I read it to him three times in that month.

Most of the time however, he was a world away. We took Dr. Ewing's advice and sought counseling as a family. It really helped us understand the disease of dementia and helped us grieve our loss; even though Pop was still alive, he wasn't the same person. I was surprised by how much it helped being able to talk to someone, and I wished I had done it sooner. There were still a lot of "mommy issues" as I called them, but with every session I made forward progress.

After weighing our options, we decided Hawaii was the best place for Pop to reside. Until they could find a facility for Pop, GamGam and Uncle Chuck stayed at Uncle Chuck's. Maui would be a beautiful place, complete with the undivided attention of Uncle Chuck and GamGam, who would also move permanently to Hawaii with Pop. We figured that given the reasons why Pop's dementia had come to fruition, we eschewed traditionalism.

I made the difficult decision to stay in HB. I was loving my job at H.S.S. and the time I was able to spend learning about the surf business. Plus, there wasn't a school anywhere near Uncle Chuck's place in Maui - my college education had to be completed.

We toured several assisted living facilities in the Orange County area to help give us an idea of what they would be like, and what would best suit Pop. Personally, I was surprised by how nice they were, but even more so when they told us how much they cost.

GamGam had to sell her home in La Jolla before moving to Hawaii. She wouldn't be able to take most of her stuff with her, and at seventy-five years-old she probably wasn't going to move back. Since Uncle Chuck had taken a leave of absence from his job in Hawaii and could stay with Pop, she and I set to work, going through everything, figuring out what could be kept and what needed to thrown away or sold off.

GamGam had managed to amass a ton of stuff. I hadn't been to her house in a long time, and I was surprised by the clutter that greeted me. She very crafty, and had knitted, carved and painted her way though inch of wall, floor and shelf space in her home. Hand-sewn quilts and blankets sat in stacks on the chairs and couches; carved figurines stood on the shelves and piano. Even the stools that lined the bar were hand-made. And there were the photos. Hundreds of them ranging in age and color of Pop and Uncle Chuck; GamGam and her sister; PopPop (my grandfather) and his family; and myself, the only grandchild, every year of my life captured and plastered throughout the house.

It was a lot of work.

On my second weekend there, I was taking photos down from the top of the piano, coming across pictures I had never seen before. There were tons of them, stacked in front of one another like dominos. I took them down one at a time, gazing at them and imprinting them in my mind - I figured I probably wouldn't ever see them again - before wrapping them up and placing them in boxes with others.

I was fine until I came across a particular photo of my mom. It made my heart catch in my chest. I couldn't stop staring at it, the undeniable beauty breaking my heart. GamGam must have felt the silence, because she walked over and peered over my shoulder at the photo in my hand. She smiled faintly. "That was the day she found out she was pregnant with you."

It was a strange feeling, standing in GamGam's house, staring at a photo of my dead mother, her face looking like no one person could ever get any happier. I looked at her left hand, a bad habit I had - I tended to stare at people's wedding bands. Her little rock shined like a flashlight in the fog.

"You can have the picture, baby," GamGam said. "You should have it."

In the car ride back to HB, I was so deep in thought I barely registered my whereabouts until my car sputtered and started to shake. It was not the place you wanted to run out of gas. I was between Camp Pendleton and San Clemente, right by the nuclear plant in San Onofre - basically in the middle of nowhere on one of the busiest freeways in the world. Thankfully, I had AAA and a cell phone.

I called in my service request and waited. It was going to be a long time before the roadside service people could respond to my call. It was dark and I was a little scared, so I called Emmett, adding to my already astronomically large phone bill. He answered as I knew he would, his voice deep and full of sleep. It filled me with intrigue; like the photo of my mom, I wondered how you could really know someone, yet not know him or her at all at the same time? I had been born by her; I had spent nine months inside of her. But I didn't really know her; I had never talked to her, and I couldn't remember her touch. The same thing went for Emmett – I knew him, I had made love to him - but I didn't have a clue what his life in his natural environment was like. What did his car look like? What view did he see when he woke up in the morning?

It all felt so weird to me at that moment. I was feeling extraordinarily emotional over it all, and I started to cry.

"What is it babe?" he asked, tenderly. His voice was so soft and soothing, and I wished more than anything that I was in his arms.

"It's stupid," I said, feeling foolish.

"Well, it's obviously something."

"I just...I found this picture of my mom. It was from the day she found out she was pregnant with me." I sighed. "She looked so gorgeous, Emmett."

"Well obviously that must be where you get it then, your beauty."

I smiled into the dark car. I could hear his blankets rustle in the background of the phone as he spoke. "It's okay to get emotional, babe. Pregnancy and motherhood, it's a beautiful thing."

"What do you mean?" It was such an oddly open thing for a guy to say. I couldn't imagine Shane ever saying anything like that.

"I don't know, I mean, you create this life together and a woman, she makes it happen. And then it's like the sweetest present ever when you finally see what it comes out like. I can't wait to be a da."

I had never seen that side of a guy before. I could picture Emmett as a father: his arms opened wide, laughing, as his child fell into his arms, scooping them up and spinning them around. Emmett was so full of life, from his laughter to his heart. I could see him passing it onto his child.

"You're right, Emmett. I'm glad we got to talk. Go back to sleep, now."

"You can call anytime, Sam. Night."

*

I spent a lot of time with Crystal who had basically replaced Rachel. She was pretty much living with some guy in Hollywood, and I'd said hardly two words to her over the course of the month. The abscess in our friendship hurt me, but I remained stubborn. She was newly immersed in a world I didn't know anything about; I figured there wasn't much we could talk about anymore, anyway

Another person I seemed to lose contact with in the course of that month was Shane. Though at first I had thought that I might be able to see him in Australia, he had succeeded in convincing his parents to allow him to travel back to England with Mags, and we had only Skyped once since Heidi and Frank had bought me the computer. I wasn't sure if it was due to the admittance of feelings we had shared and shunned, or the fact that he and I were potentially serious with other people, but that one and only Skype conversation we had shared had felt awkward forced, even.

In the last couple of weeks before I left for Australia, my lawsuit against the restaurant finally wrapped up. I had refused any further medical treatment, no matter how hard they had tried try to keep my medical care open and on-going. I went for final evaluations with my doctor and with Brian, my physical therapist. It was a bittersweet moment saying good-bye to him, someone I had spent more time with than my loved ones. All of my medical data was processed, and the Worker's Comp company appeared satisfied that we could move forward in finalizing the lawsuit. I received a call from my lawyer offering me a settlement: $22,000 and some change. I readily accepted it. I just wanted to be free from the trappings of my lawsuit and injuries.

In those final days before I left for Australia and GamGam, Pop and Uncle Chuck left for Hawaii – there was a strange feeling reeking in Pop's house. Maybe it was all the pictures taken down or the boxes that lined the walls, but even Bertie was subdued. I guessed we all knew it was the last of our lives as we had known it.

The night before my flight, we finally got to share our dinner at Captain Jack's. Pop was mellow and quiet - the latest round of medication seemed to hit him a lot harder. It seemed to curb his mood swings, and he appeared quite happy as he ate his Clam Chowder. I thought of the day in the hospital when he had tried to spoon the applesauce into his mouth. I watched him then, realizing how much progress he had made, and nostalgia mixed with bittersweet feelings for what lay ahead.

All too suddenly, it was time for me to go. The three of them – Pop, GamGam and Uncle Chuck - took me to the airport. They would be leaving for Maui while I was in Australia, so it would be our final good-bye. I hugged Uncle Chuck and GamGam tightly, promising to call as soon as I landed. I turned to Pop - who was using a cane and looking very, very frail- my vision blurred as I hugged his neck tightly. He hadn't been very alert in the car, and I knew he didn't realize the magnitude of the good-bye.

It didn't stop me from being emotional. "I love you so much, daddy."

He patted me gently. I wiped my face hard, trying to remember the man he had been and not the sick person in front of me. With a final good-bye I took a deep breath, waved at the three of them, and entered the terminal I had watched Emmett walk into six weeks earlier.

*

The flight was long and cramped. I was hot, then cold, then freezing, then hot again. There was turbulence, something I'd never experienced before, and my heart raced every time we hit a bump. I wondered how people handled flying all the time.

I pressed my forehead to the cold window, thankful for my window seat. The temperature felt good on my hot face. I stared out, hoping I would get a glimpse of the Great Barrier Reef. A nature show I had once seen said you could see it from space. I hoped that Emmett would take me to see it.

I couldn't believe it had only been a couple of months since Emmett and I had met, and then only a handful of days that we had actually spent in each other's company. It all seemed crazy to me when I looked at it point blank like that, and sometimes I felt ridiculous for the lack of substantial numbers.

Suddenly, the music from my headphones stopped and the speaker clicked on. "Ladies and gentlemen, this is your captain speaking. We will now begin making our descent into Kingsford Smith International. The weather is clear, winds light and variable with temperatures in the upper twenties. Once again, we thank you for flying Quantas Airlines."

I wasn't familiar with Celsius temperatures, so I had no idea if that was hot or cold. I took out the guidebook I had purchased before I left and looked at the little chart. Upper twenties were good- that meant eighty degrees for me. I was thrilled by my first of many Australian discoveries to come.

Suddenly, the plane tipped down and I clamped my hand tighter on the armrest. I looked around, but no one else seemed alarmed. I leaned back, breathed slowly and tried to take my mind off of my fear. I picked up the book GamGam had given me, letting my fingers trail down the smooth cover before I opened it, trying to calm down and focus on the words on the page. The flight attendants appeared and passed around customs forms to fill out, and I was grateful for something to do.

Twenty minutes later, the speaker dinged again and the flight attendant reminded us to 'put out chair backs in their upright position.' Once again, I pressed my forehead to the window. The land loomed in sight, bringing with it a thrill of excitement. I looked around at my neighbors, suddenly wanting nothing more than to chat with them but they were nonplussed, ready for the fourteen-hour flight to end. We landed smoothly, and I found myself clapping like they do in old movies, but once again I was the only one. I sheepishly grabbed my purse and papers and waited for my turn to disembark the plane

My bag felt heavy as I pulled it along the jet way. It spilled off into a hallway that led to another and then another; and they twisted and turned so many times I figured we had walked several miles by the time we ended up in a giant room that seemed to hold thousands of people.

I filed into the line I was supposed to be in and inched slowly toward the looming immigration officers. I watched one by one as the travelers answered their questions before getting a stamp and proceeding to baggage claim. I felt really nervous as I walked up, like I was guilty of drug smuggling and had an eight ball of cocaine lining my jacket pockets.

I procured documents and answered questions as the officer asked them, sweating the whole time. What if they didn't let me in to the country? Eventually, he stamped my passport and I calmed down, following the crowd toward baggage claim.

Accents and languages floated around me as I stared at a TV, trying to figure out where to claim my bags. Then I heard his voice.

"Sam!"

Emmett's hurried toward me, towering above the crowds. My nerves piqued when I caught sight of his tanned face, now home to a patch of unfamiliar scruff. He pushed through the people in front of him and wildly caught me in his arms. I wrapped my hands tightly around his neck as we hugged. He smelled clean and manly, and I marveled at the familiarity of his scent.

"Ah, baby, it's so good to have you here. Finally," he laughed.

"Finally," I agreed.

*

"What do you want to do first?" he asked, once we, my suitcases and his tools were crammed into his small work van.

"I don't care," I said, honestly. "Anything sounds nice to me."

He turned the steering wheel. "I'd like you to meet me parents," he said. "They're going on holiday tomorrow and will be gone 'til after you leave."

I hadn't expected that so quickly, but remembered he had met own family within days of meeting me. In fact, I was kind of ready to get it out of the way. The whole 'meeting the parents' thing was hard enough; the dead-brother thing just compounded it. "Okay, but I want to take a shower first."

"You sure?" he seemed unconvinced.

"Well, I have been on a flight for fourteen hours," I said. My poor attempt at cracking a joke just made him roll his eyes.

"About meeting me parents, ya shit," he reiterated.

I nodded my head enthusiastically.

The drive from Sydney to Noraville would be over two hours I was told, so we stopped and picked up some snacks before hitting the highway. Emmett informed me that his 'mum' would have a grand dinner planned for us and not to eat too much.

The whole drive I kept my eyes peeled to the road - everything was so different. I found it somewhat terrifying and thrilling at the same time: the streets ran the opposite way from the US, and it felt like we were going to drive into oncoming traffic at any moment; there were roundabouts for turning, and signs posted in kilometers; even the billboards were different, and I reveled in their unfamiliarity. I asked Emmett questions as they popped into my head, and he answered dutifully, saying at one point, "You always seem to have another question for my answer."

My curiosity was insatiable.

When I wasn't asking questions, I was listening to the radio as it played softly in the background. Every time the DJ's voice came on, I couldn't help smiling at the thick Australian accent that was still so unfamiliar at times.

The weather changed from sunny to stormy very quickly, and nearly as soon as the clouds blew in, the van was pelted with rain as we sped down the highway. But just as rapidly as the storm came through, it was gone again.

We exited the highway and Emmett said, "We're almost home."

I liked Noraville immediately. It was quaint, filled with small homes and neat yards. The shops were just that; shops, not giant shopping centers. The streets were lined with trees; it felt like it must have been the same way for fifty years.

The one thing that really struck me odd about Noraville, however, was the lack of stoplights. There was simply roundabout after roundabout. Every time I thought there might be a stoplight, another roundabout would arrive, and Emmett would expertly navigate through it, each car smoothly sailing past the other.

Finally, we pulled onto a street and into a drive. "Here we are," he said. Like the other houses in Noraville, Emmett's home was charming one-story dwelling with a small yard. He pulled his van under the carport, turned off the ignition and leaned into me, resting his lips on my own. My pulse quickened as it always did.

We weren't alone, though. A dog was running circles around the van, barking loudly. Emmett pulled away and sighed. He opened the door and yelled, "Shut up Barley, you old whacker."

I opened my own door and was greeted by a big, beautiful chocolate lab. "Oooh, look at you," I said, bending down to pet him. "This must be your roommate Natalie's dog."

Emmett carried my suitcases, affording me a chance to take in his home. The grass was browning "from the pre-mature hot summer," as he had said, but it was trim and neat. He stopped, and said, "See that?" pointing to some plants bordering the side of the house.

I clapped my hands excitedly. "Yes, those are wattle plants aren't they?"

He nodded. "Now wait until you see me garden."

I rounded the corner and gasped. Emmett's garden, or backyard as I thought of it, was the beach; his doorstep lay within a few hundred feet of the ocean. In sharp contrast to the brown plain stuff from the front, the grass was so green and healthy it looked fake. There were lush, tropical plants everywhere, and exotic flowers bordered the edges of the yard. If that weren't enough, there was a large, screened-in porch outfitted with comfortable chairs, a porch swing and more plants. We walked up the steps and into the screened-in room. He waved his arms around, saying, "Welcome to my home."

"Emmett, I am speechless."

Barley started barking again and jumping around, demanding our attention. Emmett called out, "We're here," as we walked into the living room, and I was surprised to find the room orderly and clean. The spacious kitchen was visible from the living room, and a small dining table stood to the side of the front door.

"Hiya," a woman's voice called from one of the rooms down the hall, and she emerged looking like she was from the Swedish National tennis team. She had straight blonde hair, long, lean legs and huge boobs.

So not fair.

When she reached us, she stuck out her hand and said, "I'm Nat."

"Nice to meet you, finally," I said, enthusiastically shaking her hand.

"We're happy to have you," she replied, smiling

"Brah," a male voice called. A short, blonde haired guy came into the room saying, "That's the biggest facking suitcase I have ever seen, so it must belong to the American."

Emmett and I laughed, but Natalie just rolled her eyes. "Don't start." She looked at Emmett and asked, "What's your plan this arvo?"

"We're going to mum and da's for tea, and then who knows? Depends on how tired Sam here is."

"Sam's not tired at all," I said.

"Well then let's get youse a shower." He started off down the hall, adding, "Nat, put the kettle on, will ya?"

Emmett's room was simple, with a large, four-poster bed and a wide dresser. Photographs of beaches adorned the walls, and a big mirror hung just above the dresser. I set my purse down, noticing more of the tropical plants he seemed to love. "Your plants are so beautiful. You definitely have a green thumb."

I moved over to the dresser, where there were pictures of Emmett and what appeared to be his family. One picture in particular caught my eye, of Emmett and someone else who could have only been his brother, Kyle. "Can I ask what happened to him?"

He rubbed his hand over his head as I had watched him do so many times before. "It was a surf accident, down at Bondi. He was with his mates from high school. They went out at night before a storm, the stupid pricks. It was dark...no one knew he was missing before it was too late."

I looked at the grinning teenager, who couldn't have been older than sixteen. He could easily have been mistaken for Emmett's twin, but with lighter features.

"Such a tragedy," I said wryly, thinking of my own night sessions and Pop's over-protectiveness. "Bet there were a lot of women surrounding you two very handsome men."

He sagged a little. "He was the best person ever, my best mate, my brother. God, I miss him so much it just rips a fuckin' hole through me chest every time I think of him. I know you must understand," he said, picking up the photo.

I caught sight of us in the mirror: two very different people from two very different walks of life marked by two similar tragedies. It was strange how life worked, bringing people together who might not have met otherwise.

"I want to show you something," he said, moving toward the window and opening the dark drapes.

Beyond a small scrub of bush lay unrestricted views of the ocean, and a large lighthouse in the distance. I had never seen anything quite like it, not even in California, where opulence and luxury flowed like tap water. But I wouldn't have traded Emmett's view for the fanciest house in Malibu; it was perfect.

"Can I ask another question?" I said, facing him. "How do you afford this all?"

He took a moment before answering. "It's been luck, really. Da knew the fella that owned the land here, which used to just be brush. They got on well, and we made him an offer that he accepted. The house we built ourselves."

He said it all so nonchalantly. It was one of the things I liked about him, and Australia. In California, this kind of oceanfront property would have been worth millions and the area would have been crawling with developers, scrambling to stake their claim.

"Let me show you the bathroom."

I half expected some spa-like retreat, with head-to-toe showerheads and stone tiles. But it was just a room with a tub and a toilet, like my old, crappy apartment. He turned the nozzles for me, gave me a kiss and left me alone to clean up.

*

I got out of the shower and wandered back into Emmett's room. I lay down on the bed, staring out of the open window and into the unknown. I had only intended to close my eyes for a second, but when I awoke the room was darker. For a second, I didn't know where I was. I stepped into my clothes and wandered down the hall toward the living area but found it empty. I pushed my way onto the porch, where I found Emmett sitting in one of the big chairs stroking Barley's head, who lay loyally at his feet. I sat in the chair opposite him and watched the sun make its final descent for the day. My first Australian sunset.

He looked over at me and smiled softly. "I wish you could see how beautiful you look right now."

I still wasn't used to his candid compliments. I smiled wanly.

"You looked so peaceful I couldn't bear to wake you. But you must be starving. Ready to head to mum and da's?"

Emmett's parents lived in Toukley; a town about a five-minute's drive from Noraville. We stopped at a market to pick up some wine, and just before he stepped out of the idling vehicle he looked at me and laughed. "Don't be nervous. They're going to love you."

I didn't have a lot of experience with parents, so I made a note not to drink too much. That was when I seemed to slip up the most – and where I had nearly lost Emmett before.

Chapter 14: Some People Know How to Make an Entrance

Emmett lied to me.

That was my first thought as we pulled onto a long, barbed wire-lined road that led to a spectacular three-story home, complete with a fountain.

Who actually has a fountain in their yard? I wondered to myself. If I had been nervous about meeting my boyfriends' parents before, it manifested when I saw that house. My mental image of Emmett's parents quickly became this vision of aristocratic, pinky extended, tea-sipping aristocrats waiting for me in their parlor, complete with matching lapdogs and a butler. Translation: people I had never been around and didn't know how to relate to.

Emmett put his arm around me as we waited at the door. That got me wondering: why are we waiting at the door? Why he didn't just go in? I assumed it must be another strange thing I wasn't used to, yet another facet of his English parent's rearing.

The door opened, and a teeny petite woman with disheveled brown hair appeared. She leaned out the door to give Emmett a one-handed hug, holding a pair of tongs in the other. She turned to me and gave me an emphatic hug as well.

Completely not what I had envisioned.

"Hello, darlings!"

"Hiya mum. This is my Sam."

I stuck my hand out politely to shake hers, as Nat had down with me, but she waved me off with her tongs and said, "Get in here, both of you," pulling us roughly toward her and hugging us again. "Karen Taylor," she said, as she pulled away. "Come along."

Had I met her before seeing that house, I would have pictured a small cottage, big, colorful garden, cozy cushions and lots and lots pictures. But this home contained expensive statues and bronze pieces. There were no pictures.

Nothing seemed to add up.

When we entered the enormous kitchen a hundred different smells greeted my senses: garlic and herbs, celery and tomatoes, potatoes and rosemary. Though formidable, the room was much more comfortable. Karen went to the stove and stirred some pots, patting her hair into place. She reminded me of GamGam (though much younger), and I felt myself relax a little.

I followed Emmett's lead and took a seat at the dining table. But almost immediately, he jumped back up. "Here you are, mummy," he said, holding a bottle of wine aloft. "Tom and Allan probably left you a fuckload, but 'ere's some more." He placed the bottle on the counter next to her. "Where's da?"

"He's out catching dinner." She pointed at the refrigerator with her tongs. "There is a bottle of white wine already opened. Do us a favor and pour some for us all, love. We can have the one you brought with tea."

Emmett chatted lightly with his mom as he topped off her wine and poured two glasses of wine for us. I wondered who Tom and Allan were, and what Karen had meant by "catching dinner."

It was interesting to watch Emmett and his mother. I marveled at their exchange and the difference in their accents. While Emmett spoke in his lackadaisical Australian accent and intermittent slang, Karen's accent was completely different. It was quick and efficient – like how most British people sounded - but at the same time endearing, with lilts and upswings on words.

"So, Sam, tell us about yourself," Karen said, shoveling vegetables from the cutting board into a sauté pan. "Emmett says you're a surfer as well?"

I accepted the glass of wine Emmett handed me. "I am. I haven't been out as much as I would have liked lately, but I have gotten a lot better. I'm recovering from an injury and with everything going on with my dad…" I let my voice trail off.

She paused and looked at me. "Oh dear, yes, Emmett mentioned your father. I'm deeply sorry. I can only imagine what it must be like for you and your family." She paused respectfully before resuming her stirring.

Emmett's dad appeared sporting knee-high rubber boots and a large, khaki vest. He held a line of fish in his left hand, proudly holding them aloft for all to see.

I guess that's what 'catching dinner meant.

"Dinner's here!" he said, sounding distinctly like he was trying to sound American.

I was right, because Emmett laughed aloud and Karen shook her head fondly. "Tea will be ready in no time."

He gave me a toothy grin, with surprisingly straight teeth. (These Brits didn't fall into their cliché's).

"I'd shake your hand but I've got fish blood all over. Mork's me name." He turned to Emmett. "Son, you clean the fish. I'm going to have a quick wash-up."

"Sure thing, da." Emmett said, taking the fish from Mork and heading out on the porch leaving Karen and I alone.

"Emmett mentioned you would like to go into medicine?" she mentioned, as she tried to open the stove. She kept pulling but it wouldn't budge; it appeared to be either locked or stuck. "Bloody contraption," she muttered, gazing at it quizzically.

Shane's parents had an almost identical stove, and I remembered Heidi having the same problem when they first bought it. I walked over to help her. "It's in cleaning mode, so it's locked," I said, pushing some buttons. This time, it opened with ease.

"Oh, dear me. I don't know how to operate these fancy objects, with their knobs and dials. Just give me an old fashioned cooker."

I smiled and agreed, swatting at a mosquito.

She placed a tray of garlic bread in the stove and said, "You've got to watch those mozzie's. They'll eat you alive out here. Especially with the lake out back."

I looked outside where she pointed. Indeed, a small body of water lay beyond the porch. "The lake?" I remarked incredulously.

She nodded her head. "Bloody lake. Who has a lake at their home?"

I cocked my heard curiously and looked at her. It all started to make sense. "This isn't your house, is it?"

"Did Emmy not tell you?"

I shook my head.

She picked up her glass of wine and joined me at the table, patting her hair into place. "This house belongs to Tom and Allan, clients of Mork's. They're always off traveling and they've got horses and such that need tending to whilst they're away. In exchange for the help they let us have full access to the home."

It sounded like a perfectly practical idea to me.

"Not that they can't afford to hire someone, obviously," she explained. "But they have found it easier to have friends' house-sit when they're away. I suppose it's a bit like a bed and breakfast, except you make your own bed and breakfast." She laughed. "Anyway, Mork offered to help this time around so here we are! Afterward, we'll go sit on the porch and have a cup of tea. It's beautiful out back."

*

Things continued to go well with Emmett's parents throughout dinner. Karen was sweet and gracious while Mork was humorous and booming and they both clearly adored their son. After dinner, Emmett offered to take me on a tour of the house.

I started toward the sink with my dirty dishes. Karen took the plates from my hand and said, "I've got those darling, let Emmy show you around."

Emmett's face grew ablaze. "Mu-um," he said, dragging the word out.

"Oh, sorry, love." She winked at me.

The house was the penultimate in luxury, and no expense had been spared. We passed through gorgeous, immaculate room after gorgeous, immaculate room. There was a parlor and a library and a sunroom. All rooms I had never seen in a home before.

Emmett wrapped up the tour and returned to the dining room, where Karen was piling cakes and cups onto a tray, and we all followed her onto the screened-in porch. Karen set the cups out and asked me, "How do you take your tea, love?"

"Um, plain, I guess?"

She laughed. "Oh, bless you, sweet girl you don't drink tea do you? Silly me, it's such an English thing. How about I make you a cup and you see how you like it? If not, we'll figure something else out."

Mork and Emmett chatted about a forthcoming project while I stared out at the lake beyond the porch. It was more of a pond, surrounded by small trees and immaculate green grass. The moon shined brilliantly off the water.

It was beautiful.

Mosquito's buzzed around the perimeter of the porch. I was starting to understand the screened in thing that seemed to adorn most of the homes in the area.

I accepted the cup of tea Karen handed me and took a sip. It was delicious. I was thankful for its warmth, too. I wasn't sure what Emmett meant by 'premature summer.' I was cold.

Emmett's parents asked me questions about my life in HB and I told them about my family, my injury and surfing. I was surprised when they all talked so candidly about Kyle, and it made it a lot easier to talk about my own family. When the night ended, I actually found myself not wanting to leave, something I had not expected.

Karen and Mork walked us outside to Emmett's van, and Karen hugged me tightly saying, "What a delight it's been to meet you."

I noticed she said 'been' like 'bean', too; it made me like her even more.

*

In the van, I punched Emmett in the shoulder. "Why didn't you tell me that wasn't your parents' house?"

"Hey!" he said, shrugging away from me. "I thought I did!"

I crossed my arms. "No you didn't."

He laughed, wheeled the van around, and told me about Tom and Allan as we drove back to Noraville. I hadn't been around a lot of gay men besides Eduardo, and I found myself wanting to meet them. They sounded fascinating.

When we got back to Emmett's, Natalie and Marcus were getting ready to leave.

"Fancy a beer in Toukley, E?" Marcus asked, putting on his jacket. "C'mon, I'll drive; it'll give you a chance to show your woman off."

I was curious about their nightlife, so I said, "C'mon, Emmett. We're on

vacation."

He threw up his hands. "Alright."

Marcus clasped his hands and picked up his phone. "Excellent."

Fifteen minutes later, we were all piled into Marcus's pickup truck. It was old and beat up, likely a hand-me-down or something he used for work. But Marcus didn't apologize, as I had done when I picked up Emmett, Kevin, Riley and CJ from the airport. I was quickly learning that it was much more American, the want for a new car. Natalie rode her bike, Emmett drove his work van, Marcus had his old truck. In Australia, people didn't really seem to care about their mode of transportation.

"So where are we headed?" I asked, from my perch on Emmett's lap.

"A great little tavern in Toukley," Marcus said, barely tapping his brakes as we whipped through a roundabout.

Nat rolled her eyes. "Great little tavern, my arsehole. It's a fucking shitden." She turned to me. "There's bugger all to do around here. If you want to see anything worth a shit, you need to go to Sydney."

"It's alright for a Tuesday night!" Marcus said, defensively.

"We'll go to Sydney sometime this week. Do it proper, stay a night and all." Emmett said, grabbing the handle above my head as we sped through yet another roundabout.

It only took a few more minutes before we were back in Toukley, but my butt and my back hurt by the time we arrived. Marcus careened into a spot in front of the bar, pulled the hand brake and cut the engine. We spilled out of the car, me nearly falling out as Emmett opened the door. I looked up to see that the 'tavern' was one of those small, square buildings, simple and to the point. There were no windows, and smoke and loud rock music spewed from the open door. Inside, there were the regulatory pool tables and dartboards, and in the middle, the largest sit-down bar I'd ever seen before. It could have sat at least fifty people on all three sides, and nearly did; every seat was taken. For such a small town on a Tuesday night, I couldn't believe how many people were there. I pulled Emmett toward me, yelling my observations into his ear.

"Most of them are miners," he yelled back. "They work underground all day then come out and piss their dollars away before heading home. These blokes here love their drink."

We all gathered around an empty barstool. They didn't have a lot of the fancy tap beers and liquor bottles I was used to seeing behind the bar. Instead, there were only four or five refrigerators filled with unrecognizable beers, and a couple of neon signs above them.

"What's your fancy, babes?" Emmett asked, wallet in hand.

"A beer is fine." I craned my neck closer, hoping to see a Coors Light or a Bud Light. "Something light?"

"They've got Budweiser."

I cringed.

He laughed. "How bout a nice lager?"

Moments later, I was holding a bottle of Sydney Export Lager. Feeling a bit too touristy, I poured it into the pint glass I'd been handed, leaving the bottle on the bar. Emmett led me over to a corner where several guys were sitting on barstools, all of them casual in board shorts and tank tops – typical for a beachside town full of surfers. I spied Riley, feeling relief at seeing a familiar face.

"Heya," he said, hugging me. "How ya getting' on?"

"Good, thanks. It's really pretty here."

He took a mighty gulp of his beer. "Pretty, yea, but fuck all to do. Oh, I spoke to your mate Crystal today."

"Crystal?" I repeated, surprised.

He laughed, saying, "Yea. Strange how it all happened. We started emailing when I got back to Oz, and well, ya know. She says she wants to come and visit, too."

Riley was probably the last person on earth I would have matched Crystal up with. He was much younger, and she was much more of a dreads-and-Marley hippie type to his shorthaired and clean-cut, surfer style. Notably, Crystal didn't even own a computer. I wondered where she had emailed from.

"Hereya, Sam, have a burl." Marcus said, coming over and handing me a smooth, round disc that looked like a giant macaroon. I looked at it quizzically and he proceeded to tell me the rules of Shovelboard.

Ten minutes later, I was locked in a game with Marcus, versus Natalie and Emmett. I was terrible of course, but nevertheless it was fun and the beer went down quickly. Next thing I knew, I was at the bar with Natalie ordering shots.

"To you," she said, holding up a shot glass.

"To me," I said, laughing. I threw back the shot and nearly spit it all over the place, the bitter licorice taste hitting my taste buds before the shot was down the hatch.

"Ugh," we both said.

"So what's it like, going to a new country? I've never been out of Oz." she asked, after we had ordered two more beers.

"Really? You've never left? Actually, this is my first time out of the States and it feels great. I can't believe I'm here, you know?"

"How long are you planning to stay?" she said, leaning back against the bar.

I took a sip of beer. "I'm here for two weeks."

"Right," she said, rolling her eyes. "But how long are you planning to stay?"

It took me a minute to register her innuendo. "Oh, I'd love to stay longer, but I've got school…I've got to get back.

"He fucking adores you," she said, seeming to ignore my explanation. She pointed in Emmett's direction. "Drove us all apeshit talking about you. By the way, he's going to ask you move here."

I nearly spit out my beer. "What?"

She shrugged. "I'd do it, if I was you. He's got a lot of money." Then her eyes narrowed and she said, "Oh, fuck. It's Sian."

I expected Sian to be another guy. "Who's Shawn?"

She scowled. "Not Shawn," she said correcting me, as though I was saying it wrong. "Sian, Emmett's ex."

Immediately, I noticed a beautiful woman in the corner with short curly locks and a tiny figure. Her bare legs were tanned and though I couldn't see her face, I imagined her with big, round blue eyes.

Natalie let out a loud sigh of disgust.

"What?" I asked.

"Look at Emmett, the fucking Australian Gentleman of the Year. He's going to bring her over here and introduce the two of you. I know it."

Sure enough, Emmett pointed in our direction and Sian's tight curls whipped around her face as she swiveled her head. Emmett started walking toward us and the girl followed. Natalie slapped my arm hard, saying, "Told ya so."

"Ouch!" I said, and quickly decided to throw back my beer. The alcohol made me feel fuzzy, a welcome distraction. Emmett tapped me on the shoulder and said, "Sam."

I fixed a care-free smile on my face and turned around, shocked not to be looking into two round blue eyes. On the contrary,

Sian's almond eyes were an almost iridescent green next to her bronze face, dark eyebrows and curly blond hair.

She was drop dead gorgeous.

"I'm Sian." She held out her hand.

Her accent seemed even weirder on my untrained American ears. None of her made sense to me.

"Samantha," I replied sweetly. I didn't want her knowing me as Sam. We shook hands and I retracted mine quickly, wrapping it safely around my beer.

"Uh, yeah, so there you go Sian. You've met Sam. Now can you please go back to your mates?" Emmett pointed to a pool table where a group of guys were staring back at the four of us.

While I wasn't a gossipy, jealous girl, she seemed to bring about immediate insecure feelings I'd never felt before.

"Okay, Emmett." Sian rolled her eyes and walked away, swinging her curls purposefully. After barely two steps, she turned around and came back. Putting her hand on her stomach, she asked, "Did Emmett tell you about the baby?"

Emmett's face went white with shock. Natalie spit her beer. I stood frozen. Then Emmett's face turned red with anger and he drug Sian out of the bar.

Natalie's face was full of anger. "She's full of shit. Fucking liar, that one."

Time seemed to stand still as I stood planted with my eyes glued on the door. Finally, Emmett walked back in, thankfully alone.

He came up to me and put his hands on my shoulders. "Let me explain about that."

"Fucking right, you better," Natalie said.

"Nat, please?" he said, contorting his face. "Give us a minute?"

She scoffed and walked off, leaving the two of us alone. He pulled me away to a quieter place, letting me take the lone stool as he stood next to me. He rubbed his face, looking for the right words to say. "That is Sian, me ex-girlfriend," he started. "And she's obviously a bit gone."

I didn't say anything or move. He continued.

"She's not really pregnant. This is something that has been going on for months that she keeps saying to get back together." He chugged his beer for a couple of seconds, seemingly for courage. "I probably should have warned you of her but had hoped I wouldn't need to."

He shrugged, and continued. "We were together for five years. And, well, she's mad now, really. This whole pregnant-thing started when she found out about you."

I didn't know what else to say, except, "That's, uh, weird." I couldn't imagine ever saying something like that to get back together with a guy.

He nodded. "Yeah, she shows up at places she thinks I'll be at, now…it's just, out of fucking control."

"Can't you get a restraining order or something?"

He sighed. "I don't want to do something like that, you know? No matter what, she was a big part of my life for a long time and I care about her."

I begrudgingly nodded my head, but I didn't like it.

"Look, I don't want her to ruin our night or your trip." He leaned down and kissed me, pushing my long hair back behind one ear. "Let's just go back over there and play some games with everyone. Or, we could leave if you want?"

I didn't want her to ruin my night either. "We could leave…" I let my voice trail off, trying to change my tone to a suggestive one.

"Let's go then." He kissed me again, this time more deeply. "God, I missed you."

I kissed him back, trying to match my playful tone. "I missed you, too."

But I couldn't help thinking of Sian now, too.

"C'mon." He pulled me off the barstool and led me out the door.

Chapter 15: The Unwelcome Visitor Visits

The next morning, I stood waiting for Emmett in the front yard by the edge of the gate, surfboard tucked comfortably under my arm. I was staring out at the crystalline blue water and pink sandy beach when Emmett came up beside me and shoved his own board - tip first - hard into the sand just in front of us. "Okay," he said, turning toward me. "A couple things to note about the breaks."

I had woken long before Emmett, one of the downsides – or benefits, depending on how you look at it – to jetlag. I had gone for a walk, eaten breakfast and was drinking a cup of my newly-beloved tea on the screened-in porch when he finally rose. Even then, it was still early. For awhile, we sat in silence, staring out at the lush yard and water in front of us, Emmett remarking that it was something 'he tried to do daily.'

But I had forgotten my rashguard, so Emmett kindly had popped into town to get one for me while I gathered the rest of my surf gear. We waxed our boards as he explained the breaks to me, the sun finally appearing as we were padding down the surf's edge.

We set our boards in the water and paddled out side by side. It was just he and I, and I marveled at the loneliness of the spot. It was hard to find your own break anywhere, anymore. It was both intimate and spiritual, and I paddled harder, feeling proud and strong – I had worked really hard to get to where I was at that moment.

The waves were perfect four-to-six footers, and my endurance surprised me. I felt like I could have surfed forever but my stomach had other thoughts, so I finally gave in to my human needs, looking around for Emmett as I paddled back into shore. I found him standing on the beach, looking exactly as he had that first day I had seen him on the beach in front of Pop's.

"If I thought you looked beautiful yesterday, you're a thousand times more so, today. Watching you out there... you should be really proud of yourself."

I looked away from him, feeling embarrassed. Compliments seemed so effortless for him, and his words seemed to reflect the way I felt at any given time. Yet, I couldn't seem to put them out there the way he did.

"Natalie mentioned something to me yesterday," I said, coming up to him and pressing my cold, wet body up against his.

"You're freezing!"

I kissed him hard, and he kissed me back. He pulled away first and said, "What did Nat say?"

I ran my hand across his shaved head. "She said that you wanted to ask me to move here."

He pulled back. "That cunt!"

"Emmett!" His word shocked me. "Don't be mad!"

He laughed. "I'm not, she just has such a big fucking mouth some times. I wanted to ask you that meself...but way later on, not the day after you got here."

"So is it true?"

" 'Course it is. If you want to."

Truly, I had expected him to deny the allegation. Now that it was no longer clandestine I wasn't sure how I felt. Of course I was crazy about Emmett. But, I worried that maybe we were getting in a little too deep. I grappled at straws, saying, "I mean, I still have my apartment, and my stuff...and what about school?" I couldn't believe we were having a conversation about me moving there. Why had I brought it up?

"You can buy everything you need. Crystal can help you get rid of your stuff at your flat. And Newcastle has one of the best school's around, just a coupla hour's drive from here. All easy fixes. And I figured that now that your da was gone, you may want to get away. Here's your excuse."

"Can we talk about it later?" I didn't want to bring Pop into it.

"Of course. Let's get some lunch and figure out what to do today. I'm sure you're keen to see the sights."

As we returned to the house, I looked over my shoulder one last time, taking in the landscape: the beautiful lighthouse that was the town's trademark in the distance, the large trees that dotted the steep, rocky cliff face surrounding it. The pink sandy beach and crystal-clear water. All of it different and new.

*

Emmett paused at the gate and cocked his head, looking back at me. "Did you hear that?"

I paused to listen. It sounded like something moaning. "Yeah, what is that?"

"Bet it's fuckin' Barley, ate a rotting 'roo or something," he said, pushing the gate aside to let me through.

We were crossing the yard when Emmett suddenly stopped. "What. The. Fuck."

"Well, aren't... you two, just... a picture of domestic bliss...oooohhhh," a voice said, from within the screened-in porch.

The sun was blinding me so I couldn't see inside the porch, but from the words and the tone I could only assume it was Sian.

"Sian, what the bloody hell are you doing here?"

"Emmmmett," she said, dragging out his name. "I think I need to go to hospital."

He pushed his way onto the porch. "Listen, Sian, I don't give a fuck if you're bloody dying. Get someone else to take you."

I leaned my board against the wooden post, listening to them as I peeled off my rashguard. Though I was in great shape by then, I couldn't help feeling self-conscious, feeling Sian's eyes fixed on me.

"Oh, fuck." Emmett said.

I quickly wrapped my towel around me and climbed up the steps. When I opened the door I saw Sian, curled up in a ball on one of the chairs.

"Emmett, what is it?" I asked, not understanding what was going on.

"Stay there, Sian."

He rushed into the house and I stared at her, finally comprehending what they were fussing about. She was clutching her stomach, a small drip of blood coming through the bottom of the wicker chair.

"Oh my God," I said. "We need to call an ambulance."

Emmett rushed back onto the porch, a large, clean beach towel in his hand. "Here," he said, handing it to her. "Wrap it 'round you."

She tried to stand up, doubling over when she did. Emmett quickly wrapped the towel around her mid-section and scooped her up. "C'mon, Sam," he said, pushing past me.

"Emmett, I really think you should call an ambulance."

He had already rounded the corner of the house so I raced down the porch to follow, my towel flapping wildly around my waist as I followed them. I stopped outside the van.

"Emmett, I don't want to go," I said, feeling as childish as I sounded.

He barely paused to slam the door shut. " 's okay, love. Be back in a few."

Emmett threw the van into reverse and the rocks crunched and flew as he barreled out of the driveway. I shivered, the wind blowing on me as I watched them go. Slowly, I turned around and walked back to the house.

Natalie was lying on the couch in the living room, an ice pack splayed across her face, reminiscent of Rachel. When she saw me she said, "Put the kettle on. And get the Paracetomol."

"The what?"

"Par-a-cet-a-mol. Pain medicine. Make it stop hurting."

"Um, okay. Where is it?"

She instructed me where to find the medicine and I shook out four tablets, taking two for myself and two for her. I filled the kettle with water, turned it on, and poured out two glasses of water. I sank onto the sofa next to her, popping the pills into my mouth and swallowing.

"Did you not see Sian on the porch?" I asked.

"Fucking whore, I'm not surprised. She does that a lot. I can't believe the shit she pulled last night, though. What's she saying now?"

"Emmett had to take her to the hospital."

She pulled the ice pack from off her face. "Bet she's faking."

I didn't feel like elaborating. I needed to call home, but it was the middle of the night there. I needed to shower and change. But I was unable to stop going over the last twenty-four hours I had been in Australia. Instead, I leaned back against the couch and fell asleep, waking up when I heard Emmett's booming voice coming through the window.

"Barley, move." Natalie stirred next to me, repeating Barley's name nearly inaudibly.

I looked at the clock. We had been asleep for nearly three hours. "How is she?" I asked anxiously, trying to shake the fogginess out of my head.

He threw his keys onto the table, said, "They're keeping her," and walked down the hall toward his room.

I got up and followed him. I was afraid of what came next. We both sat on the bed, and Emmett took my hand in his and said, "First, I'd like to apologize. This is your holiday and you've got enough to worry about."

"You can't help it. It's not your fault."

He scrunched one eye. "Well, it kind of is. Look, I guess what I'm trying to do is be up front. Now, all I can do is be honest with you."

I felt my head moving up and down, mechanically.

"Sian's pregnant."

I didn't speak, and neither did he. He just watched me, waiting for my reaction. My throat was dry again when I did speak. "And it's yours?"

He cast his head down. "I'm not 100% sure, but I think so. The timing is just too impeccable."

My head went to work doing calculations. We had been dating for around two months - it was unlikely she could have become pregnant in any less time than that.

"How many weeks is she?" I asked, adopting pregnant-speak.

"About twelve. Look," he started again, "It was one time, and it was a mistake. Sam, look I swear, nothin' ever happened again after I returned to Oz from Huntington Beach. Once I met you, everything with her ended."

I wasn't accusing him of anything and I wasn't mad. Yet, the more he seemed to apologize the more I grew suspicious that there was more to it than just a fluke; a minor, drunken hook-up.

"I am in love with you, Sam. And I want to be with you. I want to make this work. Please don't let it change anything between us."

I laughed uncomfortably. "Well, it sort of does."

He lowered his head once again. "I'm so sorry."

Despite my dislike for her, I couldn't help but ask, "Is she… and the baby… going to be okay?" I nearly choked on the word baby, remembering Emmett's words about wanting to be a father.

For a second, I wondered if they had both let it happen, for their own selfish reasons.

"About that..." he started. He put his head in his hands. "It's twins."

"Twins!"

"Yea. They're keeping her in hospital to keep an eye on her."

"Twins." Suddenly, I didn't feel so forgiving. "I mean, this just sort of changes everything, even more." I felt panicky, like the time we had brought Pop home from the hospital. I needed to run. "Give me a second, Emmett."

I left him sitting on the bed and walked through the living room past Natalie, who was muttering, "More... Paracetomol." I ignored her, stepped onto the porch and walked to the front of the house. I broke into a jog, heading toward the lighthouse. For some reason I felt drawn to it, like it was a place of respite from the nightmare that was quickly transpiring.

I tried not to hate Sian. Between Emmett's looks, budding surf career and fabulous home, who wouldn't have gotten caught up in Emmett? Just as I felt things were starting to come together for he and I, there Sian came along with her life-changing bombshell and suddenly, everything was a mess.

Though I wanted to place all the blame on Sian, I couldn't forget that Emmett was just as much to blame. I couldn't stop thinking about what he had said to me over the phone when I was stranded in San Onofre, his words about pregnancy and fatherhood. Had he purposefully gotten her pregnant?

*

That night, I finally had the chance to talk with my family. It was GamGam who answered when I called.

"Hi, GamGam," I said.

"Hi, baby!" she said, excitedly. "Oh, it's so good to hear your voice. How's Australia?"

Though I omitted some of the obvious details, I told her about Noraville, Emmett's home, his friends and family. Finally, I got to the reason for my call. "How's Pop?"

"Darrell has been doing really well since you left. Not all together there, of course, but he's doing well."

Wildly, I wondered if I was the reason for Pop's dementia.

"Oh," she added, "We're not going to be leaving for Maui right away, as planned. There's some things we need to be here for, regarding the sale of your father's home and my own; we're going to put Hawaii off for a few months, dear."

We talked some more and then I said hello to Uncle Chuck, but decided against talking to Pop. Whether he was actually doing better because I was gone, or for some other unknown reason, I didn't want my voice to send him back into a downward spiral. I said good-bye to my family and called Crystal, but hers went straight to voicemail.

Thankfully, Sian's big pregnancy announcement was the only excitement that came about for the next few days, and we got to have some normalcy. She was released from the hospital, and Emmett and I agreed not to talk about it anymore until we had to.

And I let Emmett talk me into taking the semester off from school.

I figured, if we were going to make things work it was worth it to spend some time together then while I was still there, rather than mess school up six months in because I wanted to move to Australia. Emmett obviously wasn't going anywhere, not with the babies. And I had enough money to last.

So I finally got the chance to do some of the things I had been dying to do for years. For two months, Emmett and I surfed our way up and down the east coast, from Brisbane in the north to Canberra in the south. Most places weren't within driving distance, but the flights were usually short, between two to three hours. We would leave for a few days before returning to Noraville, where Emmett would drive over to Sian's place and check up on her. It was important for him to stay connected with the babies, I knew that much.

Just as our two months were coming to a close and he was getting ready to return to work, Emmett mentioned checking out the University of Newcastle, home to one of only eight medical schools on the whole continent. It was driving distance so we made a day of it, opting to take the longer route on the Central Coast Highway.

As Emmett steered the van onto the bypass (their version of a highway), the crystalline blue waters surrounding Noraville gave way to dense, scrubby brush, more of what I expected Australia to look like. The weather seemed to change with it; while the sun had brilliantly sparkled off the ocean, the clouds gathered and the sky darkened as we moved inland.

The university more than paid for the ugliness of the day. Maybe it was because I had never set foot on a college campus before but I was awestruck upon first glance. Modern, brick structures vied with older, majestic buildings set amidst blooming flowers and astonishingly green lawns. As if on cue, someone whizzed by on a bicycle as I climbed out of Emmett's van.

It was like stepping into a brochure. "Wow," I said, looking at Emmett wide-eyed. It felt thrilling, the thought that I could add a place like that to my resume.

He grinned at me and took my hand. We wandered aimlessly up the path toward one of the older-looking buildings. We hadn't booked a tour or spoken to a counselor about our arrival; I wanted to experience it on my own, not be told facts and figures about a place by someone who was paid to do so.

Thunder roared. Inevitably, the skies opened up and it began to pour. Emmett pulled me onto the porch of a building, and along with several other students we sought refuge from the surprise storm.

He swept his arm in front of him and said, "Welcome to Oz."

He was soaking wet, and his thin shirt stuck to his rippled chest. Raindrops dotted his eyelashes and hair, and when he smiled his teeth gleamed next to his tanned, chiseled jaw.

The thunder roared once more and the rain pounded the pavement heavily. I ran my hand along his spiky head, brushing off some lingering water. I said, "I think I've seen enough."

He shook his head like a wet dog. "But we just got here."

"I know. And now I know where I'm going to school." I leaned in close to him and said, "I want to move here, with you. I'm ready."

He leaned back, his smile stretching from ear to ear. "Yea?"

"Yeah," I said, confidently.

In the months since we had met, we had weathered and come through many challenges, some that most couples didn't encounter for years – if ever. Yet neither of us had been deterred.

"Let's go home," I said.

"Home, eh?" He kissed my lips lightly.

"Home," I confirmed.

*

The sun was fading into the cloudy horizon when we pulled up to Emmett's place. The rain had cooled the air drastically, and I shivered as I stepped onto the screened in porch, where I found Natalie and Marcus swinging lazily on the porch swing, Barley snoozing at their feet. They were both holding cans of beer, their lit cigarettes the only light on the porch. It was the kind of clichéd scene you might imagine some young Hollywood screenwriter scripting out.

"Hi," I said, falling into a chair facing the two of them.

"How was your trip to the Uni?" Natalie asked, snubbing out her cigarette in the ashtray.

"It was beautiful!" I said, clasping my hands together excitedly. "I really can't believe I'll be going there in just a few short months."

"So you're going to be staying?" she said, reminding me of our conversation back at the pub in Toukley.

"I hope that's okay?" I said, realizing that it was her house too.

" 'Course it is!" she said, lifting her beer up. Marcus bumped hers, and they toasted the air together.

*

It was one of the first nights we had all been in the home at the same time, and we chatted excitedly about the forthcoming months. Though school was only a few short months away - and there was plenty to do to prepare for it - the Australian summer was just on the horizon. Natalie, Marcus and Emmett talked about all the things they wanted to do and all the places they wanted the four of us to see. Though Natalie and Marcus argued incessantly, they were a riot to be around and I couldn't wait to do all the things they talked about.

Yet, I still found myself wanting to get to Bondi.

Chapter 16: Screw Reality

On a hot Tuesday afternoon, I was in the kitchen making myself a cup of tea when Emmett came in looking bedraggled after a visit to Sian's,

I immediately crossed the kitchen to meet him at the door. "What is it?"

He sighed deeply and ran his hand across his head a few times. "I need to talk to you about something."

My heartbeat quickened as I took a seat at the kitchen table across from him. He took my hands into his own. "As you know, Sian's getting on in her pregnancy, and is now at a point where she needs complete bed rest. She's going to need me help more, and it's going to become harder and harder to split my time up between the two houses so..." his voice trailed off. He cleared his throat. "I've had to invite Sian to come live with us."

Deep down inside I had expected something to happen. Everything was going so swimmingly between Emmett and I, but still, I hadn't expected that.

"Live...where?" There were only three bedrooms in the house: ours, Natalie's and the office.

"For the mo she'll stay in the office. I'm going to get it all sorted as soon as we finish talking here. I've been wanting to start an addition on the house for when the twins get bigger anyway, so I guess there's no better time than now to start. Once that's done, Sian can move into there."

The thought of Sian living in the same house as us made me want to barf. Yes, I understood that she needed his help and it was his responsibility to take care of her. But I was still irritated that he hadn't even consulted me, especially considering it was both of our future's impacted.

"Did you say 'have' invited her?"

He nodded. "I had no choice, babes."

I flinched with anger, but the fact remained that it wasn't my home to open or not open to people. The situation was delicate enough as it was, so I decided to keep my thoughts to myself.

If I thought I was mad though, it was nothing compared to when Natalie found out. She stormed out of the house as soon as he told her – just not before a few choice words and her announcement that she would be moving out. I had to wonder if maybe he had expected that reaction from her, because he certainly didn't try to stop her.

For the first time since we'd met, there was a distance between Emmett and I in the bed that night.

*

The next morning, Natalie announced that she would be moving out in two weeks. The time passed slowly, and it was so awkward between Emmett and her that I made a point to stay away as much as possible. I simply couldn't imagine how Emmett and Sian had dated for so long, when clearly no one liked or respected her place in his life.

I spent my time either surfing or hanging out on the grounds just outside of the lighthouse, my new refuge. Sometimes I would sit for hours, just thinking, wondering how things had fallen apart so quickly and if it was truly worth salvaging. Eventually though, I came to the conclusion that I wasn't ready to give up on us. He appeared to be making a concerted effort to accommodate both Sian and myself, and had taken a more senior role with his family's construction business, so as to not be off traveling with the pro-circuit and away from us.

Sian had gone from not-so-pregnant to very, very pregnant within weeks. Since Natalie had refused to let Sian live in the office while she was still living there, Sian had moved in with Emmett's parent's. Sian needed to be waited on hand and foot, and Karen, Emmett's mom, didn't work, and they had the space. Secretly, I wondered why she couldn't just stay there for the duration of her term – it seemed to work out better for everyone, anyway. Mostly, I wanted to ask where Sian's family was and why she couldn't stay with them. But in the interest of remaining detached I kept my mouth shut and stayed out of the way.

Finally, the inevitable day came round and Sian moved in. Emmett, to my chagrin, appeared delighted.

That's where I started to notice that I was losing him.

At first, Sian stayed in her room and left Emmett and I alone. Not that Emmett and I were spending much time together, anyway. If he wasn't working with his dad, he was fully absorbed in the new addition to the house. Between the two, I rarely saw him.

I started to look forward to school as an escape.

One afternoon, I was surfing the break outside of Emmett's house when my surfboard broke in two. I had only brought one with me to Australia – after all, I had originally intended only to stay two weeks. As Emmett's boards were too big for me, I would have to go buy a new board. I looked up a good surf shop in the area, deciding on one within biking distance, in Toukley.

It took longer than I anticipated to bike over, but that was kind of part of the point - anything that took me away from the house for a long period time was welcomed. I parked the bike outside the store and wandered inside, feeling right at home as I walked through the rows and rows of surfboards, and between them and the smell of the new clothes and shoes – it was ecstasy to me. I was examining a board when a guy with short, wavy blonde hair approached me.

"That's a Star Ekoff, one of a kind. You familiar with his boards?"

I ran my hand up and down the smooth fiberglass frame. "No, I've never heard of him. Is he a local?"

"Yea, he's from Budgewoi."

I'd always had a soft spot for no-name local shapers. It reminded me of Pop. "How much for this one?"

"I don't know offhand, but I can check for ya. Give me just a mo." He turned and disappeared amongst the boards.

I continued to look through the boards, at one point even considering a longboard, but I kept coming back to the Star Ekoff. After ten minutes, the sales guy finally reappeared.

"Took a bit of research, but I finally got the deets on it for ya. This seems to be the only one we have left and I can't get rid of this 'ere floor model. Star's a buddy of me dad's though. I can probably get youse his mobile number, if you're interested."

"I would love that."

"You're American, are ya?" he asked, his nose crinkling as he asked the question. The Australian's seemed to take on an accusatory tone when they asked where you were from.

"Yep," I confirmed. Tearing my eyes from the board back to the young guy, I said, "I need some other gear as well. Do you think you can help me? I just moved here and I didn't bring much with me."

" 'Course, I can get youse outfitted. I'm Drew," he said, extending his hand. I shook it heartily.

Drew set me up with way, way too much stuff and I knew I didn't need a lot of the things he offered. But it was therapeutic being there, and Drew was a good salesman. We both said goodbye happily.

When I walked outside, I remembered I had no car to put my new purchases in. I was just about to call Emmett when Drew came outside and offered me a ride. After my new gear and bike had been loaded into his truck he asked, "Where to?" putting the vehicle in reverse.

"Norah Head, right by the lighthouse. I don't know the exact address but if you can get to the neighborhood, I can steer you to Emmett's."

He nodded. "So who's your mate you're crashing with?"

"Emmett Taylor" I said, looking out of the window at the scenery I was beginning to love.

Drew's eyes got wide. "You're mates with Emmett Taylor?"

"Actually, he's my boyfriend," I said, noting I didn't feel as proud as I should have.

He let out a low whistle. "Way to arrive in Oz in style. So where's he?" He motioned to all of my stuff in the back of the truck.

I shrugged. "He's working a lot, and I'm pretty independent. I just forgot about the part where I needed to get it all home." I laughed.

I noted with some relief that Emmett's van wasn't in the driveway when we pulled in. But another storm seemed to be building, so I quickly moved my purchases to the porch with Drew's help.

"Thank you very much," I said. "That would have been one sucky bike ride home."

"No prob," he said. "Come by the store sometime, even just to say hi."

Once inside, I tried calling the number Drew gave me for Star, the shaper, quickly realizing I didn't know how to dial locally. I gave up and plopped down in front of the TV and watched a re-run of Friend's.

It was nearly dark before I heard anything from Emmett, or Sian, for that matter. I grew increasingly worried, so when the phone rang and I heard Emmett's voice on the line, I breathed a sigh of relief.

"I've been at hospital with Sian. We're on the way home," he said, fatigue present in his voice.

"Is she alright?" I asked.

"Yea, she's fine now. We'll see you in a bit." The phone cut off abruptly. As I hung up, a loud crack of thunder made me scream. I felt very, very alone.

*

I awoke to darkness, feeling stiff as a board and disgruntled. I pressed the light on my watch: it was three am. Panicking, I jumped up and immediately banged my knee into the coffee table. I raced to Emmett's room, finding him lying face down on the bed beneath the covers. I breathed with relief, rubbing my sore knee.

I crept over to him and gazed at his handsome face, debating if I should wake him up. I sat lightly on the edge of the bed and reached my hand out to rub his spiky head.

"Emmett," I whispered into the darkness.

"Hm?" he grunted, sleepily.

I softly rubbed his back. "Hey, why didn't you wake me up?"

He didn't say anything, just rolled away from me. I swallowed hard, feeling his rejection. I took off my clothes, slipped into the bed and molded myself against him.

Neither of us moved the rest of the night.

*

The second time I woke up it was light out, and Emmett was already out of bed. I wondered just how I managed to sleep so heavily with all that was going on, as I threw back the covers and slipped into my robe and slippers. I walked around the house, searching for Emmett when I heard laughter coming from Sian's room. I crept up to the partially opened door.

"Babe, we don't know what they even are yet," Emmett said, laughing.

"I know, but I think it important we start bouncing around names now," Sian's high pitched voice said.

"Well if it's a boy, I want to name him Kyle, obviously."

The room was quiet. Immediately, I felt like I was intruding. I started to turn away when Emmett said, "I got you a massage. That should help with the pain in your back."

"It would be heaps cheaper if you just rubbed it youseself," she said laughing.

That whore! I almost threw open the door but the phone rang, dragging me away.

It was Natalie, asking me if I would like to have lunch with her. It was a welcome distraction, I hastily answered yes. I showered, stepped outside and set off on my bike.

I met Natalie at a small pub for lunch, where I found her sitting at a picnic table outside, smoking. I sat down across from her and asked, "Can I have one of those?" pointing at her pack of cigarettes.

" 'Course." She shook one out and handed it to me. "Didn't know you smoked."

I lit the end and inhaled deeply. "I don't anymore," I said, letting smoke out as I spoke.

She nodded, pulling the sleeves of her sweatshirt down. The afternoon air was chilly, and I regretted not having a jacket of my own. "So where are you living?" I asked, realizing I had hardly talked to her since the night Emmett and I returned from Newcastle.

"With Marcus. Actually, we're going to go work in England, make some cash and hopefully come back and get a bigger place. I'm glad I moved out of Emmett's. This whole Sian thing - I don't want to be any part of it."

Neither do I, I thought wryly, wishing I had more of choice.

I felt dizzy and put out the cigarette. "I have some errands I need to run today. Is there a bus system you can recommend?"

She shook her head. "Bus systems a bit wonky out here in the bush. We'll go round and get Marcus' truck, I can help you with them."

I thanked her, and we both picked up lunch menus. The conversation remained light after that, mainly talking about her plans in England.

After lunch, she handed me a helmet and said, "You can ride with me. The construction site is only a mile up the road. You can sit on the handle bars."

I stared at the helmet and at her new dilapidated moped.

"Do I have to? I have my own bike."

"Don't be such a girl." She slapped the helmet on my head and fired up the engine.

*

One scary moped ride later, we were finally in Marcus' beat up old truck and were moving across town. Natalie took me to get a "mobile" and to "the chemists," which was what they called the pharmacy. I had run out of toiletries and had been using Emmett's, so it was a nice to know that I wouldn't smell like a guy anymore. She showed me how to operate the phone, which was a bulky, ancient-looking Nokia thing, resembling my first cell phone nearly ten years prior. But it was cheap, simple to operate and was pay-as-you-go.

I pulled out the paper with Star's number on it and asked her to help me dial. As I pressed the phone to my head, I marveled at the strange-sounding beeps as it connected with the person on the other end.

" 'ello?"

"Uh, hi, is this Star?"

"Who the fuck do you think it is?" he answered gruffly.

I swallowed. "Okay, hi. My name is Sam, I was given your number by Drew. I'm looking into getting a surfboard made."

"Well, what else would you be calling about? A diamond fucking ring?" he laughed, his voice crackly from years of smoking.

I vowed not to smoke any more cigarettes. "Can you help me?"

"Why don't you come by love and I'll set you right up," he said, his voice softening.

I took down his information and hung up the phone. I felt proud – my first Australian phone call – and Natalie laughed at me and shook her head. It started to pour, so we ran for the truck. Natalie threw the windshield wipers on high but the poor old truck could hardly hold up against the battering. She inched the truck up the road to Star's, and just as we turned onto his street the rain stopped and the sun started shining. "Typical." Natalie grumbled.

Star's shop was nothing more than a house. There were no advertisements or signs, so I had to check the address twice just to make sure we were in the right place.

I knocked hard on the door and heard the sound of two yapping dogs. The door flew open, a trail of smoke preceding the voice of a woman. "Yea?"

"I'm here to see Star," I said, timidly.

"Who the fuck are you?"

"I'm Sam. Samantha...er, Samantha Dane."

"Well which is it? Samantha, Sam or Dane?" she said, cackling as she finished.

"C'mon, c'mon in," she held the door open for us to enter.

These people sure have a weird since of humor, I thought, looking at Natalie. She rolled her eyes back at me as we pushed through the screen door.

Cheap surfing posters torn from magazines hung haphazardly on the walls, much like I had adorned my own back in high school. The smoke was stagnant in the air, and was so thick I probably could have reached out and felt it. The rooms were bare, with old, barely-functional furniture. And as for Star's wife, girlfriend or whoever she was, she reminded me of the crazy cat lady from The Simpsons. Every few feet she walked, she would randomly start cackling, and then stop just as suddenly. Just as I was asking myself what the hell I was doing there for the fifth time, we entered the garage, a room not much more different looking than Pop's. But it was crowded with more boards than I had ever seen together in one room before. There were longboards and shortboards, some finished, some not. It was like Willy Wonka and the Chocolate Factory for surfers.

Star himself was a slumped mess of a man that looked much older than I suspected he actually was. He was tanned and wrinkly, wearing nothing but a pair of dilapidated board shorts, his protruding beer belly seeming out of place against his muscled arms and back. His hair was almost iridescent, the little tufts matted on his forehead with sweat. A homemade cigarette sat dangling between his lips, depositing little flakes of ash as he moved this way and that around the board he was working on.

" 'ey!" the lady called, poking Star harshly on the shoulder, making myself and Nat jump several feet. "The American is here."

Star removed the cigarette from his lips and studied both of us. After a moment, his eyes settled on me. "You're the yank."

"Uh, yes sir." I shifted uncomfortably.

"So what kind of board are ya lookin' for?"

"Longboard, I think. Something to use while the waves are small and flat."

He raised his eyebrow. "Do I look like I don't know what a longboard is for?

How long have you been surfing for, because I've been surfing me whole fucking life!"

His anger was sudden and intrusive. I shook my head and started speaking rapidly, explaining where I was from, why I was there and what I was looking for. When I mentioned Emmett's name, his whole demeanor changed.

"Your boyfriend is Emmett Taylor? I've been shaping for the Taylor lot for years. Shame about the brother, though. Why didn't you say so in the first place?"

After that, we had no problems. Star took my information and the specs for the board I wanted, promising to have something made for me at the end of the weekend.

In the truck, I sagged against the seat. The whole afternoon had sucked the energy out of me. I was exhausted, and I was doing less than I ever had in my life.

*

By the time I got home, it was late. Emmett was missing, as was Sian, and I was becoming so depressed about the situation that I didn't even bother calling him or texting him. Natalie and Marcus had dinner plans, and didn't feel up to calling anyone else. There wasn't even anything on TV worth watching.

So I went to bed. When I awoke, Emmett was in the bed with me, snoring quietly. Again, I wondered how I had slept through his coming home.

But I couldn't go back to sleep. I lay awake for hours, going over everything in my head. I continued to worry about Pop, who I had firmly refused to talk to. He was doing better than he was when I had been home, and I attributed it to myself; somehow, it must have something to do with me. I worried that things with Emmett were on the verge of collapsing. I was rapidly losing faith in our relationship.

Though Emmett was partially to blame, I mostly blamed myself. I was so passive and inexperienced with relationships, that I didn't know how to say what I was feeling and I was afraid that if I didn't soon, I might explode. After only a few months of dating I didn't feel the promise I had felt before; now, the uphill battle with Emmett and his baggage was just exhausting to me. I didn't feel like we were winning anything by that point.

Deep down inside, I knew something had to give, and forced myself to think clearly through some tough questions. Did I move back to the states if Emmett and I split up, or did I stay in Norah Head? With each passing day I fell more in love with the quiet seaside town. I wasn't sure I was ready to give it up. I wondered if I could live in Newcastle, but I didn't know anyone there. Then there was my financial situation. I was burning through money, so if I wanted to stay in Australia I needed Emmett or I would have to get a job. Without a visa, that would be difficult.

Eventually, I drifted off into an unfit sleep.

*

As usual, when I woke up Emmett was gone, and it was cold without him in the bed. It was Saturday, and I shivered as I tried to get warm, vaguely wondering where he was but too tired and cold to get up.

My stomach growled and I needed to use the bathroom. Resignedly, I threw back the covers and quickly stepped into some sweatpants. It was very quiet; there were no deafening storms beating at the windows, no sounds from Sian or Emmett.

Just me and my thoughts. A dangerous combo those days.

I loped into the living room and found Emmett asleep on the couch. It made me really angry; I wanted to shake him awake and demand some answers. Instead, I went back to the bedroom, quietly cleaned myself up, and slipped out of the house.

I hopped onto my bike and rode into town. It was a pleasant ride, albeit a chilly one. There weren't a lot of people out on the early Saturday morning and I reveled in the peace of it all: the birds chirping, the cool wind on my face, the open space.

I saw a coffee shop, pulled up to it and climbed off the bike. I leaned it against the building, wondering for a second if I should lock it up. Sizing up the one patron reading his paper, I figured it would be okay and went inside to order a complicated coffee drink, feeling very, very American. As the young barista prepared my beverage, I wandered over to the message board that seemed omnipresent in all coffee shops. There were the usual Tree Trimming, Real Estate and Babysitting services offered, but one ad in particular caught my eye:

Surf Lifesaver needed

Soldiers Beach
Please enquire at:
52 Sanders Road

 Surf Lifesaver? I could do that. It had been years since I had been a lifeguard, but I still surfed, and I always kept up with my CPR training. I pulled out my new cell phone and dialed the number.
 "G'day?"
 "Yeah, hi, I'm calling about the lifeguard position-- er," I gazed at the ad, "Surf Lifesaver."
 "Do ya want to come by now?"
 Everything in Australia seemed so informal. "Sure."
 The man rattled off some more information and hung up.
 I figured that if I got a job, I could buy myself some time.

Chapter 17: When the Shit Hits the Fan, You Better Have a Poncho

Since I had already told the man over the phone my qualifying skills for the surf lifesaving position, I was surprised when I was given a grand speech about how surf lifesaving wasn't a job to be taken lightly, and that it was absolutely required that I have a Bronze Medallion or something similar that took months to obtain. I would also be required to obtain work experience in a pool, with kids, both things I hadn't done in Australia.

Those were both things I didn't have. Obviously, school was starting for me shortly thereafter, and it would be pointless for me to do the months-long training – I just couldn't finish it in enough time.

So I thanked them for their time, and started to leave, dejectedly. I was almost outside the door when a guy walked in, probably in his late twenties, tanned and lean with thinning, faded blond hair spoke up and said, "Hang on, did you say you were a life saver back in America?"

I relayed everything once more, informing him that I had been surfing my whole life, that I was a Junior Lifeguard in Junior High and High School, and informed them of my CPR qualifications (something I had always kept up with). They asked to see some identification, asked me my intentions in Australia, had me demonstrate my lifesaving abilities via a blow-up doll and a mini-CPR routine and finally, they seemed satisfied enough to let me tag along with a girl – much younger than myself – down to the beach to get familiarized with the turf. On my way out, I was asked to report to the beach Monday morning at six a.m.

*

Star had left me a message informing me that my board was ready. As I still didn't have a way to pick it up with the bike (and was barely talking to Emmett), I texted Natalie to see if she could borrow Marcus's truck and help me out once more.

When I returned to Emmett's, Sian was gone but Emmett was there.

"Where's Sian?" I asked, not even bothering to greet him when I came through the door.

"One of her mates picked her up. She's getting a massage."

I flinched, thinking of the morning I had heard them talking about baby names in her room. "Isn't she supposed to be on bed rest?" I asked, thinking that was the whole reason she was supposed to be at Emmett's in the first place.

He shrugged. "I suppose once every few weeks is okay to get out of the house. She said she felt okay." He came over and put his arms around me. "I feel like it's been so long since I've seen you." He surprised me by kissing me gently on the neck.

I laughed awkwardly. "Well, I've been right here."

He pulled away. "So I've called a few mates over for a bbq this arvo."

"What about Natalie and Marcus?"

"I, uh, left her a message." He looked away, and his tone told him he probably hadn't bothered.

I took off my shoes and started toward the room. "I got a job."

"You did?" he replied, sounding incredulous.

"Don't sound so surprised. It's nothing big, just a gig lifeguarding. I start Monday morning at six a.m. Oh, that reminds me. Can you do me a favor? I got a new board made and I was wondering if you could drive me over to pick it up."

He nodded. "Yea, we have to go into town to get some stuff for the barbie anyway. Where'd ya find a place to make a board?"

"I went to the surf shop in Toukley and was given Star Ekoff's name. So Natalie and I popped over to his house, and he made it for me."

He nodded approvingly. "Good bloke, he is. Mad as fuck, but he'll set you right up."

I was angry with Emmett for his negligence and his coldness, and the warm encounter was making me lose my resolve. I didn't want him to think it was okay to keep treating me like that, so I left the room before I rushed over and threw my arms around him like I wanted to do so badly.

*

The bbq turned out to be exactly what we needed. Everyone, with the exception of Natalie and Marcus, was there: CJ, Riley, Kevin, even Emmett's parents came by. There were some others I didn't know and hadn't met yet as well, but all in all, it was a good time. And Sian stayed away all night.

I found myself talking to Kevin more than I had before. He was the one person I had known as long as Emmett, yet we had exchanged maybe twenty words. I wanted to get to know him better, but he was so quiet. I would just have to drag it all out of him.

I found him strolling on the beach in front of the house. "Care if I join you?" I asked, coming alongside him."

"No prob."

We walked quietly for a few minutes before he asked, "How's your dad doing?"

It touched me that it was the first thing he asked. But it was still a painful subject, especially since I had decided not to talk to Pop over the phone. "I think he's okay. I haven't really talked to him,, or anyone back home, lately. I've been really disconnected…" I trailed off. "All of this stuff with Emmett and Sian…" I didn't want to elaborate and put myself in a bad mood.

"I know," he said. "It's fucking bizarre. You're handling it well though."

I laughed awkwardly. "I guess so. I'm just not sure how much more I can take."

He didn't add anything and we continued on, alone in our thoughts.

Suddenly, I absolutely had to get it all off of my chest. Kevin seemed as unbiased as anybody could be in the group, so I said, "I think there is something going on between Sian and Emmett. Again, I should say."

He stopped walking and turned to me. "What makes you think that?"

I told him about the distance between us, the intimate conversation I had overheard between the two of them. I even told him about the conversation I'd had with Emmett back in Cali, how Emmett had said that pregnancy was beautiful and he'd love to be a 'da'. I finished saying, "I think he's just getting really emotional from it all. Maybe it's just clouding his judgment. But I could be wrong. I don't have anything 'concrete'." I added, hastily.

"Sometimes, intuition is your best tool to discovery."

There seemed to be an underlying message. "What about you?" I asked. "Are you interested in any special ladies?"

He cocked his eyebrow suspiciously and I wondered if I had offended him.

"Sorry, I didn't mean to pry," I said.

"No, it's just that... well, I figured E would have told you. I'm gay," he said.

What?! I had not expected that. "You are?"

He nodded. "Not many people know, so keep that between us."

The short beach ended and we turned around, heading back toward Emmett's.

"So I guess I should amend my question and ask if there are any special men in your life?" I said, hoping he caught my playful tone.

He shrugged. "Not really. Surfing's me main priority at the mo."

Emmett came jogging toward us.

"Don't saying anything about what I told you," I said quickly.

"Sam, Nat's on the phone for ya." Emmett held out his cell phone.

I wondered why she hadn't called my own. Maybe she had forgotten I had one by then. I took it from him, and he jogged back to the house. "Hey, Natalie," I said.

"Sorry to call you on Em's phone but I couldn't find your mobile number anywhere. We're going to Sydney tonight. Wanted to see if you want to join?"

Mid-conversation, Emmett's phone vibrated annoyingly. I pulled it from my head to see what it was. A text.

I put the phone back to my head. "Er, I think I'm good, Natalie."

It vibrated again, so I pushed a button to stop the vibrating. It opened up the text, reading simply, "Come in me room when you have a mo."

"You sure?" Natalie asked.

The phone vibrated again and I pulled it away once more. This time, my heart stopped. "I love you, too." It read.

I looked ahead, registering Emmett running toward us once more. We caught each other's eye.

"Hang on, I might have to call you back, Natalie."

"What'd she have to say?" he asked lightly, holding his hand out for the phone.

"She said to come into her room and that she loves you, too," I replied, giving him a cold look. How dare he treat me so stupidly, especially after we both knew what was going on.

The color drained from Emmett's face. "Okay, wait." He held up his hand. "It's not -- it's not what you think."

"You fucking asshole," I said hatefully, ignoring his explanation. My eyes burned, tears blistering my eyes as they threatened to boil over like a volcanic eruption. I ran past him, toward the house.

"Sam," he yelled, running after me.

I made it into the yard, where everyone was staring at us. I ran past them up the steps and onto the porch, the screen-door slamming in Emmett's face.

"Don't do anything crazy, Sam," Emmett said, opening the door.

I ran straight to Sian's room and threw open the door, banging it on the wall in the process. She looked up, terror plainly reading across her face.

I took a minute to catch my breath. By then Emmett was behind me, trying to pull my hand. "Let me explain, Sam." Guilt enriched his tone as he pleaded with me.

"Don't touch me!" I yelled hotly.

Sian was sitting up on her bed, her burgeoning belly hanging out inappropriately of her out of a too-small top

"You're lucky you are pregnant," I said, through gritted teeth. "Because if you weren't I swear I'd beat the shit out of you." Turning toward Emmett, I said, "How could you do this to me?"

He didn't say anything.

"I trusted you. I trusted both of you." I looked back and forth between the two of them.

Sian dramatically placed a hand on her belly and scrunched her face. Emmett pulled my hand. "Please, Sam, let's not upset Sian. The babies…" he trailed off.

I never would have imagined myself as one of those women, but his words hit me so hard that I slapped him right across his face. He barely flinched, but I cried out in pain. It actually hurt me more than it hurt him.

"How dare you!" I was bawling by then, and shoved past him to his room, locking the door behind me. I grabbed my suitcase and started throwing my stuff in it.

Emmett didn't come after me. I could hear him talking in quiet tones with Sian, soothing her. I pulled my cell phone out of my pocket and dialed Natalie's number.

"Natalie? Can I get that ride to Sydney with you?"

I gathered all of my paperwork and documents and shoved them in a large tote bag. I threw it and my purse over my shoulder and pulled my suitcase toward the door just off to the side of Emmett's room that up until that very moment had never used. I was so grateful for it, because it meant I wouldn't have to say good-bye to Emmett or see any of his friends or family.

Natalie and Marcus were waiting in the driveway. I threw my suitcase in the back of Marcus' truck and yelled at them, "Go, go, go!"

Squeezed between Natalie and the door, I reached into my tote bag and rifled around until I found exactly what I was looking for.

Reggie McIntosh's phone number.

I sent a quick text, placed the phone next to me and waited.

*

I didn't cry like I thought I would. In fact, once I was in the truck and out of Emmett's house I was strangely calm. Natalie and Marcus didn't badger me with questions and left me to my thoughts.

Any other logical person would have gone straight to the airport. There was no reason for me to stay in Australia any longer. But I wasn't ready to go, and told myself that if Reggie returned my text before we got to Sydney, I'd meet him. And if he didn't, I would go home. It was illogical, but it was how I figured I could hurt Emmett most, and right then I wanted nothing more than to hurt him the way he had hurt me.

Reggie could have been out of town. He could have been anywhere in the world on the circuit but halfway through the drive to Sydney he texted me back.

Bondi Beach wasn't far from Sydney, and Natalie and Marcus were kind enough to drop me off at Reggie's without passing judgment.

I thanked them and climbed the stairs to the oceanfront flat.

*

Reggie had texted and said there was no key needed to gain access to flat. I knocked politely, twice, but didn't hear anybody. So I walked into the messy apartment, finding two guys sitting on a couch smoking a bong. I started to regret my decision and nearly took my phone out to call back Natalie, when one of them turned around and said, "Hello."

"Hello," I responded, tentatively. "I'm--"

"A friend of Reg's?" The other guy finished for me, smirking. "Second door on the left."

Reggie said he lived with four guys, but it was easy to find his room with their directions. Thankfully, it was tidier than the rest of the house, although it was a complete 180 from Emmett's. XXX pictures, torn from magazines hung on the walls. There was a miniature refrigerator that had bottles of liquor on top and some glasses stacked next to those. A big fish tank stood off to the side of the room.

But I went straight to the liquor bottles and poured a shot of bourbon.

And then another.

Finally, I felt ready to face the two guys again. I walked out and asked them where I could get a taxi to the restaurant Reggie had given me the name for. They helpfully called one for me, and even offered me a beer.

"So, where ya from?" the guy on the right asked.

"California. Huntington Beach." I clipped my words and sipped my beer.

"Wicked," the other said, offering me a toke from the bong. I shook my head, muttering, "Thanks, though."

"So what brought you to Oz? Reg?"

I didn't feel like giving any details. "I was here visiting a friend in Noraville."

The two looked at each other. "Are you Emmett Taylor's--"

"Former ex-girlfriend? Yes."

They both laughed. "Oh, fuck."

A horn beeped. I stood up, grateful.

"There ya go. See you around." But they didn't bother to wave.

*

I spotted Reggie before he spotted me. It was dark by that time, and he was sitting at a table with a bunch of people, four very pretty girls flanking him on either side. I smoothed down my jean shorts, pulled the rubber band out of my hair and shook out my hair.

Just as I started to head toward the table, Reggie saw me. He stood up and came over to greet me. "Sam! Hiya!" He pecked my cheek and stood back, admiring me. "You look more gorgeous than ever."

"Thanks." I half-heartedly smiled.

He smiled back, his ten thousand white teeth gleaming against his tanned skin. "C'mon, I want you to meet some people."

Reggie was definitely the star of the show. The girls that had been sitting by him previously had been shoved out of the way to make room for me. They now sat across from us, sulking and smirking at me every chance they got. People asked me questions pertaining to surfing, the States and what I thought of Australia so far, but it all became fuzzy after a certain point. Drinks continued to appear in front of me and I continued to drink them, trying not to think of Emmett.

I barely registered someone mentioning dinner, and at the sushi restaurant I drank more, not bothering to eat. I pasted a smile on my face, pretending to laugh at jokes I didn't really get. But by then, I wanted nothing more than to cry it out although I felt like that meant Emmett had won.

Reggie didn't bothering asking about Emmett or why I was suddenly there. In my drunken state, I let Reggie take advantage of my fragility.

As dinner was wrapping up I excused myself. I bought a pack of cigarettes and moved outside to have a smoke. As soon as I was alone, tears came and I sobbed as I smoked. I checked my phone, but I knew there wouldn't be any calls. I hadn't even remembered to tell Emmett I had the phone.

I had barely stopped crying when Reggie appeared.

"Finally, a moment alone with you," he said.

This time, I ignored his advances. I lit another cigarette. Feeling bold I asked. "Why does Emmett hate you?"

He took the cigarette from my hand, took a drag and handed it back to me. " 'Cause I'm better at everything than he is."

I rolled my eyes. "Don't be such a dick."

"Seriously. I've always beat him at everything. Better grades in school, better scores in competitions, and why I think he hates me most, I got the girl he wanted."

"Me," I said, sadly.

He looked at me and laughed. "Not you. This sheila from school. It was so fucking long ago, but he never got over it." He looked at me, finally serious for once. "What happened between youse?"

I didn't answer. Instead, I kissed him. He didn't pull back. So I kissed him harder. Finally, he did pull back and said, "He really fucked you up, huh?"

I moved toward the door. "Yep, he and Sian... whatever. Everybody wins, I guess." I didn't really know what I meant by that, but I was drunk and I didn't care. "You ready to go back inside?"

*

I didn't remember anything the rest of the night. But when I woke up the next morning, I was naked and in bed with Reggie.

I felt awful. I felt beat up. Hungover. Exhausted. I finally wished I had just gotten on a plane and gone home.

Reggie woke up with a boner and kept trying to pull me on top of him. It repulsed me, so I got up and started pulling on my clothes, barely stepping over a used condom on the carpet. I felt bile in my throat. I wanted to throw up.

"You know I've fancied you since I met you at Tim's shop," he said, watching me dress.

I didn't say anything, just tried to remember what happened from the sushi restaurant to Reggie's bedroom. I drew nothing but blanks.

"You wanna grab breakfast? Get a surf in?"

I realized I never picked up the board from Star Ekoff's. I would probably never see it.

"Reggie..." I said, searching the ground for my underwear. Spying them, I shoved them in my suitcase. "Listen. This was a mistake." I wasn't worried about hurting his feelings, but I wanted to get the right words together. "I'm not ready for this. I loved Emmett. He may have fucked me over, hard, but I need some time to like...let it set in."

He got out of bed and started dressing. As he put on his watch, he asked, "Do you know how many girls would KILL to be with me? Huh? Lots. And I blew off a few yesterday arvo to be with you."

I cast my eyes down. "I'm sorry." I felt tears well up in my eyes.

Where was I? Who was this awful piece of shit I had just slept with, and what was I crying about?

He sighed. "Look, I'm sorry. Why don't we go eat, or talk or get drunk. What the fuck ever."

What the fuck ever, I thought miserably.

*

Bondi was just as big and touristy as I had imagined it would be, but Reggie seemed to know people everywhere and took me to the best breakfast spot in town. We sat down, ordered Mimosas and talked about absolutely nothing but surfing.

"So how serious are ya about getting back into surfing? Word has it you're pretty decent. When was the last time you gave it a burl?"

"Actually, I've been surfing daily. I'm almost a hundred percent again."

"And are you planning to stay in here, in Oz?"

I looked around. Everywhere, there was laughter, and sunshine and the beautiful landscape. The beach glistened below us, the tiny dots of people laying on the sand and bobbing in the water. I didn't have to see Emmett in Bondi, and I wasn't ready to go home and be all alone. Pop was almost gone by then and....

"Indefinitely," I answered, stopping my train of thoughts.

"So, try out to join the Women's circuit," he said, simply.

"I'm not Australian. You know I can't join the Australian women's circuit and compete internationally."

"So? You can compete within the country."

Up until that point, I hadn't done much more than dream about professional surfing as a goal, anymore. But I was healed, and I was stronger than before my injury – I was in the best shape I'd been in for nearly five years

"C'mon. We'll go out this arvo. I'll take a look at ya and see what you've got to offer. If you're as good as I hear, I know all the right people to get ya started here in Oz."

We finished breakfast and went back to his place to grab some gear. Reggie was a lot shorter than Emmett, so I was able to use one of his boards. We piled up Reggie's SUV and went just to the south of Bondi where the bigger waves lay. Though I was hungover and dehydrated, and definitely not in my best form, I made a concerted effort to put everything else out of my mind and focus on surfing, my one true love.

Reggie stayed on the beach and watched me while I paddled out and took on every wave that came my way, no matter what it looked like. But it wasn't hard; it was the perfect time of day and it was a fantastic break. After about twenty minutes, he gave an ear-piercing whistle, signaling me to come in.

"You look fuckin' berko out there. Sick as shit."

I guessed it was a compliment. "The waves were perfect. Look at those barrels." I said, pointing at the idyllic tubes just off shore.

"I've seen all I need to see. You'll have no problem getting on the circuit."

It was great to hear. Reggie joined me and we paddled back out, spending the afternoon tearing up the waves. He might have been a lot of things, but he was good at what he did. There was a reason he was as popular and successful at surfing as he was, and I figured I could suck up whatever I was or wasn't feeling long enough to get myself somewhere back in the professional surf realm.

*

I missed Emmett, his friends and Noraville, desperately. And I felt bad about not showing up for the Surf Lifesaving job, too. But I put continued to force myself to put it all out of my mind and lost myself in Bondi, becoming completely disconnected from everyone and everything outside of the beachside town. Bondi Beach was like the Malibu of Australia; everyone was gorgeous, rich and talented. It was like I had re-wound three years and was at the top of my game again.

I fell into a drunken, sex-fueled relationship with Reggie. When I wasn't surfing, I was drinking. When I wasn't drinking, I was sleeping with Reggie. Between my newfound success in surfing, the majestic beauty of Bondi Beach and Reggie's (and my own) escalating popularity, I lost track of everything else.

In addition to surfing constantly, I had become a member at a local gym. Though I was leaner and stronger than ever, my knees were starting to give me some trouble once more, and I knew I needed some time with my old friend, the elliptical machine. I refused to let another injury sideline my future. So I ignored the pain.

True to his words, Reggie put me in touch with the right people and before I knew it, I had an official sponsor - a local surf shop just outside of Bondi. It was bitter-sweet, reminding me of the years when I had nearly ascertained sponsorship from H.S.S.

The only thing missing was Pop, and I felt the abscess more than ever. One night while Reggie was sleeping, I crept outside, took my phone out and called home.

"Hi Uncle Chuck," I whispered.

"Hi Sammy," he whispered back. "Why are we whispering?"

"Oh, it's nighttime here. Everyone's asleep. How's everything going?"

"Well, you called just in time. We're getting ready to leave in two days."

I gulped. Guilt flooded me once more.

I should be there.

But I quickly remembered why I wasn't. "Hey, is Pop around?"

"You ready to talk to him?" He sounded surprised.

"Yeah," I said, softly.

"Okay. Hang on." He put the phone down heavily, and it was a few minutes before I heard Pop croak into the phone.

"Yello?" he said.

My throat caught. "Pop, it's me," I said, crying.

"Honey...Hi."

"I miss you. So, so much."

"I miss you, too. Where are you?" His throat was scratchy.

"I'm still in Australia. Guess what? I'm surfing again." I struggled to clear my throat.

"But you never stopped, did you?"

"What do you mean?" I pulled my knees to my chest.

"In your heart, you'll always be a surfer."

I smiled into the darkness. "Too right you are Pop."

"I'm getting ready to leave, honey. I'm so glad you called."

"You're going to like it there, Pop. It's going to be so beautiful."

He didn't speak right away. "I know."

I shivered. It was chilly outside at night, just like in Huntington Beach. It was almost like I was there with him. "I love you, Pop."

"I love you too, Samantha Helen. Sweet dreams."

We hung up, and it was a long time before I went back in the house.

*

The next morning when I woke up I knew it was time to move out of Reggie's flat. With more and more competitions in sight and money starting to flow into my bank account, I knew I could afford my own place.

That same day, I found something I loved right away and in the same area as Reggie's. It was tiny, to say the least, maybe six-hundred square feet at most. But it was furnished, and offered one-hundred-eighty degree sweeping ocean views. That alone was enough. So I took it.

*

One afternoon, I was walking – and texting - down the stairs from my flat when I tripped on a small box and came crashing down on my troublesome left knee. Pain shot through it immediately. I stood up and tried to continue descending the stairs.

I simply couldn't.

I pulled out my cell phone, called Reggie, and asked him to take me to the hospital.

Not even in my darkest nightmares could I have imagined re-injuring myself so badly. In the fall, I had managed to successfully tear not one, not two, but three ligaments in my knee. The mounting pain I had been feeling in the preceding weeks had been wear and tear. Slowly, I had weakened my knee to the point that one small fall had done me in.

It was over. I was done surfing, forever.

Chapter 18: The End Is Near

Once Reggie realized I was done surfing and was therefore useless to him, he bailed out immediately. But I didn't bother trying to get in touch with him, either. I didn't care about Reggie. I guessed we had gotten exactly what we needed out of one another.

I knew by then I finally had to go home. I couldn't afford the flat, I couldn't return to Noraville, and most importantly, I needed surgery once more. Feeling lonelier and sadder than I ever had in my life, I booked the quickest (most inexpensive) flight home - three days from then. And without any competitions on the helm, I wasn't sure if I even had enough money to get home.

I was sitting on the porch when someone started pounding on the door. Figuring it was Reggie, drunk or possibly coked-up, I didn't answer right away. But the knocker persisted. Finally, I gave up and threw open the door. "Reggie--"

It was Natalie.

"Oh. Hi," I said, casting my eyes down.

"Sam, I've been bloody looking for you for two days. What happened to your mobile?"

"I had ran out of credit. I don't have any more money to top it up..." I trailed off. I had planned to say my good-byes to my Australian friends via email, once I was safely back home. "How did you find me?"

"Reggie told me. Sam," she started, her tone softening. "It's your dad."

My heart stopped.

"You need to go home. He's in hospital."

"How bad?" I asked.

"I don't know. They called Emmett so he has the rest of the details. He couldn't leave, em...what with the twins now born, he couldn't get away." She looked very uncomfortable.

"Whatever," I waved my hand. "You've done enough, but can you take me to the airport?"

She finally registered the bandaged knee. "Oh, Sam." She leaned forward and hugged me.

I started to cry. I had made so many stupid mistakes. And now, I had no idea what was going to happen to Pop. She pulled back and gruffly said, "Well, call the airline, then!"

She started throwing stuff into bags while I tangled with airline red-tape. It took forever, but I was able to pay just a small fee to change my flight, given the emergency. By the time we had arrived at the airport, I had barely managed to hang up with the airline.

There was also no time for questions or lengthy good-byes. "Thank you, for everything." I said simply, but meaning so many things in that one statement. "Good luck in England."

I tried to call my family and Crystal before my flight left, but I literally was out of money. My credit card declined. I didn't even have change for a soda. I stumbled through security, hurt, scared and in pain. What a stark contrast to how I had arrived in Australia.

The flight home was the longest fourteen hours of my life. I spent the entire flight with my forehead pasted to the window, a steady stream of tears pouring down my face as I feared the worst for Pop.

As soon as the wheels touched the ground, I retrieved my American cell phone from my purse. There were several messages, but I didn't bother listening to any of them. I called Pop's house straightaway, but there was no answer.

Customs was a busy, tangled mess, and the long lanes frayed my patience. Finally, my injury actually worked to my advantage, and got to jump the line I started in.

I had just enough American dollars to get myself a cab. I called the hospital Pop had been admitted to previously, but to my frustration I couldn't get an operator. I finally realized it was Thanksgiving, and there were probably hundreds of stupid, turkey-carving mishaps, with relatives and loved ones calling the hospital and tying up the lines. Neither GamGam nor Uncle Chuck had cell phones - unbelievable, considering that it was 2010. I kept trying the house, hoping that someone would answer. Just as I was trying to call the Baxter's cell phones, my own phone died. I gave the name of the hospital to the cab driver and instructed him to head straight there.

There was nothing else I could do but wait.

*

For the third time in too many months, I raced into the ER. I wondered if it was some kind of fucked up plan by God to prepare me for a career in medicine, because between myself, Pop and Rachel, I was far too familiar with the associated motions of emergencies.

I was ID'd, given a nametag, and referred to the Intensive Care Unit. I limped through the halls on my crutches, past hospital staff and rooms, finally finding Pop's room in the farthest fucking place from the entrance it could possibly be.

I stopped abruptly when I saw Pop in the hospital bed. "What happened?" I dared to ask.

GamGam came over to me. "Baby…"

She didn't say anything for a couple of minutes. She held on to me, crying. I continued to state at Pop.

"But what happened?"

She sniffed. "He… he tried to commit suicide."

I gasped loudly. My crutches fell as I rushed to the side of the bed.

"How could you? How could you do this, Pop?" I whispered.

All at once, I was screaming. Arms enclosed around me but I didn't know whose they were or where they came from. I struggled out of their grasp and back to Pop's bed.

"Do you see me?" I screamed at his lifeless body. With the tubes and the respirator and IV hooked up to him, he looked like he was some kind of Matrix experiment. "Do you see your, daughter, Darrell?" I stomped my foot, pain flooding in my knee. "Like it wasn't enough for one parent to die, you have to make it two?" I sobbed. "I hate you, I hate you! I hate you! You've always been selfish. You've never even TRIED to get over her. Ever!" I sobbed again, wheeling around to face my frightened family. "He never even tried," I whimpered.

"Sam, just calm down. It'll be okay," someone said.

"How do you know?" I screwed my face up, sniffing loudly. "How can you say it's okay? It's your fault! You two!" I pointed at Uncle Chuck and GamGam, wanting to place the blame somewhere, even it meant hurting everyone around me. "How could you leave him alone?" I wailed. "How?"

I turned around again and looked at Pop. "I should have never left you for Australia. I should have called more. I should have visited more. But I thought it would be worse." I babbled on and on. "Pop, just come back to me, we'll--" I could hardly speak. "We'll get through this. We'll do whatever it takes." I said, beseeching him. "Pop," I fell onto him, succumbing to my grief as I felt the rise and fall of his chest. "Pop," I said, quietly, and I murmured it over and over again as if the words could build themselves and make him whole again.

*

Sometime later, I pulled myself up. Holding his surprisingly warm hand, I looked at all of the monitors that surrounded him, framing his frail body. I memorized the sounds of the beeps and let them numb me. I took a deep breath and turned around, ready to face my family. GamGam, Uncle Chuck and the Baxter's were standing across from me, and I felt like it was me and Pop versus the world. Ironically, it was they who looked dead to me, unmoving and unblinking with their sunken cheeks highlighted by tears.

I asked thickly, "How bad is it?"

GamGam just shook her head and Uncle Chuck sighed. Then I finally recognized Shane. It was he who had said that everything would be fine, earlier. He held my gaze and finally said softly, "We don't know how long he was out for. Chuck found him."

I cut in, needing the gory details to somehow make it more real. "How?"

"Sam," he shook his head sadly.

"How?" I asked again, firmly.

Uncle Chuck spoke up. "I found him hanging."

I slapped my hand across my mouth, surprised by how good the pain felt. "I don't understand." Tears flowed as fast as the questions that raced through my head.

Shane came over to me and he took my free hand, talking as though he were a grief-translator. I looked into his handsome face, the face I had looked into for so many years, that was nearly unrecognizable at that moment. "Listen, you don't need to hear all of that."

I shook my head vehemently. "I need to know."

He sighed. "Really?"
I nodded silently.
"Chuck found him in the garage," he paused.
"Hanging," I said for him.
"Chuck found him in the garage, hanging."
"From what?" I felt sick asking, but I couldn't explain why I needed to know so bad.
"From a leash to a surfboard."
I sobbed, and the unwelcome human emotion made me angry. "Of course, he would have to be so fucking melodramatic, to tie surfing in somehow."
Uncle Chuck tried to speak, but he was crying, too. I had never seen him cry before. "I tried everything to revive him, I did,"
"Chuck kept him alive while the paramedics came," Shane continued.
A nurse came in to do a vitals check on Pop. Her presence felt so obtrusive to me, I wanted to scream at her to get out, but this time I controlled myself. We were all silent until she left again.
"So how bad is it now?" I asked, feeling like I could talk again. "Does this mean he's going to have to be in a home?"
GamGam started to wail. In slow motion it dawned on me. "No," I said, pulling my hand from Shane's and placing it on Pop, as if I could protect him from death. "No," I begged.
"Sam," Shane said, and he put his arms around me, this time not letting me pull away. "It's going to be okay," he said again.
"How?" I asked. My eyes flashed around the room wildly. But no one had an answer.
Shane held onto me, while I held onto Pop. For a long time, we stood there awkwardly. It was dark in the room by the time GamGam spoke up.
"We need to make a decision."
I immediately knew what she meant. I didn't know if I had the strength to make that decision, but I pulled myself out of my insanity long enough to hear snippets of their words: "long time without oxygen," "extensive brain damage," "may never regain consciousness."
I realized what a selfish, needy brat I had been. I let go of my anger toward GamGam and Uncle Chuck and we sought comfort in one another. I knew they needed me as much as I needed them.

I wasn't the only one losing someone, after all. GamGam was losing a son. Uncle Chuck was losing his brother.

GamGam procured a note from her purse and I trembled when she handed it to me. I read the note silently, hating the unfamiliar penmanship, the stroke having changed even Pop's writing style.

> To my beautiful daughter,
>
> These moments are now very rare, where I am coherent enough to look upon the world I once lived in. After hearing your voice, I realized that these brief glimpses will only become more and more brief. I have tried to live for you as long as I could; I wanted nothing more than to be there when you walk down the aisle, and to be a grandfather, to watch you grow old and become successful. I know you are going to be great at whatever you do, and I don't think I have said it enough: how incredibly proud I am of you. You have always given 110% to everything you do. Your mother would have been just as proud, and it pains me every second of every day that she couldn't be around to know our daughter.
>
> So it is with great sadness that I admit to not being the man I always wanted to be. I can't live another day without Helen, and I know now that you will be okay. You have all of your mother's strength, and none of your father's weakness.
>
> Don't forget about the people who have always loved you. Open your heart to them.

I'll never, ever stop loving you. And I'm sorry for having to leave you.

Love,

Your Pop

I knew right then it was the right decision to take Pop off of life support. He didn't deserve the pain that he was in, and I knew that all he had ever wanted was to be free of it. I knew that my own love wasn't enough to save him.

Still, it was hard to let go.

That night, lying on my makeshift bed in his room, I prepared myself for good-bye. Occasionally, I would look over, my heart skipping if he grunted or made a sound. But I knew the real Pop wasn't there anymore, and had not been for a long time. I had to let go of this unrecognizable body that lay in the same room as my own.

*

On a cold November evening, with my family and best friend by my side, I gave the okay for the doctor to pull the plug. It felt like I was watching an execution, morbid and wrong. It wasn't natural for a person to make a decision for someone else's life to end. I listened numbly as they said the time of death and stared at his body underneath the eerie grey light, as if I could watch the life leave his body. I stayed with him until the warmth left his hand.

My grief felt interminable. Once I said the final good-bye and left the cold, sterile hospital I lapsed into blind shock. Pop had made his own final arrangements: all we had to do was execute them.

His wish was to be cremated and spread at sea. I found this surprising – I thought surely he would have wanted to be buried next to my mother. He didn't mention anything about a tribute, but I wanted to have one for him, anyway. Someone suggested a video collage of Pop, and I thought that sounded nice. It was even somewhat cathartic selecting old photos, and I even let myself laugh once or twice.

On the morning of his memorial service, as I picked out a dress I knew I would never wear again, I remembered one last thing I needed to do. I drove over to Pop's house, hating that I would have to step into the garage where he had tried to end his life but I knew I had to be the one to remove the peeling photograph stuck to the refrigerator. I walked into the cold, empty room where mercifully someone had removed the surfboard leash. Sure enough, the brown, fading photo was still taped to the fridge. I peeled it off and slipped into the plastic baggie I had brought with me, placing it delicately in my pocket. I walked next door to the Baxter's and found all three of them waiting for me in the newly remodeled parlor.

"Hi," I said, my voice wavering as I tried to smile bravely.

We drove in the Baxter's suburban to the hotel and picked up GamGam and Uncle Chuck, who had taken up residence there since Pop's hospitalization. Suddenly, I wondered where Bertie was, but I couldn't muster the energy to ask. Heidi chatted incessantly as we drove to a little church in La Jolla. I wasn't sure why it was so far, but again, I was just too exhausted to ask. Though I found her non-stop conversation tiresome, in a lot of ways, I was happy for her chatter. It meant I didn't have to speak. Speaking led to crying, and crying led to pain. It was better to remain quiet and numb.

But on that morning, even though I was silent, unwanted tears trickled hotly down my cheeks. I kept my eyes trained on the road, one hand clutched on the plastic bag in the pocket of my sweater, the other onto Shane's hand.

Frank pulled the Suburban into a spot at the church and we all climbed out. I was shocked to see how many people were there: some I knew, some I didn't, but it seemed like they all knew me, for there were faint waves and greetings as Shane steered me up the steps and into the church.

I saw shapes of people sitting in pews and heard a woman wailing, but I couldn't see who. As I moved toward the front of the church, where Pop's remains were sitting in a little box, I stopped and said to Shane, "I can't do this." I tried to turn around.

"You can." He squeezed my hand encouragingly.

My body shook and I bowed my head, praying for the first time in a long time. I prayed for strength - I wanted, needed to expunge my grief, yet I felt myself holding onto it somehow. Like Pop had with his depression. It was one way in which I didn't want to follow in his footsteps, so I took a deep breath and kept moving forward, taking a seat next to Uncle Chuck and GamGam.

I clutched tightly onto the photograph in my pocket. Uncle Chuck leaned over and asked for my hand. He turned it, palm-facing up and dropped a ring in it.

"Your father's wedding band."

I looked at it reverently. I was holding the last material item that bonded my parents. I pushed my finger near it, just to see if it was real. It was all I had left of them that I could touch.

A woman played the organ softly as more and more people filed in. The air smelled of carnations, a smell I immediately hated and knew I would liken to funerals forever.

At long last, the pastor called everyone to attention. I tried to listen to his words, but all I could do was stare into blurred space, thinking of nothing, really.

The pastor left the podium, and two girls, long distance cousins of Pop's, sang Amazing Grace. I didn't know who they were, but their singing was beautiful.

Before I knew it, Shane was tapping my shoulder.

"Sammy, it's your go."

I walked up to the podium behind the little box that was left of Pop. I looked out at the audience, unable to recognize anyone through my blurred vision. It had been like that for days on end. I wondered if it was going to stay that way, permanently.

And then something just kicked in and I was able to speak. I had written a speech down, but it felt inadequate. I crumpled the note in my free hand, opened my heart and the words started to tumble out.

"You all knew my father," I began, "And we all know he wasn't a perfect person. He was guilty of loving my mother more than life itself. But he was also guilty of loving me, and my family, and his friends, and the ocean. And I know he did everything in his physical power to try to stay here with us, until he couldn't take anymore and his body gave up on him." I felt myself choke up once more and accepted the fresh box of Kleenex the organist handed me.

I steadied my voice and continued. "No one could ask for a better father. Pop was the most loving, gentle person I ever knew and he carried my mother's memory until the day he died. I know he's finally got the peace he spent his final years trying to seek." I wrapped my finger tightly around his wedding band and looked at the picture of him someone had mounted next to his remains.

"So when you think of Darrell Dane, remember that person," I said, pointing at the photo. It was one of the few pictures of us as a family, taken just weeks before my mother's passing. Pop was holding my tiny, sleeping against his chest, his arm protectively around my mother as she gazed adoringly up at him and he back at her. He was wearing one of his beloved Hawaiian shirts and a pair of chinos, and both their smiles were as big as the ocean we had loved. The picture summed up everything that Pop was. "Remember my father, your son, your brother, your friend, and when you see the ocean, think of him up there riding the ultimate wave."

Quietly, Surfer Girl, by the Beach Boys, started playing. I looked at the picture one last time.

He was finally back with his own beloved surfer girl.

*

Following the service, I copied GamGam's lead and stood at the front of the church, waiting to greet and thank everyone for coming. One by one, people hugged and kissed me, paying their respects. I was surprised when I saw Greg and Tim and wondered who had told them about the service. Behind them, came a whole slew of Pop's old surf buddies, some I hadn't seen in years. As they said their condolences, it made me proud to realize that Pop had touched so many people's lives.

*

On the drive home, the heavens opened and rained poured down on the car. It felt like a miracle - rain didn't just appear in Southern California like that. I don't think I could have handled anymore sunshine, and I thanked God for that small gift.

We drove straight home. The Baxter's were hosting a luncheon at their home, and as much as I didn't want to be, I knew I had to be there. The bratty kid in me wanted to run, but if there was one thing I'd taken from my time in Australia it was that it was more than time to take on my responsibilities and grow up.

Dutifully, I ate lunch with everyone, idly chatting, though I had no clue what was talked about. When people started leaving, I grabbed Shane and we ducked out of the house. I removed the small box from the back of the suburban and we walked down to the beach to fulfill Pop's last wish. It was raining and it was cold, but it didn't matter to me.

I took a seat on the wet sand and placed the box in front of me.

"Pop," I started, talking directly to it, as though it really were him, "I know how much it hurt you to be here." I procured the faded photo from my pocket, the one I took from the refrigerator. "I know you're with mom now, and I want you to know that it's okay; I'm going to be okay. But I'll never stop loving you, just like you never stopped loving her." I removed the photo from the baggie and held it up, as though showing it to the box.

I closed my eyes, willing myself to say my final good-bye. I stood up, waded into the freezing cold surf and waited for the wind to die down. With the cold water churning, I shook the ashes out and quickly stepped out of the water to let them intermingle.

I stood there for some time. I watched the waves wash out to sea, carrying my father away from me forever. When I felt I was ready, I took his wedding band from my pocket and threw it with all my might.

"Good-bye, Pop."

When I turned around, Shane was waiting with his arms outstretched. I put my arms around him and breathed his scent, so, so grateful for his friendship.

My whole life, I always thought I was alone. But more and more, I realized that my own life was filled with nothing but life. I had GamGam, Uncle Chuck, the Baxters, Crystal, and sometimes, Rachel. And a million memories with Pop to last me a lifetime.

I thought of my mistakes in Australia and guessed I was glad for them. They were behind me. I could do nothing about them but move forward.

It was time to let go.

*

"How are you feeling, Sam?" Shane asked tentatively, coming over to where I was laying on a couch in the den.

"Tired. Really, really tired."

"Are you ready for more news?"

"No." I shook my head vehemently.

"Well...I think this is a good surprise. Emmett's here."

I sat up. "Oh, God." I didn't have the strength to fight. "How did he – "

"I called him. He told me everything that happened."

I looked down sheepishly. "What about – "

"The other guy? Yeah, him too."

I looked down again.

"It's not a big deal, Sam. People do things. They make mistakes. I didn't ask Emmett to come here, he made that decision on his own. But you should talk to him, at least."

"Where is he?"

"He's staying at the Hilton. Here, call him." He took out his cell phone and dialed for me.

Emmett answered right away. We agreed to meet at his hotel in an hour's time.

*

I almost walked away when I first saw him. With his short, shaved hair, his broad shoulders and his long legs protruding from under the table – it was like the first time I met him, and his betrayal felt fresh all over again. Combined with everything else, I wasn't sure I had the strength to deal with it right then. But when he saw me, his face was soft, and he stood up and walked straight toward me, crushing me in the biggest hug.

"I'm so sorry, love. You're heart must be breaking." He stroked my hair, and I instantly started to cry into his chest.

"You were so brave up there, talking about your Pop."

I pulled back. "You were at the service?"

He nodded. "I was upstairs where you couldn't see me. I wasn't sure…if you'd want to."

"Can we go outside?" I let him lead me through the doors and out onto the terrace. I always felt better when I was facing the sea.

"You know, it's true what they say." I began, turning toward his heartbreakingly handsome face.

"What's that, love?" he asked, softly.

"That with every death comes a new life. In your case two…" I trailed off.

"About that," he said, rubbing his spiky head. "We have a lot to catch up on." He took a deep breath. "First of all, I am truly sorry for being such an aresehole. You didn't deserve any of what you got from me. I took advantage of your trust, and I threw it back in your face. I hope you can forgive me for that."

"Yeah, but I-"

He held up his hand. "Please." Suddenly, his shoulders sagged. "All along, she was playing me."

I raised an eyebrow. "Sian? What do you mean?"

He nodded. "She was lying. She knew all along. The babies aren't - weren't mine."

My mouth flew open.

"I know," he said, a light smile on his face. "That's what I did. Yea, as it turns out, she knew who the father was all along. But he fucked off and left her. So, knowing me like she did, she knew I would take care of her," he shook his head, "And she was right. She admitted it all right after you found out about us. She felt very, very guilty."

"You should have told me," I said, furrowing my eyebrows.

"I didn't know where you were for a fair bit. Nat wouldn't tell me. But once I promised I wouldn't go near you, she informed me you were with Reg. She said you needed to make your mistakes first."

I couldn't help but smile.

His face clouded over. "And then I found out about your Pop. I just had to be here."

"Thank you," I said, whole-heartedly. "And I'm sorry too, Emmett. You were right all along, about Reggie."

"Doesn't matter now." He took my hands into his own. "I made a mistake, Sam. A massive fucking mistake. Can you forgive me?"

"Of course, Emmett." He reached for me, and I hugged him tightly. His smell brought back so many memories. That first night on my rooftop deck. Spinning around in the airport when I first arrived in Australia. Our decision to live together, on the beach. Kissing in the rain at Newcastle.

"Of course I forgive you, if you can forgive me, too."

"It's done." He waved his hand passionately. "But I have another question to ask you."

My pulse quickened.

"Will you come home with me, back to Noraville? Please?"

I let go of him. As much as I wanted to, as much as I probably needed to, I just couldn't. "Not right now. I need some time to settle some things in here," I patted my heart. "I need to learn to love number one, first."

He nodded. "I understand. I'm massively bummed, but I understand. So what will you do next?"

"I don't know." I thought of the apartment in Bondi Beach – the apartment that I was still renting. With no money. "Stay here for awhile. Sort out Pop's stuff. Have surgery, again." I laughed dryly.

"I spose I should be letting you get on."

I stood up. I hugged him again, feeling sad this time but knowing I was doing the right thing. "We'll stay in touch, won't we?" I asked.

He grinned, his eyes crinkling at the corners. "Abso."

*

Shane was due to return to England to be with Mags, but he stuck around much, much longer than was necessary. I told him to leave, but he said wouldn't until he was 100% sure I was going to be okay on my own. "Like that's going to happen anytime soon," I had told him.

The day after Pop's funeral, GamGam called and asked to have lunch with me, alone. She didn't wait until we had ordered – she started talking right away.

"Baby, there is something big I need to tell you."

I braced myself, having no clue what it could be about.

"Don't look so worried. It's good news this time. Upon following your mother's tragic death, your other grandparents, the Macy's, filed a wrongful death suit against the railroad company that was responsible for her death. They won a very substantial settlement, and that settlement was turned into a trust fund in your name."

"But they've been dead for years. I mean, how did I never know about it?"

"Well, your father didn't want you to know."

"I mean, how much is it?" I felt lightheaded.

"Five-and-a-half million dollars."

"What!" I had to take a second to digest the news. "But why didn't Pop use the money?"

She took a dainty sip of coffee. "It wasn't his to use. Ultimately, he didn't want your life to be about money, sweetheart."

"I don't want the money," I said decidedly.

"We expected you to say that," she said with a smile. "But why don't you think about it first?"

I appeased her by saying I would. But what on earth would I do with so much money?

*

As Shane and I sat on the rooftop deck of the apartment, I told him about the money.

"What do I do with it? I don't want to keep it." I said, staring out at the horizon.

He drummed his fingers on the armchair of the porch swing and said, "Are you still thinking about college?"

I nodded vehemently. "Like, ASAP. And I definitely still want to be a doctor."

"Then put enough aside for school, take care of your knee and then give the rest away to dementia research or something."

I looked down at my heavily wrapped knee, wondering if I would ever surf again. I'd wondered that before, but this time, it felt final. Yet, I couldn't imagine myself falling into the downward spiral that had culminated in my discovering Pop's dementia. There just had to be a way I could incorporate surfing with healing.

"What about Australia? Do you plan to go back?" Shane asked, bringing me back to the present.

I thought of the beautiful campus of the university in Newcastle, that I was still enrolled into; of Emmett's home in Noraville, the beautiful beaches and bustling nightlife of Bondi. But how could I go back to Australia without a visa? I absolutely refused to use the money for anything selfish – and I wasn't going to use Emmett.

Then it came to me. I sat up, rapt.

"What if I set up a mentoring program...like, something for little groms, or people who have lost loved ones, something like, where we can use surfing and the ocean as a tool for healing? Like a YMCA or Big Brother, Big Sister program meets Junior Lifeguards, but in Australia?"

He smiled big. "You'd have to iron out a lot of logistics, but I'm sure you could make something happen.

"We could do it in Noraville, by Emmett's place. That way, I'd have my visa, I'd be using the money for a purpose and I'd be giving back, all while doing something I love!"

It made so much sense. Suddenly, I felt so much hope.

"That's a start, babe." Shane said, patting my leg.

"You know how much this means to me," I said, gruffly. "You being here with me. You've always been great like that. Mags is a lucky, lucky girl."

"You're not..." he started.

"Oh, don't flatter yourself, Baxter. I'm not interested in you anymore." I stuck my tongue out at him playfully.

He stood up. "Well, I suppose you're healed now. My work here is done."

I smacked his leg playfully. He laughed, and I laughed, too. It felt so, so good to laugh.

Somewhere out there, Pop was smiling down on me. I could feel it.

Epilogue

I spent the week prior to my surgery in a flurry of activity. Despite my resolve to start my new journey as a single woman, I talked with Emmett constantly, collaborating and mulling ideas for how best to build my mentoring program. We began cementing a new friendship, and I felt proud by how well we had handled everything.

GamGam, Uncle Chuck and I began the process of going through Pop's stuff and putting the home on the market. None of us could stand to be around it any longer, and for me, all of my good memories were tainted knowing it was the place Pop had tried to take his life at.

GamGam's house in La Jolla still hadn't sold, but she decided to stick with her initial plans to join Uncle Chuck in Hawaii. I think she too felt the emptiness without Pop around.

Shane had returned to England and proposed to Mags. The wedding was set for the following summer; I hoped that Natalie and Marcus would still be there.

Almost immediately, I reconciled with Rachel. Our friendship wasn't the same, but neither were we. Truth be told, I really, really missed her. She had moved out of Crystal's house and up to Hollywood, where she was pursuing acting full time.

Crystal had an unlikely new roommate: Riley. The two of them were madly in love, and both newly Vegan. Riley was going to stay with Crystal through the summer and see how things went. From there, they would figure things out. (I think everyone had learned a lesson or two from Emmett and I about rushing into things).

There was only one person I had not seen by then and was dying to see: Eduardo. I hadn't even talked to him since I'd been fired from Scarpulli's, and the night before my surgery he met me for dinner in nearby Sunset Beach.

"Sweetie!" he shrieked, when he saw me. We hugged and laughed giddily.

Once we had sat down, he said, "Tell me everything!" as he slipped both hands around his Mai-Tai.

"Eduardo, your hands!" I exclaimed.

"What?" he nearly screamed, staring at them.

"Their beautiful! You got the job at Sephora, didn't you?

He blushed. "Yes, I deed. The money is no as gud, but, I get to look at preety ladies…and preety men…all day now." He preened happily, and begged me to tell my story once more.

We took a long time to catch up, and I culminated my story with, "I wish I could take you with me." Then I had a thought. "You should! It could be you, me and Bertie!" I pictured myself, the injured American surfer, the gay Latino and the parrot, starting a new life in Australia. It sounded like a reality show.

"Who's Burdy?" he asked. "Is he sexy?"

I laughed. "Bertie's my dad's parrot."

"A parrot? No! I want heem! Just like from my home. I come see tomorrow."

"Her," I corrected.

"Oh!" he squealed. "Speak of her, I almost forgot. Maria," he said, enunciating her name, "Ees fired."

I gasped. "No!"

"Jess, she was steeling lots of money from Scarpulli's. I got to see her be an escort."

"You got to see her be escorted out?" I translated, laughing.

He nodded. "I think of you when I see that happen." He pointed at me. "I mees you, and now you leeve again!" he sighed. "Okay, I go with you! Find me a nice Ostrian boy."

*

The day of my surgery, GamGam and Uncle Chuck drove me to the hospital and stayed with me while I was admitted and prepped. Though it was my sixth surgery, I still was fearful every time.

As it was an outpatient surgery, I was sent home a couple of hours afterward. I slept most of the night and woke up the next morning to a whole slew of people in my house. I opened my eyes, and surprisingly, the first person I saw was Kevin, Emmett's best friend from Australia.

"Emmett sent me," he explained.

I would have laughed had I not been so groggy. "Haha," I said.

"Don't worry, I'm not here to try and get youse back together. I was passing through, and Em was worried."

"I have Crystal, and Riley," I said thickly. My mouth was insanely dry.

He rolled his eyes. "Those two would put ya on the wrong flight." He picked up a cup of water next to my bed. "Here." He held the straw to my lips. "Oh," he added. "Since I've been sitting here both Emmett and Shane have called. Twice." He rolled his eyes. "What is it that ya do to these blokes? Emmett, Reggie and Shane? Maybe I should take notes."

I managed a smile. "Emmett and Shane are just my friends."

He snorted. "Yeah. Just friends."

THE END

Thank You's

Firstly, my utmost thanks must go out to Raymond Obstfeld. You're candor and stark analysis of my many, many first chapter drafts kept me in a constant state of editing over the years. Between those marathon Tuesday night classes and Writing Retreats, I learned the discipline to become the writer I am today.

To my friends and former classmates from Ray's Novel Writing Workshop. Truly, could not have gotten to where I am today without you all. Your invaluable advice and helpful hints gave me the extra boost my work needed.

Abra and Chad, you were my first "real" critics. If not for your surprisingly good review (even in the hideous early drafts) and preceding low expectations (haha!), I might not have continued my writing journey. Most importantly, thank you for leading me to the uber-talented Lauren Wise at Midnight Publishing, LLC.

Lauren, your expertise and advice has been priceless. Without your watchful eye and anecdotal suggestions, this would have remained a manuscript and never became a novel.

Leanne Sergeant, my family, my friend, my illustrator. You took my cover vision and made it into a masterpiece. Thank-you for creating the most piece of art I have ever laid eyes upon.

Dave Szych and Huy Nquyen, thank you for your advice on the technical aspects of surfing. Most importantly, years and years of friendship. Dave, also for the opportunity to freelance for ACTravelagent.com, a journey I hope to continue on.

Mark Kirsch, MPT of Mariner's Physical Therapy, you were more than just a physical therapist. At times, I wonder if you might have been a sort of psychotherapist as well.

Special thanks to Katie Leighton, Teri Roberson, Jen Dorward and Monica Richter. Your unwavering support kept me going. Rocks, you are.

My impossibly loyal friends, some past, some present, and some unknowingly that helped shape these characters and concepts I have come to love: Illiana Edney, Shelly Miller, Danny Thomasson, Demyon Wright, Ben Crosbie, Lucy Lewis, Pamela Amaral, Alicia Kozma, Linda Mena, James Lucente, Nikla Albertini and Ryan Johnson.

Dan Jones and James Lucente, unlikely fans who read without bias.

The fam: The Stuarts, Deadra Gardenhire, Jenny Lambert, the Scherlers and the Robersons . I love you all.

Most notably, to my brother and sister: My life wouldn't be what it is without either of you. Every iota of the person I am today is because of you. Thanks for picking up the pieces our parents left and righting so many wrongs.

About the Author

Hannah Shelton comes from many places. Though born in rural Oklahoma, she was raised in Southern California where she lived until she was sixteen, when she decided to emancipate herself from her guardians. She homeschooled herself through her last year of high school before taking a five-year hiatus from her education to travel, and has lived in England on three different occasions. She loves (in no certain order): travel, wine, food, St. Bernard's, her cat, Napoleon and is a maniacal Minnesota Vikings and Oklahoma Sooners fan. She currently lives in Northern Virginia.

Hannah Shelton has been editor for ACTravelagent.com. This is her first novel.

CONNECT WITH HANNAH

Hannah is an avid Facebooker, Twitter-er and Blogger. You can keep up with her crazy adventures and stay informed with her latest news at:

Twitter: @gohannah1234
Facebook: 'Like' Hannah Shelton's Author Page
Website: www.hannahshelton.com

Made in the USA
Charleston, SC
10 December 2011